I0685088

A Drew Morrissey Thriller

Wire

A Drew Morrissey Thriller

The theme of *Wire* is Watergate meets *The Fugitive*. A spunky investigative reporter uncovers a conspiracy involving a Presidential candidate. Soon, she finds herself stalked by a pro hit man. She lives on the run, a fugitive. To survive, she must solve the crime that shattered her life. Drew Jennifer Morrissey fought her way from stringer at *Rolling Stone* to reporter for *The New York Chronicle*. She is in a mess at work. Getting her articles kicked out of the Metro section has become normal. Drew leaps at the chance to redeem herself by chasing a breaking story. Instead, the assignment turns her life inside-out. She becomes the sole witness to politically motivated homicides. The only thing keeping Drew Morrissey alive is her quick wits. She lives on the run, chased by an assassin code-named Elijah. His connections reach everywhere Drew goes for help, including the FBI. Jake Balducci, head of the FBI's New York bureau, insists Drew go undercover, working for the people trying to kill her.

UN-TIED ARTISTS

Based in Silicon Valley, these authors write comic fiction, thrillers, mysteries and adventures. Un-Tied Artists donate proceeds from sales of their books to Doctors Without Borders.

In 1999, the Nobel Peace Prize was awarded to Doctors Without Borders for their work in relieving the suffering of underprivileged countries. Why a peace prize for doctors? Because terrorists find eager recruits among the despairing millions of this world, living in unthinkable conditions.

See more about Un-Tied Artists and their books at
www.SiliconValleyNovel.com

Other books by Un-Tied Artists

Satan's Touch is a Cold War spy thriller, based on the author's real life experiences working for CIA. The novel is a tale of malice and greed, the fast-paced action of Ludlum spiced with the sinister logic of Le Carré. *Satan's Touch* is the story of a man trained by the KGB and still having its power behind him. Driven by twisted obsessions, he's determined to find something he was forced to abandon years ago.

Everest is Hollow is an adventure novel, featuring a teenage Indiana Jones-style archaeologist. His nickname is "Trouble." Together with his friends Nuru and Tattoo, Trouble climbs Mount Everest's difficult West Ridge. Trouble enters a cave and realizes Everest is hollow. He discovers an abandoned city, the key to a lost civilization built on treasures of the past.

Why is Paris burning? For money, a lot of it, more than you can possibly imagine. A serial arsonist killer is loose and American Interpol agent Nicki Foster fights to stop him. To stay alive, Nicki and Fire Captain Paul Denis race to solve a puzzle leading to an immense fortune. Lose the race and a flashover fire will burn them alive, leaving only an x-ray of them behind.

Stir outrageous characters in a thick sauce of greed and you have the recipe for *Silicon Valley Game*. This is a humorous, naughty book that really dishes. Everyone searching Google is curious to peek inside lives caught in the Silicon Valley Game. What will they find? Answer - backstabbing, gossip and juicy scheming.

Wire

A Drew Morrissey Thriller

This book's story and characters are fictitious. Some well known public agencies, locations and establishments are discussed. But the characters in this novel are entirely imaginary.

ISBN-13: 978-0-9817702-6-0
ISBN-10: 0-9817702-6-6

Published in the United States of America by Un-Tied Artists

1

Inside

The New York Chronicle, the plastic sign on my desk reads "Drew Jennifer Morrissey." It should say "Stressed Morrissey." I was buried in problems, shredding a Styrofoam coffee cup in frustration when my boss walked in the newsroom. From my chair, I could only see the back of Saul Morgenthal's head, where a laurel wreath of tightly cropped hair ringed his bald skull. The wreath was all that remained of a 1960s-style crew cut. Morgenthal once told me if he hadn't become an editor, he'd have been an astronaut. Time and job pressure hadn't been kind to Saul's body. Twenty years ago, he might have been in shape for astronaut training. Today, Morgenthal's frame wouldn't fit through the narrow door of the Space Shuttle.

Saul's daily stress was showing itself in a working breakfast, where he ate the sandwich he couldn't eat during his noon meeting with the Executive Editor. A corned beef on rye was jammed in his talking mouth. Typical of his pressured life, food was inhaled at the same time Morgenthal scanned the newsroom, looking for someone. I hoped it wasn't me. I shrank in my chair, trying to be invisible. I failed.

Morgenthal spotted me and bellowed. "Where's that piece on the Garment District fire. We got deadlines, Morrissey."

I jammed my hands into tight jeans pockets. "I finished the Garment District piece an hour ago. It's sitting in your email."

Saul immediately lost interest. "Doesn't matter." He mumbled through bites of the deli sandwich. "Got a better story for page one. You're bumped, Drew."

I wasn't surprised. Having my articles kicked off the front page of the Metro section had become normal. To say I was in a political mess was an understatement. I was learning a lesson I'd never forget – don't mix sex with work, even if he sits at the other end of a 39,000 square-foot newsroom. The lesson began when my boyfriend Jamie was fired for stretching the truth in an article. *The Chronicle* has zero tolerance for made-up interviews.

Now I was under suspicion, due to my intimate relationship with Jamie. People were whispering … perhaps I'd encouraged Jamie to lie … maybe I also made up facts instead of researching them. To survive the rumors flying around, I needed to prove myself, like a rookie. In fact, I was worse off than a rookie. Politically, Saul Morgenthal was safer firing me than keeping me. He just needed an excuse. I was fighting hard not to give him one. I was losing the battle.

"Uh, Saul." I talked quietly, hoping he wouldn't hear me. I hated dealing with him. But he did hear me. Saul cocked an eye in a question mark. It was his way of saying this had better be good.

"Who are you looking for? I mean, you're standing here, gazing around the newsroom. It's not like you're taking a stretch break, is it?" There, that wasn't so bad, Drew. You can talk to Saul Morgenthal after all. Maybe.

"I'm lookin' for a reporter, Morrissey. You see any? I don't."

Ouch. Chill out, Drew. Don't let it hurt. I dared another question. "You got a story needs covering?"

"Another hit on an election headquarters. Third one this year."

"How'd you hear about this?" I was astonished.

"The killer phoned our switchboard. They transferred him to me. Now he's on the air talking to Howard Stern, the shock jock."

"Where'd this killer do the hit?"

"Across from MOMA. Five minutes by taxi this time of morning." He looked at me like I was in kindergarten and didn't know what MOMA meant. "MOMA, the Museum of Modern Art. You mighta heard of it."

Saul pivoted, scanning the floor for someone he could put on the story. For once I got a break. It was too early in the day for other reporters to be inside the newsroom. Saul had nobody else to assign. He glowered at me. "OK, it's yours. Don't mess it up by faking something. This is your last chance. I'm sending Benson to take photos. Wait while I find him."

"Flashbulbs" Benson was the only photojournalist left in the world who still used a film camera instead of digital. *The Chronicle* put up with film because Benson was only a year from retirement. I rolled my eyes in amazement at Saul's choice of photographers. It would be a miracle if Benson caught even one picture Saul could print. With a dozen rolls of film in his photo vest, Benson wasted every frame on sickening gore, stuff no editor could show to the public.

Waiting for Benson meant wire services like Reuters would beat me to the scene. Saul getting his article from the wire services would be the death of my job. Morgenthal would say I was slow and missed his deadline, forcing him to run the same bland stuff printed by every paper in the country, even though the story happened in his backyard. But there was something I could do about it.

I could lie. "I'll wait for Benson downstairs." I pulled a linen blazer over my Eminem T-shirt. The shirt was a freebie when I was a stringer at *Rolling Stone*, so I wore it. Free clothes fit my wardrobe budget. I pushed my stool back and stood up. Then I rolled out of there and hit the elevator bank.

I jogged through the blue-shirted security guys in the lobby, not giving Benson a second thought. I passed a bust of George R. Jennings, founder of *The Chronicle*. Mr. Jennings scowled like he'd read my dead column on the Garment District fire. "Don't worry," I assured him, "I'm getting you a better article." I gave him a high five and spun through eggbeater doors.

Outside, the neon of Times Square blasted me with ads louder than the honking taxis. I shut it all out and focused on saving my job. A cab stopped in front of me and I decided to splurge. Get there first, Drew, I told myself. Saul will reimburse the taxi fare when he sees your write-up. I yanked the cab's door open and flopped on the back seat. "How fast can you get to MOMA?"

The driver didn't say a word. He hit the gas, the door slammed shut and I was thrown backwards in the seat. Damned fast was his answer.

Muted sunlight leaked through the muggy sky as I got out of the taxi. Nearby, a frankfurter cart hissed with boiling hot dogs. Their steam lingered in the warm summer air. Church-goers leaving the morning service at St. Thomas wove through fat pigeons clogging the church's steps. Brooks Brothers was ignoring the heat wave and shifting to an autumn wardrobe, dressing window mannequins with corduroy and thick flannel.

Across the street, a blue Suburban dressed in red and white crepe paper marked the election headquarters of a small, independent party. Bumper stickers covered the SUV, declaring solutions to all problems, just vote for us.

The only sign of trouble was a police cruiser angled to the curb, indicating a fast stop. Bursts of police radio squawked out its open windows. More cop cars must be in an alley behind the building, I told myself. I assumed it was safe to go inside. It was another lesson to me. Never assume Drew.

I crossed the busy street, approaching a storefront with windows plastered in slogans like the Suburban. Humid air clung to me like shrink-wrap, sticky and cloying. Fifteen seconds in that midtown steam bath and dark stains spread down the armpits of my blouse. I was pumped when I pressed a shiny aluminum doorknob into my fist and twisted. I'd sweet-talk my way past the official yellow tape, get vivid comments from witnesses, write my way to page one and save my job.

I had it all planned out, but the doorknob wouldn't cooperate. The blasted knob didn't turn, so I pressed on the door. It didn't budge. I found a TV camera peering down and waved. "Buzz me in, will you?" What was taking the cops so long? Were they going to keep me outside until the rest of the press arrived?

My stomach began to churn. I'd missed breakfast, such as that ever was. Lunch was really my only meal. My stomach was telling me to find a Mickey D's somewhere and appease my hunger with a cholesterol bomb of a hamburger. Salt and grease, my kind of health food.

I bent toward the shiny windows, trying to peer through reflections of the street. Seeing inside was impossible. Finding no intercom, I rapped on the glass and waited. My feet shifted and I felt a shoe drag on the pavement. Something sticky was oozing under the door. I shivered when I looked at the fluid on the sidewalk. It was blood. Saul hadn't been kidding. This part of the story I could do without. People getting hurt wasn't necessary. But there were shattered lives here to report and I'd do the job.

There was a sliver of alley between the office building and its tall neighbor. I told myself it didn't make any sense to go through that alley. I'd just get my new blazer dirty and have to send it to the dry cleaner. I'd spotted a Donna Karan jacket at 80% off when I researched the Garment District piece. But a moment later, I found myself carefully moving down the alley, trying to avoid its soot-coated walls. I waited at the end, standing in dark shadow, quietly brushing gray soot off a coat sleeve.

Why was I so worried? The police must be here. But where were the other squad cars? I saw only a UPS truck idling near a green dumpster. I glanced at the truck and saw a driver inside, chatting on a cell phone. There was no way I could know the UPS driver was Richie Shaw and five minutes ago he'd been talking with Saul Morgenthal, claiming he'd done a bunch of killings. Now Richie was bragging to Howard Stern, but I couldn't hear the details of Shaw's conversation from where I stood.

I peered at the back door of the election headquarters. Everything looked safe, didn't it? I walked toward the door, feeling myself breathing a little too fast. Calm down, Drew. You have to get that story. You can't go back empty-handed. Saul will fire you.

I took a deep breath and faded into the dark hallway. The loud clatter of midtown Manhattan was muted to a dull surf of traffic along the boulevard. The only loud noise was a chattering jackhammer, ripping up sidewalk for another of the ceaseless repairs needed to keep a giant city running.

Halfway down the corridor, a short man in UPS uniform backed out of a room. We collided with a mutual grunt. When he turned, the gleeful look on his face twisted my guts. His cold eyes seemed wired straight to an icy mind. A gun came up and pointed right at my face. There was a slight click, followed by another. His eyes showed irritation. A clip fell out of the gun, clattered against the floor and a new clip of bullets appeared in his hand. The gun barrel seemed huge to my eyes, made even larger by the silencer at the end, looking like the thick foam windscreen used on microphones to interview people in bad weather.

It slowly dawned on my scattered brain that I'd walked right in the middle of things. The taxi hadn't hit a single red light. I'd gotten to the election headquarters so fast the killers were still there. I stumbled, trying to back out of the hallway. I looked for a place to hide and saw none. On one side, the corridor opened into a stockroom. Metal industrial shelves held bathroom tissue, bottled water, coffee in foil pouches and campaign banners. I turned around. The gunman's face was contorted and his gun was coming up again.

I threw myself at a door and it mercifully flew open. When I slammed the door closed, it was pitch black inside the room. The killer's footsteps came to the door and stopped. I groped for the lock and found it before he did. I felt his violent twisting, fighting against me as I locked the knob.

He whined sadistically through the door. "It won't do you any goo-ood."

The gun, I thought. He's going to shoot off the lock. Oh God, he'll go right through that door and get me. I twisted around and tripped over a mop. I was about to kick the mop away when I realized the handle could be jammed against the door. It worked. The broomstick acted like a brace you bought for your front door, preventing someone from breaking into your apartment, even if they tore out the lock. Just like cramming for a test in college. I was always best under pressure. A crazy thought when someone was trying to kill you, but that's the way my mind works.

A burst of silenced gunfire spattered wood chips into my hands. The splinters burned my fingers. Light poked through bullet holes in the door. The pencils of light shot at me like daggers. I knew the bathroom was tiny, but I still tried to run away. I slammed into a metal wall. The blow sent pinpoints of light darting across my eyes. I was stunned for a moment. He opened up with the gun and I tried to get on the floor, slipped and fell hard against cold tile. My temple collided with a toilet, shocking me with a bolt of pain and making me dizzy.

I lay on the floor and realized it was quiet. No, there was another sound, one that gave me comfort. Sirens. Police were coming to save me. It was safe now, it had to be safe. Finally, the cops were here and this clown had to leave. I told myself to get up, even thought I was getting up, but cold tile still pressed into me. I managed to lift my face. I heard two men arguing with each other, screaming.

The UPS driver's voice quavered in the hallway. "Gimme the automatic."

"Right," the gunman drawled in sarcasm.

"What do you mean?" The UPS driver sounded like a child simpering at having a favorite toy taken away.

"Get back to the truck," the killer insisted. "I'm doing this hit. You can do the next one."

"Why?"

"Because you're too hopped-up, that's why."

"I can do it," the UPS driver whimpered. "I shot good in Jersey, at that gun club. You said so."

"You hit targets. People ain't paper targets, kid. You gotta be calm and make sure there's no witnesses. So I'm going in there, not you."

"Then I don't get credit. I want credit for killing them."

"Relax. You get the credit," the gunman snorted.

Then the submachine gun started again, cutting the room like a ghostly chainsaw. Each bullet hit the wall with a soft poof, sending chips of metal divider and tile flailing around my head. I curled in a ball, tight as I could make it. Just when I knew it would go on forever, knew I couldn't stand any more, the gunfire stopped. Footsteps ran along the hallway and clanged into the UPS truck. But I didn't move. I just lay on the floor, trembling, grateful to be alive.

In a few minutes, I got off the bathroom floor and stumbled into the reception lobby. At first the area looked normal, just another office with filing cabinets, chairs and desks. But this reception area had a security guard sprawled over a glazed planter. A potted palm lay crushed beneath the guard's body and spilled dirt buried his hands. There was a gory trail smeared on the wall, left as the guard slumped to the floor. I tried to pretend the guard was an illusion, a bad dream like the dead receptionist toppled over a desk, arms flopped like a rag doll. But this rag doll had a shattered head. My eyes focused on bullet holes in her face and my stomach lurched. Bile etched my throat, burning like acid searing a pattern into glass.

I collapsed into a chair and looked at my fingers. They were torn. Clotted blood scabbed the knuckles on both hands. A dandruff of tile chips speckled my blazer and it was smeared with white dust. I exhaled a brief, ironic laugh. In the alley, I'd worried about getting a little soot on my new blazer's cuff.

I stared vacantly through mini-blinds on the front windows. I needed to see reality. Where I was sitting couldn't be real. It was too insane. I looked at brilliant orange streaks of light, the sun painting the glass cubes of the Museum of Modern Art. The beginning of the lunchtime crush was on the sidewalks, flowing out of doorways. How could I reconcile people walking past me, going to lunch, with bits of flesh scattered across the floor, blood running under the front door? I couldn't.

My dull musings were ended by heavy footsteps tramping along the hallway, chased by their echoes. Everything seemed to be a dream.

The dream spoke. "Hey Drew, you OK?"

I tried to straighten my posture and couldn't. I saw the dream's black orthopedic shoes and talked to them. "OK? Who can be all right in this place?"

A shadow moved in front of me. I heard the leather squeak of an equipment belt and realized the shadow belonged to a police officer. I forced myself to look up. The policeman was wearing mirrored sunglasses, the kind peepers use at the beach for staring at string bikinis, thinking they're being subtle. I saw my distorted reflection in his silver lenses, curved like a funhouse mirror. I looked drowsy from shock.

My eyes refocused on his face and I recognized him as a black police sergeant I knew. My lips were so dry I could only mutter. "Hello, Sid. We have to stop meeting like this."

He drawled, "What happened to you, Morrissey? You're supposed to report crimes, not get in them."

"Very funny, Sid. I thought you guys were here already. There was a cruiser out front. What was that cop doing? Hitting on some babe?"

"He was me, Drew. I was on break in a Starbucks around the corner. I didn't know you needed me or I would'a run over and played Vin Diesel."

Footsteps rumbled along the hallway again. I turned to see Benson running down the corridor, fumbling with his camera. There was a sudden flash and shocking white light stabbed my eyes.

Sid frowned. "Hey, Benson, cut that out. I'll catch hell if they find you here, before techs go over the scene."

I had a suggestion for Benson. "*The Chronicle* can't print photos of bodies, anyway. Why don't you go outside and take a picture of the building?"

Benson sulked away. He knew I was right. I twiddled the wand on the mini-blinds and looked out. I saw chaos. Ambulances were stopped in the middle of 53rd Street with their dome lights strobing. Paramedics yanked out gurneys. NYPD patrol cars screamed down the street and flung themselves around the ambulances. A half dozen police rushed ahead of medics and pounced up the stairs.

Sid's radio squawked. I asked him, "Did you get the guys who did this?"

"Yeah, Drew, we've had all of five minutes. They been tried and convicted. Made the front cover of *People* magazine. You guys from *The Chronicle* are behind."

"I wasn't ragging on you, Sid. One of them was in a UPS truck out back. He was talking on a cellular. Ask the precinct what they know, will you? I'll make sure you get mentioned in the article. Front page."

Sid rolled his eyes. "Me and the President, real front page stuff. If I call, you and Mr. Flash Bulbs leave, right?" Sid talked into a radio mike on the collar of his NYPD jacket.

Police were banging on the door. I opened it. The cops ran past, guns pulled. They checked every room, looking a little sick. It was exactly the way I'd felt coming down the hallway, turning my head into open doors. Each room had a tragedy written on walls, floors, tables.

In my mind, I walked down the hallway again. I saw killings that were done in an exact, professional style. The shooter was no Gulf War vet blasting random bullets. The people had been shot in the forehead, twice. Nothing was chewed up except the bathroom where I'd hidden.

"Excuse me," I whispered, pushing past the cops milling in the hallway.

One of them stopped me. "Hey Miss, where're you going?"

"To the bathroom. I don't want to throw up on the floor." I twisted my face.

"Don't touch anything. We haven't dusted for prints."

"Don't worry. Hands off." I wagged my hands to show I wouldn't disturb anything.

I went past rooms strewn with bodies, straight to the shattered bathroom door. I had to see it again. It didn't feel real. But my ordeal definitely happened, only a few minutes ago. A brass chunk of doorknob lay in the sink. On the floor was a mop, the handle cut in pieces, chewed by bullets. Ceramic shrapnel was scattered across the floor. The stall door twisted on just the top hinge. Drops of my blood on the toilet hadn't yet dried. My temple throbbed from colliding with the porcelain toilet.

Sid punched my arm. "I checked with precinct like you wanted."

"And?" I waited.

"They got nothing. Not yet, anyhow."

"Great." I sagged against the bathroom doorframe.

"Hey, Drew, don't mess up the fingerprints," he complained.

I turned to face Sid. "I don't think you'll find any prints, Sid. Whoever did this was a pro. Look around. He knew what he was doing."

Sid looked at me like I was crazy, then jiggled his bulk down the hallway.

I called after him. "Thanks for checking with the precinct, Sid." I stared again at the bathroom. There was a large area on the floor with no chips in it, the outline of where I'd been lying. Why would someone hire a pro to hit an election headquarters for a small political party with no clout? My mind didn't have an answer for that question. The carnage in this election headquarters made no sense to me.

I shook my head to clear away cobwebs and walked out the back door into the alley. The UPS truck was gone, replaced by police cruisers. There was no point in hanging around. There were no leads. I had no way of pursuing the story. I decided to go home and clean up. I could at least be well dressed when Saul fired me.

2

After showering, I stood in an open apartment window and closed my eyes, letting summer rain soothe my face. I knew I was feeling better when my stomach growled, demanding food. I had a lone Butterfinger in my laptop bag, but a candy bar wouldn't touch the hunger I felt. The smell of burnt olive oil drifted through the open window, courtesy of a cheap Italian restaurant on my block. The eatery was a storefront with a single waiter and plastic tablecloths, doing a brisk neighborhood business. The food wasn't bad, but I couldn't "go Italian" unless I paid for the meal – and a lot of others. I'd worn out my credibility as a *New York Chronicle* reporter and the owners were no longer willing to put lunch on my "tab."

My roommate Donovan could help me out. He owed his share of this month's rent and I debated confronting him. That wouldn't be a nice way to treat an old friend, someone I'd known since high school. Besides, the time to ask Donovan for money was early Sunday morning, when he dragged home from tending bar in SoHo. He'd be flush with tips from the weekend scene, where people drink for hours and flip the bartender a twenty to impress their date.

I opened my eyes and looked down. Benches edging Central Park were filled with gang kids in windbreakers. They glowered at me and put their plastic boom boxes on a stone wall. Angry rap music thumped from the boom boxes, bringing the gang-bangers' sullen rage to me. Thanks, guys.

My place had its drawbacks. Still, it was 800 square feet of rent-controlled space overlooking Central Park West. I'd leased it straight out of college and hung on desperately, with the help of roommates. I loved the place, even if gang-bangers gave me a "concert" when I least needed the hassle.

I shut the window and walked barefoot across the cool hardwood floor. In 1930, maple was cheap and the wood of choice for my then-elegant art deco apartment building. My stereo was mixed between books and discs heaped on cheap particleboard shelving. The boards rested on cinder blocks, a student decor I'd hoped to toss out years ago, at the magical moment when my real life began. It was frightening to admit the truth – this was my real life.

Still in shock from the election headquarters violence, I didn't check the stereo's volume after selecting a favorite FM station. Bass riffs reverberated like cannons and a neighbor thumped the wall in protest. I lowered the sound and blew my law-school neighbor a loud "sorry." One day he'd graduate and sue.

I moved to a dining table that doubled as my living room furniture, leaving the lights off. Normally music eased my anxiety but this time it didn't work. Madonna's latest try at making the charts failed to compete with a kitchen light shining on a clutter of unfinished projects. It was amazing how well a distant 60 watt bulb spotlit thwarted goals.

The dim bulb highlighted a stack of cardboard tubes holding Metropolitan Museum of Art posters. Unframed Impressionist Masters languished next to paint cans and roller trays. My ambitious "someday" tasks were strewn across a door propped on sawhorses. The door served as my desk in college and was now a workbench for refinishing the apartment. I consoled myself, saying I was a great opener, while others shined in reaching closure. On honest days, I admitted I'd never paint these depressing walls. I was too busy scrounging a living.

Clearly the music was no help in unwinding. I walked along the hallway, following the stare of the bare bulb in my kitchenette. My computer niche was squeezed in the kitchen pantry area, where I plugged my Apple laptop into an Internet connection and a printer-scanner-fax combo machine. In my grand plan, the computer gear was relocated to a spare bedroom. I wondered how many years it would be before I could afford this apartment without roommates, so there'd be another bedroom to use as my office? True answer was probably never.

A wall phone blinked in the pantry, counting unanswered voicemail messages. The light winked four times and paused. I replayed the messages, hoping one was from Jamie. That got me a broken heart again. The first call was a guilt trip from my mother. Luckily, it was too late to call her back. She was at work. Megan had Knicks tickets and a blind date for me. I winced, recalling her last fix-up, an accountant with sweaty palms. The vet asked me to authorize surgery on Nintendo, my cat. His leg was broken on a fire escape, chasing the neighbor's white Persian in heat. The last call was my heavy breather with threatening sexual innuendos. If he ever quit calling, I'd lose my daily laugh. I hung up the phone, more stressed than when I'd entered the apartment.

A little TV hunkered on a plant shelf above the kitchen sink. Maybe there was an update about the election headquarters killings on a news broadcast. I watched a perfect, hair-sprayed anchorwoman announce, "The noon lead story is the sad conclusion to this morning's fatal violence at a midtown election headquarters. Nine people died and now a tenth. We replay our News Cam footage of Detective Lindquist giving a press conference at police headquarters."

In a video effect, the anchorwoman shrank away and I was looking at a rugged, masculine face. Staring over a bundle of microphones, Lindquist cleared his throat and spoke. "This morning, SWAT units forced entry to the suspect's apartment in Chinatown. They found him without pulse or respiration. SWAT team members found an Israeli-made submachine in the apartment. Ballistic examination of the gun proved it was the weapon used at the crime scene. This concludes our case. We wish it was possible to resolve all homicides in such a prompt fashion. Certainly the NYPD is glad we could do it in this case."

There was a barrage of questions screamed at the detective. Lindquist palmed the crowd to quiet down and pointed at a reporter in the front row.

The reporter stood. "Lieutenant, was it this man who called a radio program and claimed credit for the killings?"

"Yes." Lindquist didn't blink. He looked confident.

"How do you know that?"

The Lieutenant didn't consult his notes before answering. "Verizon logged a call to the Howard Stern Show from the perpetrator's cellular phone at exactly the time corresponding to the show's recording of the event. Also, the caller gave his name as Richie Shaw, same as the dead man found in Chinatown."

Another reporter shouted, "Lieutenant! What was the motive for the killings?"

"He discussed his motives with Howard Stern and CNN *Headline News* before he died. I'm not a psychiatrist. I can't speculate on what causes people to commit violent crimes. I just arrest them."

A woman in the second row asked, "Was Shaw's death murder or suicide?"

"It appears Shaw committed suicide. He left no suicide note, however. The Coroner's office concluded the suspect died from heart seizure induced by an overdose of methamphetamines, combined with high alcohol intake. An empty champagne bottle containing traces of meth was found on the premises, confirming the diagnosis."

"What else can you tell us about the killer?"

Lindquist recited facts from a sheet of paper in front of him. "Suspect was a Caucasian male, age 19. He went by the name of Richie. Mr. Shaw was a UPS employee with the election headquarters on his regular delivery route. Shaw had undergone psychiatric therapy twice, but had no priors, that is, no previous arrests. He was a member of a Jersey gun club. They confirmed Shaw had taken the murder weapon out for practice. He shot a dozen clips the weekend before this incident occurred."

The anchorwoman returned, with her co-host. I didn't hear them. I was stunned Lindquist didn't mention an accomplice. Could the cops be withholding that data because they were checking out a lead? Yeah, that was it. So why was I feeling queasy?

The news played out with its normal assortment of entertainment fads, weather and sports, punctuated by loud commercials. Finally, the anchorpersons came back. "Now as we close, we'll play for you a sort of requiem for our times. Here's the audio of Howard Stern's interview with the late Richie Shaw. For WABC, have a good day. We'll see you again at five."

Credits rolled. I recognized Howard Stern talking. "Why are you so proud of yourself? It's murder in the first degree. You're making even me believe in the death penalty."

The next voice belonged to a brassy, nasal Brooklyn kid. It was the same voice that screamed inside the election headquarters, "We've got to leave. The cops are here." But it wasn't the killer talking. I flashed on another voice, a flat monotone saying, "Bang, you're dead" as a gun came up and pointed at my face. It was dumb luck his submachine gun was out of bullets or I'd be on a stainless steel table in the morgue.

Lindquist said Richie Shaw died of champagne laced with methamphetamines. To me, that meant the accomplice killed Richie, probably forced the kid at gunpoint to drink the entire bottle of champagne. The meth flavor would have been noticeable, but Shaw had no choice. He was going to die one way or the other. Why? Because Richie knew too much about the accomplice and he wouldn't hesitate to kill me for the same reason – I could identify him. I'd seen his face. I could pick the accomplice out of a police lineup. That made me a prime target for murder. What did Richie call this other guy, the one who almost killed me? The name floated just out of reach.

I scanned the New York telephone directory to get an address for the midtown precinct. My gut instinct screamed how important it was to tell Lindquist that Shaw had an accomplice. I knew Lindquist would hate reopening a case after bragging on TV, saying he'd solved the crime. My mother didn't raise a total fool. I needed juice, clout to help me persuade Lindquist to reopen the case.

I called the midtown station and asked for an appointment with the precinct chief, Captain O'Shaughnessy. They fit me into O'Shaughnessy's busy calendar. It helps to say you're from *The New York Chronicle*.

I got dressed, full of righteous confidence. I was going to get help and be safe – or so I thought. Dream on, Morrissey. Nothing is ever that simple.

3

I sat in Captain O'Shaughnessy's office and let my eyes roam the walls, where bright sunlight glared off awards and photographs. The walls were covered in photo-ops of O'Shaughnessy in the company of VIPs, snapshots taken at St. Patrick's Day parades and other ceremonies. Image quality varied from amateur to pro, yet the pictures were always mounted in the same cheap frame, plastic tinted to resemble wood.

O'Shaughnessy's office wasn't painted the same color as the rest of the precinct station, an institutional green. The Captain's personal space was bright yellow and his carpet was new, though his rug was the generic type that can only be supplied by a least-cost-bidder. New carpeting was the lone modern item in O'Shaughnessy's office. A 1950s executive desk bent in an arc echoed by a curved sofa and round chairs. All the furniture was wrapped in orange naugehyde upholstery. The style was state-of-the-art fifty years ago, when people watched *Leave It To Beaver* in black and white on round TV screens.

Now the furnishings seemed aged and distressed, which was how I felt at that moment. The Captain was forty minutes late for his appointment with me. I took a sip of coffee from a thick porcelain mug and held it for encouragement. The coffee cup was empty long before the door finally opened and O'Shaughnessy shook my hand. "The Mayor, God bless him, is always rearranging priorities for me. I apologize, Ms. Morrissey, I do, but it couldn't be helped."

O'Shaughnessy was a burly man with the restless eyes and careful movements of a politician. He worked his bulk around the desk and sat in a tall-backed executive chair. The Captain reached in his parade-dress uniform for keys to unlock the desk and pulled out his calendar. He stole a glance at today's page and winced, letting me know how lucky I was to have an appointment with him, without saying anything.

O'Shaughnessy folded his hands on the calendar and gave me his most charming Irish smile. His tobacco-stained teeth explained the heavy odor of cigarette smoke lingering in his office despite "no smoking" signs plastered across the precinct station. Captain O'Shaughnessy talked in a respectful tone he'd practiced many times. "I understand you're a key witness to today's tragedy at an election headquarters. We certainly want to know about your experience, Ms. Morrissey."

"Yes, Captain. I was there when –" I stopped as the door opened behind me and the Captain looked up.

"Perfect timing," O'Shaughnessy said, partially standing. "Ms. Morrissey, may I introduce Sam Lindquist, our detective in charge of investigating the election headquarters shooting?"

I turned to see the same face I'd watched on TV, blinking at dozens of microphones. Curly gray hair covered Lindquist's head like steel wool. He shook my hand and mumbled, "Pleased to meet you." He was at home on the crime scene and putting on manners to greet me was a strain for Lindquist. The detective sat on the sofa and his sports coat fell open, revealing a badge clipped on his belt and an empty holster. Inside the station, cops keep their handguns in a safe to prevent accidents. Lindquist crossed his legs, exposing a scuffed shoe in need of repair.

Captain O'Shaughnessy gestured a large hand at me. "I was just telling Ms. Morrissey how the department is very interested in her impression of the election headquarters homicides. She was on the scene and has information that could be helpful to us." O'Shaughnessy added with a very unsubtle change in tone, "Ms. Morrissey is a reporter for *The New York Chronicle*."

At mention of *The Chronicle*, Lindquist's eyes brightened. His face turned away from me and toward the Captain. Lindquist nodded, acknowledging that he understood O'Shaughnessy's warning to be careful around me.

Captain O'Shaughnessy locked his desk, pocketing the keys. "Detective Lindquist, would you sit in for me? I'm afraid, Ms. Morrissey, that I must leave. I know it's rude to be going so soon, after just getting here and making your acquaintance. But I'm afraid it can't be helped."

The Captain rose and carefully skirted between the massive desk and Lindquist's shoes, jutting from the sofa. "Sam, feel free to use my chair. That way you can take good notes." O'Shaughnessy gave me a generous smile and shook my hand.

The door closed and Lindquist sighed. He rose from the couch and went behind the desk. Lindquist sat on the edge of the Captain's chair and took a spiral-bound pad from his coat, flipping lined pages to find a clean sheet.

"May I have your full name, Ms. Morrissey?" Lindquist stared at the pencil in his hand, not at me.

"It's Drew Morrissey." I spelled my name, gave my address and the phone numbers for home and work.

"What exactly did you see?" Lindquist looked at my face, sizing me up.

"Richie Shaw didn't do the killing. He was in a UPS truck parked behind the election headquarters, talking on his cell phone with Howard Stern. There was a second man inside the building, using a submachine gun with a silencer."

He didn't want to believe me. It meant reopening the case after announcing on TV that the crime was solved. An enigmatic smile played on his lips, then his face went blank again. "Really? You're certain you witnessed a second man?"

"Yes." Be cool, I told myself. He's baiting you.

"Who was the second man?" Lindquist's voice was flat as a corpse in the morgue.

"The gunman was shorter than Richie. Built like a jockey. At least ten years older than Shaw. I ran into the real killer in the hallway. He tried to shoot me, but I jumped in a bathroom."

"You saw both men together?" Lindquist poised the pencil, as though to take a note.

"Well, no . . ." I was upset with myself for sounding defensive.

"So you never really saw the two men together." He said it politely, yet there was a razor edge on the words.

"No. But I heard them talking. Two very different voices, a pair of men. I think –"

Lindquist interrupted. "Excuse me, Ms. Morrissey, but how would you know what Shaw sounded like?

"They played Shaw's voice on TV this morning. Shaw spoke with a Brooklyn accent nobody could miss. The gunman's voice was flavorless, like he'd been coached how to speak, the way a TV news anchor is trained. It's what they call mid-Atlantic."

"When did you first see this accomplice?"

"I entered the election headquarters through its back door. I ran into the gunman in the hallway."

"Why didn't he kill you?" Lindquist stared at me.

"He tried to shoot me. But his gun just clicked. He stopped to put more bullets in the gun and I ran into a bathroom, shutting the door."

"Can you ID this guy?"

"Yes."

"OK. Go on." He nodded, but the pencil still wasn't making any notes. " You ran in a bathroom and ...?"

"I locked the door. I was afraid he'd shoot me through the thin door. I looked for a place to hide. Then I slipped and fell. That was actually lucky, because I was lying on the floor when he fired through the wall. I thought the gunshots would never end, but eventually he ran out of bullets. That's when I heard Shaw talking to the killer." Suddenly I remembered what Shaw called the other man. "Richie called this other guy 'Elijah.' Maybe that's some help in tracing him."

Lindquist finally made a note. "Elijah was probably a code name unique to this job and can't be used to trace the hit man to other crimes. Still, it was worth mentioning. Go on. What happened next?"

"I don't know exactly." I thought for a moment. "Oh, yes, I heard sirens and Shaw —"

"Police sirens?" Lindquist was staring at me now. "So there were more people in the area at this point?"

I knew what Lindquist was thinking. He could sweep this second man away by saying Morrissey was scared and confused. She mixed up the good guys and the bad guy. There was only Shaw at the election headquarters. The other man Morrissey heard was a cop.

"Look," I said firmly, "there were no police inside the election headquarters when Shaw and Elijah were there. After they left, I went down the hall and saw the dead security guard. A police sergeant I know, Sid Hawthorne, found me sitting in the reception area ten minutes later. He was the first cop on the scene and Sid is all Harlem. He doesn't talk like a TV news anchor."

Lindquist nodded and made more notes. Finally, he looked up from the pad. "How much time elapsed between when the killer shot at you and when you left the election headquarters?"

"I don't know. About fifteen minutes, I think."

"You didn't wait to file a report with us?"

"I told Sid what happened – and I'm here now to file a report."

"Yes, I see. Is there anything more you'd like to add to your account of the election headquarters?"

"Elijah is out there. He may try to kill me. Are you going to do something about it?"

"Try to kill you … why?" Lindquist shrugged. He wasn't stupid. He knew why. He just wanted me to tell him.

"I saw Elijah at the election headquarters. I can ID him. He's better off with me dead."

"Has he tried to kill you since the election headquarters? Made an attempt on your life?"

"No. But it's not like Elijah's had a lot of time. It's only been a few hours."

Lindquist closed his notepad. He leaned back, debating what to do. Finally, he picked up the phone and buzzed the intercom. "Ask Sally to come in here. Yes, now." He hung up and twirled the pencil for a while.

The door opened and a policewoman walked inside the office. "What do you need, Lieutenant?"

"Have a seat." Lindquist pointed to the curving sofa. He turned to me and talked slowly, being careful with his words. "Ms. Morrissey, you've been through a lot. I appreciate your coming to see us. We'll do what we can to track down this accomplice, but there isn't much to go on. We got a partial print from the back door for Richie Shaw, but nothing else we couldn't identify. In fact, you're listed as having been at the election headquarters, matched from your driver's license fingerprint, but we thought nothing of it at the time." He got up and the policewoman also rose. "Sally will show you out."

I stayed in the chair. "I'm not crazy, Detective. I saw the real killer at the election headquarters. He was a short man with curly hair, in his thirties. Richie called him Elijah."

Lindquist was unfazed. "You never really saw both men together. You said there were sirens. The second voice could have been a police officer in the street."

"I'm not confused. I know who did the killing. It was Elijah, not Richie Shaw. I saw Shaw's picture on TV and he's not the killer. Look, Elijah murdered Richie Shaw so he couldn't identify Elijah as the gunman. I'm next to die, for the same reason. I need help."

Lindquist glanced toward the policewoman, then back at me. "Ms. Morrissey, I can offer you protective custody. It's the standard treatment we give a material witness to a major crime. You stay with us at the city jail, in a cell. It'll take us a few days, perhaps a week, to check out your lead on Elijah."

He looked smug. Lindquist had a right to feel cocky. In case anything happened to me, he'd covered his tail beautifully. I'd been offered absolute protection at no cost to the city. It was my problem if I refused to spend a week inhaling drunk tank smells – urine, vomit and worse. When I got out, the meager personal items on my desk would greet me in *The Chronicle* lobby, shoved in a cardboard box by Saul.

I shook my head in amazement. "You have the case closed and you want it that way, no matter what."

Lindquist didn't flinch. He stood there, blankly. I felt the policewoman's firm hand on my arm. I shook her off and turned for the door. "I'll print my story in *The Chronicle*. Maybe that'll get your attention."

He just shrugged. The policewoman pressed on my back. I was to leave. Sally trailed me to the front door of the precinct house and shut it behind me.

I was alone. Captain O'Shaughnessy did his politician's dance and left me in Lindquist's tender, loving care. Lindquist covered his tail and kicked me out. A second killer made Lindquist into a fool, after holding a TV press conference saying the case was closed, wrapped in a ribbon.

I didn't hate Lindquist for his attitude. He and O'Shaughnessy were trying to survive in their jobs, like I was trying to survive in mine. Helping me meant admitting they'd made a mistake.

So I was on my own, me versus a professional hit man. Needless to say, pepper spray seemed inadequate. Elijah would laugh at the mace can. Then he'd turn my face into a shattered mask, like he did to the receptionist in the election headquarters. I was screwed and there was nothing I could do about it, which made me furious.

I let my rage wear off over scalding coffee from a sidewalk cart. While the java cooled, I bought a giant pretzel and painted it with mustard. I ate in my usual rushed style, smearing mustard on my chin and burning my tongue with boiled coffee. Mid-pretzel, my pager went off, playing its electronic version of Mozart. I read a text entry on the little screen and felt sick. It was a short message from my boss, Saul Morgenthal – where's my story?

I had to call Saul back. I couldn't say there were no leads. I had to be working an angle to get some slack from Morgenthal. A professional killer shooting at me wouldn't faze him. Saul was always bottom line – do you have a story for me or not? So could I get Saul his story? The only fact I had was Richie Shaw lived and died in Chinatown. I had to visit Shaw's apartment in Chinatown and see if I could turn up something the police missed.

Coffee and pretzel went in the trash instead of my stomach. I moved briskly toward the nearest subway entrance. Several near-misses with pedestrians brought me to reality. I was running, not walking. My legs slowed but my heart rate didn't. It was a toss-up who frightened me more, Elijah or Saul. Getting fired by Morgenthal would also kill me. It'd just take longer to die. In that respect, Elijah was merciful compared to Saul.

4

NYPD still had Canal and Baxter sealed with barricades, staffed by a dozen cops I'd never met. With these guys, my press credentials were useless, as was my girlish charm. Even residents couldn't get past the barriers. I leaned against the cleanest building I could find, watching sunlight fade across the Schwab brokerage pagoda. The brokerage was closed but its neon tickertape still marched like army ants, ticking off prices in Hong Kong, Singapore, Cairo, London, you name it.

A Starbucks in the pagoda's ground floor became my "office," where I nursed a Java Chip Frappuccino and tried to call Saul. Mercifully, the battery on my cell phone was dead. The unhappy store manager made a point of asking every few minutes if I wanted to buy another drink. I ran out of cheerful ways to say no and resumed my watch outside, elbows resting on a police barricade.

It was almost 6:00 P.M. before NYPD cleared out and I could talk to the manager of Richie Shaw's apartment house, Lech Ulaklowski. I wheedled the use of a phone from Ulaklowski. He made me feel like I was in jail, using my one call to plead with a bail bondsman. I stood in the narrow entry hall, holding a 1970s princess phone, trying to look "important." It wasn't easy to look important when Saul Morgenthal was running over my ego with his steamroller personality.

I fought back. "Saul, I'm in Chinatown, about to get into Richie Shaw's apartment. You know, the guy who confessed on Howard Stern. I've been stranded for hours while police techies went over the place. I got an angle no one else has. I was there, at the election headquarters. They shot at me in the hallway. You still need these election killings covered and I –
"

"We already did a piece on the election headquarters." Saul bit through a crisp deli pickle and chomped into the phone. I knew he was doing it to annoy me. His rudeness didn't hurt. It was cutting me out of the story that sliced me like a kitchen knife.

"Who wrote the column?" I let more of the hurt show in my voice than I should.

Saul Morgenthal bellowed in my ear. "Just another reporter. We got a few at *The Chronicle*. I took most of it off the wire. Reuters has shooting details in neon on the front of their building. Morrissey, let me remind you of something. Cutoff is normally at 11:30 A.M. sharp. Then I take the story to the noon staff meeting, where our charitable and beloved Executive Editor presides.

I wedged in a one word protest. "But –"

Morgenthal ignored me and continued his lecture. "I'm the desk head for New York City local, in case you didn't realize it. I don't just drop your prose on a plate and run the presses. I edit it first, before the page one meeting, not after. Lockup for page one is at 6 P.M. For big stories I can get an exception. They grant damned few exceptions, but I can get 'em. That Garment District fire was going to be a big story, Drew. You remember how you promised me it was a big story, Drew?"

"Saul, it just didn't break that way. Don't be so small minded. I can email a portrait of Richie Shaw before you start printing at –"

"We cut plates in three minutes, Morrissey. Write fast. Email it and I'll see. Maybe I can put a postscript on page ten. Some local color. Better yet, I'll put it on the society page. That's where old gossip belongs."

"No one at the *Daily News* even followed this lead. Oh Saul, I got a big one all to myself. I –"

"Did it ever occur to you, Morrissey, why no one is there? Richie Shaw isn't worth covering."

I persisted like a drowning woman paddling in the middle of the Atlantic Ocean. "I'm in the manager's apartment. He wants a hundred bucks for a private look at Shaw's place. You're gonna cover me on that hundred, right Saul?" I'd work the cab ride in later – if there was a later.

"Try *The National Enquirer.*" There was a click and the dial tone buzzed in my ear. My stomach sank like a concrete block.

I had to bluff my way through this one. My only hope for redemption was to find something unique inside the apartment. If I went back empty-handed, I'd be covering lost dog stories, assuming I covered stories at all. I winked at the apartment manager and continued like I was still talking to Saul. "Yeah. Great. Four piece series, front page. Runs this week, right? And I can have mister, uh, hold on Saul." I covered the mouthpiece and shrugged at the manager. "Sorry, I forgot your last name . . ."

He dragged out the name so I'd understand. "Yoo laaa klowww skiiii."

"Uh, Saul, Mr. Ulaklowski will be coming in tomorrow. You'll have the petty cash at reception, right? OK, yeah. I'll give him a voucher. I don't have the form, but my signature will do, right? Great. Love ya too, Bro. Bye."

I rummaged through my pockets for a scrap of paper. The only clean piece was the back of a note on the Garment District fire. I smoothed out the wrinkles and wrote a pretentious-sounding IOU. I hoped it would impress Ulaklowski. "There." I handed him the paper fragment.

Lech Ulaklowski squinted at my IOU through watery eyes. Sausage-like fingers handed the scrap back. "Not enough."

I groped for something to say. "I can't ask for more. It's settled with the editor."

"You write about this place, I'll never rent it again. No one wants to live where a corpse was found. Who wants to sleep with a dead man's ghost in the room?"

I had to persuade Ulaklowski this was all to his benefit. "Risk publicity? Are you kidding? You can double the rent because Shaw died here. People are fame suckers. They itch to breathe the air where something important happened."

Ulaklowski scratched the stubble on his chin. "I can't rent the place after you write about it. Six months, maybe a year, no money. I'm out one thousand dollars." He folded arms across his chest, standing firm on the thousand dollars.

His arithmetic didn't make sense. A year's rent was more than a thousand dollars. But it didn't matter. The guy saw his moment and figured I could sign for a hundred, so why not a thousand? I had to cave. Still, I didn't want Ulaklowski demanding more to see each room in the apartment. "Five hundred max and I go in alone."

"Seven fifty and I watch you every step. The cops will have my ass if they find you here."

"Five hundred is tops. The editor will fry my ass a lot worse than the cops for that sum." I bluffed for the door.

A firm hand grabbed my arm. Ulaklowski pushed the chit in front of me. "OK, five hundred. I go with you. Don't leave prints."

I grinned. I pulled cotton photo lab gloves from a pocket and flashed them. Benson's film fixation was good for something.

I scribbled an indecipherable sum on the paper, hoping I could contest it as being a mere two-fifty. Then we headed for the door of Richie Shaw's apartment. Ulaklowski pulled out a key ring tethered to the metal case on his belt. He knew Shaw's key by heart. The lock clicked. Ulaklowski lifted yellow police tape so I could duck under and push the door open.

Ugly smells came from the dark interior. Shaw lost control of his bowels when he died. The police hadn't aired the place out. I felt for a wall switch, flipped it and a weak fluorescent bulb flickered, spreading dingy light around the room. I stepped across the chalk outline where Shaw's body was found and went to the front window. I snapped the latch and cranked the window open for some air.

Ulaklowski shouted in a hoarse whisper. "Hey, you can't do that. Close it up."

"This way you hear the cops if they pull up. I'll close the window before I leave."

Ulaklowski scowled. "OK, I guess."

I stood in the open window where I could breathe without gagging. Red neon flashed Chinese characters in my face. An owner pulled a rusted grating across his restaurant. He secured the fence with a huge chrome padlock. Enough "ambience." I took a deep breath and turned around, surveying the room.

A mattress was shoved in one corner. Richie's sleeping bag lay wadded on the soiled mattress. The dirty edge of his pillow jutted from the messy pile. Magazines were crudely tossed in a plastic milk carton. I ventured closer and switched on a gooseneck lamp.

All the magazines were thumbed like Yellow Pages at a pay phone. Their glossy covers showed oiled bodies with rippling stomachs and popped biceps. A plastic barbell sat at the foot of a weight bench. On the wall was a cork bulletin board, thumbtacked with health articles. There were also clippings of election headquarters violence. When a state congressman was shot in Florida, the murderer had center stage. The killer's picture was circled in red.

I stepped around underwear piled on the floor. In the closet, I pushed aside three sets of brown UPS uniforms. There was a pair of jeans and a white dress shirt. Then a muddy jogging suit. On the closet floor, generic running shoes had worn bottoms and the insides were rotted from sweat.

I turned to the manager. "This Richie Shaw, you ever see him do a workout?"

"All the time. Crazy kid ran laps at night, even in the rain. At the end of the month, I worried he'd get mugged and I'd be out the rent."

I noted Ulaklowski's concern for his renters and swallowed a sarcastic comment. I pointed to the weight set. "Seems Richie didn't just run. Pumped iron, too. Am I right?"

"Yeah. You stand in the hall, you hear him grunting. His neighbor once complained to me. The kid was thumping weights in the middle of the night. I told Richie to knock it off and he knocked it off. Muscles don't impress me."

I ignored his bragging. "Anybody ever visit Shaw? Girls maybe?"

"Nobody. Weird loner. But he paid on time."

I walked around Ulaklowski and jerked the bathroom door open. There was a chain dangling from the ceiling and I pulled. The naked bulb showed a toilet like gas station restrooms I'd been forced to use when driving cross-country. The filth was unreal. I lifted the lid of the toilet tank, the way narcs do in movies. There was no baggie filled with hashish, but then the cops might have taken the drugs.

"Any strangers come into the apartment building today, around the time Richie Shaw got home from work?"

The manager shuffled toward me. "Nobody to see him. I already covered that with the police."

"I gave you five hundred, remember? How about covering it with me?"

"The people who live here come and go. I don't pay special attention. I'm no snoop."

"Yeah, I'm sure. But was somebody else here today?"

"Say, there was someone. A Con Ed guy."

"Why did Con Ed come out? You call them?"

Ulaklowski scratched his belly. "No. It wasn't even the day to read the meter."

"You mention this to the cops?"

"Yeah."

"They check it out?"

"Naw, said it didn't matter."

"The Con Ed guy, was he carrying anything?"

"Yeah, a cardboard box. About the size of a shoe box. No, larger."

I fingered the stem of a plastic champagne glass and accidentally pulled the stem out of the bowl. I quickly jammed bowl and stem together under Ulaklowski's hot scowl. "You said the Con Ed guy carried a box. Was it big enough for a champagne bottle?"

"Yeah, that would fit."

"Did he leave with the box?"

"No. I figured he replaced somebody's meter 'cause they bitched about the bill."

"Thanks. That may be important. I'll call Con Ed, check it out. What did he look like?"

"Don't remember the face. Small, like a jockey. Quick movements."

I flashed on the sick face of the hit man in the election headquarters, dry firing his submachine gun at my head. He'd been small, like a jockey. He'd had quick movements. I felt electricity trickle along my spine. "You let the Con Ed guy in?"

"No. Someone else buzzed him in."

"Here long?"

"No. Fifteen minutes max."

I picked my way around a bug-eyed Bart Simpson doll and Blockbuster DVD's strewn over the floor. I squeezed into the kitchenette. The refrigerator was tiny, sitting on a wooden counter. The white cooler blocked a window venting to an air shaft. I opened the refrigerator. "Yogurt, carrot juice, alfalfa sprouts, a vegetarian burrito. Didn't this kid eat any real food?"

Ulaklowski snorted. "Wouldn't eat at Chinese places around here. Said peanut oil was lethal. Gives you bad cholesterol. Plus you can get a stroke from all the MSG. Me, I take the wife out every Friday night. Never bothered us."

I pulled open a microscopic freezer compartment, hardly large enough for the Lean Cuisine jammed inside. I went through kitchen cabinets, then started on the drawers. A potato peeler, a baster with cracked rubber bulb, three Game Boy cartridges. No photos of family, no scraps of handwriting. The place had the eerie unreality of an anonymous life. I tugged at a jammed drawer and forced it open. The bin was filled with napkins from Integral Yoga Natural Apothecary and Juice Bar. Another dead end. I tried to close the drawer and it stuck. I slapped the drawer in frustration.

"Hey, I told you. Don't wreck nothing." Ulaklowski glared at me.

"OK. Sorry."

I gently lifted the drawer to shut it and realized there was a color pamphlet at the bottom, under all the napkins. I took the brochure out and started reading. A smile bent the corners of my mouth.

"Hey, don't take nothing." Ulaklowski moved toward me, trying to look menacing.

I put the pamphlet back, but left my hand on it. "The police will never know if I take this brochure. Come on, Lech, be reasonable. You're getting your five hundred."

"Well, maybe. Long as I don't see it done." Ulaklowski turned toward the window and I folded the pamphlet into my coat pocket.

"You're making me nervous." He fiddled with his key ring. "Let's go. You got your money's worth." Ulaklowski hovered over me, clicking the keys on his ring.

I took a last look at the room. Richie, you stupid, needy kid. You had no idea you'd die, did you?

Ulaklowski escorted me out, worried I might take something else. He unlocked the worn outer door. I said an unrequited, "Thanks."

I stood in the apartment building's colonnade, looking at a parade of narrow facades, where rusting fire escapes marred the tired brick of walkups. Garish red and yellow signs blared this was Chinatown, in case anyone missed it. If they did, they read books in Braille.

God, how I needed Richie Shaw to be a real story. To make that happen, I'd have to tie the pamphlet in my coat pocket to the killings. The image of a short, quick Con Ed guy carrying a cardboard box flashed in my mind. That was a lead. I was sure he was the gunman who shot at me, in the election headquarters. It was time to go back to the office and search the on-line morgue, where old stories were kept. Maybe that would jump start an idea in my brain.

5

Problems hit me the moment I walked in the lobby of *The New York Chronicle*. I approached the bank of entry gates and ran the magnetic stripe on my ID badge through a swiper. The bars didn't retract with a whoosh like they usually did. Instead, a buzzer squawked and the barrier stayed in my way. The bars were made of a composite material used in Air Force stealth jets and harder than steel. Blue-shirted guards looked at me like I was a terrorist, not a reporter. I swiped my badge again, with the same result.

"You have to sign in, Ms. Morrissey." A guard at the desk waved me toward the guest register. She confiscated my badge and gave me a temporary ID. "It's only good for an hour. Guess they don't expect you to stay in the building."

"How reassuring," I said. I swiped the temp badge and it worked. Gate bars retracted with a pneumatic whoosh. I walked through the barrier on wobbly knees. I knew Saul was upset, but I hadn't expected it to be this bad. At least the elevator bank was still around the corner and hadn't moved. That much remained the same since I'd left the building this morning.

The first person I met in the newsroom was Harry Styman, known as "the Beak" for his bulbous nose. His eyes seemed pitying, but then they always looked watery and sad. The Beak turned his impressive nose in the direction of Saul's glass-walled office. "Morgenthal wants to see you." The Beak talked like a funeral director discussing "future arrangements" with a ninety-year-old widow.

My hand was in a coat pocket, nervously clutching the wrapper of a Butterfinger bar, last night's dinner when I couldn't afford real food. But I didn't let the Beak get to me. "Of course Saul wants to see me. It's that big raise he promised."

"I don't think so." Styman dragged his words out sarcastically. Then he shook my hand. "Been nice workin' with you, kid."

"Thanks Beak," was my irritated reply. The Beak walked away, searching for the next victim to receive an injection of his melancholy.

I headed for my workspace to make a quick call and check out a few facts in the "morgue." Then I left the island of crowded desks and walked toward Saul, watching Morgenthal through his office's glass wall. He was talking across his desk to Donna Pimberton. I bet she'd stolen my election headquarters story. I glared at Pimberton. If looks could kill, she'd at least be wounded. But Donna was too busy to notice me. She was practicing her "organizational advancement skills." Pimberton sat with a benign, daughter-like expression on her face, listening to Saul's every word and taking notes. Donna's thin legs were crossed and she bobbed a huge boot, moving it up and down like a pumping oil rig, matching the pace of her fast note-writing.

Pimberton hadn't totally caved-in to the establishment. She was still wearing trendy pants instead of business slacks. The beltline was so low-slung it must have forced her to shave pubic hair. Donna's clingy blouse stopped at her navel to expose a tattoo inked around her bellybutton. Donna's rocker-groupie looks were quite a contrast with Saul Morgenthal's conventional appearance.

I waited for a break in their conversation and got it when Saul quit talking so he could inhale. Even Saul Morgenthal needed to breathe. Never one to waste time, Saul overlapped breathing with writing a note to himself. His large hand picked up a pencil and made it look like a toothpick. I pretended I wasn't intimidated by his size and barged in the office. Courage Drew, I told myself. Make it look positive, like everything's going your way. "Hey, Saul, I got it. Took a while, but I got the story."

Morgenthal turned away from Donna and his face assumed a scowl. He spilled my name with sarcastic mock amazement. "Drew Morrissey? I heard you'd quit, so I ordered your desk packed. Your stuff's in a box somewhere. Don't worry about your severance pay. I gave that to mister, uh, what's his name? Yeah, Mr. Ulaklowski. He taxied over after talking to you." Saul dug through papers scattered on the desk. "You promised him $500. I didn't."

"It was worth ten times that Saul. I've got to talk with you for a minute." I motioned toward Donna, indicating Pimberton should leave.

He ignored my gesture. "So talk." He looked at me with amusement.

"See you later, Donna," I urged.

"She stays. In case you did get something and I need it written up, a detail you don't understand, Morrissey."

I shuffled my feet and thought about pushing the privacy issue. I decided I wouldn't win. My best shot was to keep going, fighting for my job. "Look, Saul, I know someone's sponsoring hits on these election headquarters. Richie Shaw was a health nut and exercise freak, not a druggie. OD'ing doesn't make sense. Someone murdered him."

"I like your style, Morrissey. Never mess up small. Donna, will you excuse us while I fire this asshole, formally?"

Donna's spiral-painted fingernails snatched up her notepad. She gave Saul another sweet, daughter-like smile. Pimberton turned toward me and the pencil lines of her lips froze in a red smirk. Donna kept the smirk focused on me as she strolled out of the office.

I ignored Donna and persisted. "Saul, that punk Shaw didn't do the hits at the election headquarters. It was a pro gunman. The midtown victims were all double-tapped in the head. Shaw was a rattled kid. He didn't have the cool to shoot people twice in the forehead." I leaned over Saul's cluttered desk. "What'd you think?"

"Hot air, theory, conjecture – that's all you got." Morgenthal crossed his arms and rocked in his chair. But I had his attention.

I sat on the edge of his desk. Out of the corner of my eye, I caught Donna staring at us. When I glared at her, Pimberton walked away. I turned to Morgenthal. "Saul, a Con Ed employee visited Richie Shaw shortly before he OD'd."

"So?"

"I think the Con Ed guy wasn't really an employee of Con Ed. It was the killer, disguised in a Con Ed uniform. The Coroner found champagne mixed with uppers in Richie's stomach. The pro hit man forced Richie to drink a lethal combination of alcohol and methamphetamines. Whoever sponsored these hits wanted Shaw to look like a nut acting on his own. They didn't want him talking to the cops, so they killed him."

"How do you know this, Drew? You gonna tell me Con Ed is owned by fanatics?" Saul wagged his head from side to side, chortling. He leaned forward, rummaging through a mountain of paper strewn on his desk.

I knew he was looking for my firing slip. I accelerated my words, burbling them out like an auctioneer. "Ulaklowski said the Con Ed guy was carrying a box large enough for the champagne bottle."

"Or a new meter." Saul quit searching for my pink slip, found a pencil and chewed on it. He looked at me.

My stomach unclenched. "No new meters. Con Ed sent no one to that building, Saul. I checked. Shaw dies and the real killer leaves, dressed in a Con Ed uniform. Better yet, a Con Ed meter reader was found dead two days ago. Guy was short, built like a jockey, same as the killer I saw in the midtown election headquarters. So the dead meter-reader's uniform would fit the pro gunman. Let me run with this one, Saul. I'll go to the other cities and look at the Coroner's reports. I'll find a link."

"What about these sponsors? How are you going to tie them in?"

"I don't know that yet."

"Can you prove *anything*, Morrissey?" He resumed his search for the one piece of paper I didn't want him to find.

My eyes skittered between his hands and face. I raced to convince him. "Look, why not run the conspiracy link as a theory, stir the pot, see who can't take the heat?" I showed him the pamphlet I'd found in Shaw's apartment. "Put these guys on the spot. See what they do."

Morgenthal chortled. "Shit, yes. I love lawsuits, don't you? You ever go to school, Drew?"

All I could do was nod and try to swallow. I couldn't. Luckily, my fear seemed to appease him.

Saul stopped his search. "Go to school again, Morrissey. Do your homework. Do it in one week. But this is the last time I ever relent on firing your ass." Saul waved a piece of paper at me. "This is your termination notice. I hold it one week only – and the $500 for the landlord still comes out of your pay."

I beamed. "You won't be sorry, Saul. Oh, I need my ID badge back. They, uh, took it away downstairs. Must have been a mix-up."

"I'll extend that temp badge seven days, no more." Saul grabbed his phone and dialed security.

I started to protest and his glare stopped me cold. "Sure," I said lamely.

Always believing a good front helps you, I went out whistling. I flipped a glowing smile at Donna, who winced in response. Then I found the Beak and patted him on the back. "See ya."

Nice style, I thought to myself, but all bluff. This story was my last ticket to ride and it better be good. Wished I'd talked to you first, Richie Shaw, before Elijah put a gun to your head and told you to empty a champagne bottle. I bet you would've told me killing those people wasn't your idea.

It came from others and they had great plans for Richie Shaw once he proved himself.

I had one lousy week to put this story together or lose my job. Would it take Elijah a whole week to find me and put a bullet in my head? Besides that minor concern, I was chasing a story without a lot of leads, like almost none.

I headed for the Howard Stern Show. Maybe Richie said more than I'd heard on the air. It was one good thought. I only needed a hundred more smart ideas like that one and I'd be safe from Saul Morgenthal. Elijah was another matter. Well, one threat at a time.

6

Yesterday's coffee and perfume clung around me, trapped in the stale air of a tiny room. Howard Stern's talk was lavish and his show spanned the world. Yet typical of Manhattan's overpriced real estate, the staff crammed themselves into submarine-tight quarters. Matty Davis' office was about the size of a walk-in closet and packed with enough electronics to fill a moving van. I was closed-in by racks of studio equipment, stacked floor-to-ceiling, radiating heat that probably felt good in winter but not on this muggy summer day. The walls of sterile electronics were embroidered with film characters, like a dangling Spiderman and a *Shrek 2* donkey, who chattered non-stop when I squeezed him. Next to me, Matty punched a line on her phone set. She drably announced, "Howard Stern Show, king of all media … I'll transfer you."

Matty Davis had a jet black business card naming her "Call Screener Number Two at the Howard Stern Show." Her face was vampire pale, no makeup except dual slashes of purple gloss lipstick. One ear was tucked under her hair with a gold earring dangling from the lobe. Matty's other ear was pierced with a diamond and peeked out from a Pompadour hairdo cellophaned with orange and green highlights. She was wearing a leather biker's jacket over a white T-shirt, tucked into skin-tight toreador's pants. I should lose enough weight to look like Matty did wearing those pants, rivaling nineteen-year-old Audrey Hepburn in *Breakfast at Tiffany's.*

Matty popped the lid on a glass bottle of Snapple and took a sip. She ignored flashing lights on the PBX and asked me, "So what does a person of your eminence want from a lowly call screener at the Howard Stern Show? I thought *The New York Chronicle* knows all."

"I'm into this Richie Shaw thing. You remember him?"

"You kidding? I had to keep the brat entertained until Howard could wedge him in."

"So you talked to Richie personally. I mean, you took the call?"

"None other. You want me to play it back?"

"I heard what Richie said on the air. Did you record more? Like what he said before you cued Howard?"

"Yeah. I made a copy for the police, but I kept the original." Matty shuffled through a litter of micro CDs in front of her. She pulled one from the pile, popped the small disc in a recording deck and handed me a pair of huge broadcast earphones. I put them on and she jabbed play.

I heard Richie Shaw saying, "I wanna talk to Howard."

Matty answered, "You bet. You just gotta talk to me first. For a little while, 'til Howard gets done with his current gig. What you got for Howard?"

"I just did the hit."

"Sorry, Howard doesn't talk to druggies."

"I didn't take a hit, you asshole. I did a hit. I just killed a bunch of people."

"This some fantasy you're gonna do 'cause you hate your boss, co-workers, what?"

"No, bitch, can't you get it? I did the hit on a midtown election headquarters, across from MOMA, in case you didn't know. Now put Howard on."

Matty's voice changed. She was no longer sleepwalking. "What's your name?"

"Richie Shaw. What is this? Fifty questions?"

Matty stalled. "I'll check it out. If you're for real, I guarantee Howard'll talk to you. Just hold a minute, OK?"

Shaw grunted. "Hurry it up. I haven't got all day."

"This won't take long."

I hit pause on the deck and asked Matty, "What'd you do while Richie was on hold?"

Matty dragged again on her Snapple bottle. "I called the midtown precinct and asked if they knew anything about the killings."

"Did they?"

"No. It was news to them. Said they were immediately dispatching a SWAT team and backup. They wanted me to keep Richie on the line long enough for Verizon to trace the call. I figured we might get lucky and Richie'd get busted while he was still on the air with Howard. But it didn't break that way."

"How'd the call end?" I was very curious. This had all become personal when I was groveling on the bathroom floor, bullets zinging around me.

"Richie stopped mid-sentence, after a few minutes of drivel. We normally would have chopped the guy, but Howard knew the game was to have Richie caught on the air."

"You hear anything in the background when the call ended?"

"Yeah, sirens, like the cops were coming."

I nodded. "If they'd been a minute later, I'd be dead. I walked into the whole thing. Shaw had an accomplice named Elijah. He was pumping rounds at me from a submachine gun. I was hiding in a bathroom and Elijah was sawing the door in half so he could get to me. Meanwhile, Howard was talking to Richie."

"Wow." Matty took a real hit of Snapple on that one. "I didn't know. Howard might like an interview. You want on the air?"

I thought it over. "Not yet. I can't really say anything definite. I don't have enough proof."

"You gotta do it today or tomorrow. After that, it's old news."

I laughed. "I'm familiar with how fast news ages. I'm a reporter, remember? Sure you didn't hear another guy's voice before Richie hung up?"

"No. Just Shaw."

I pulled the pamphlet from my jacket pocket and unfolded it. "Did Richie mention these people at all?"

Matty glanced at the pamphlet and laughed. "A United Tomorrow, otherwise known as AUT. How suffocating and conformist can you get? Nobody's more uptight than AUT."

"They ever contact the show?"

"No, Drew. They aren't exactly in our demographics, as our ad manager would say. They're more the Rush Limbaugh type. Take everything seriously. We don't take anything seriously around here."

I put the pamphlet back in my coat. "Well, thanks anyway." I listened to the rest of the Shaw interview, but there wasn't anything useful in it. He was a perfect loner – paranoid, alienated, scared. It would be easy to convince him violence is the best solution to the world's problems. I gave Matty her earphones back. I didn't know how people wore those things eight hours a day. I'd get neck cramps. Well, each job has its downside. I thanked Matty and rose to leave.

"Hey, Drew, you gonna quote me?" Matty chuckled, but behind every joke is the truth, as they say. Matty wanted her minute of fame or she wouldn't be apprenticing at the Howard Stern Show. "Sure I'll quote you. What'd you want to say?"

"Tell the world I think Richie Shaw is an innocent victim." She laughed. "That'll shake 'em up at A United Tomorrow."

"More than you think." I shook her hand. I agreed that Shaw was a dupe. Richie had been a scared kid, alone in a huge city. Like Matty, Richie was seeking a minute of fame for his anonymous life. Richie got his sixty seconds and Elijah collected the bill. Settling the tab cost Richie Shaw his life.

I wandered along a white hallway filled with doors to tiny offices like Matty's. Finding the door marked "exit," I rode the elevator down and drifted into the street. On the sidewalk, I stood looking at everything and seeing nothing. Who could tell me more about A United Tomorrow?

I had an inspiration. George Halliday owed me a favor and it was time to collect. Halliday was policy advisor for the senior Senator from New York. I'd covered Senator Cort's re-election speech last month and made an interesting discovery. When I needed to use a bathroom, I opened a closet door by mistake. Inside the closet, George Halliday was proving the power of Viagra with a young intern. She didn't seem to mind being watched in the act of sex. Perched on a shelf, skirt around her waist, legs spread, the intern actually gave me a competitive smirk. We all have our ways of getting to the top.

Halliday's reaction had been somewhat different. George turned crimson and pulled out. He stuffed his erection into silk boxer underwear, then zipped his pants. Outside the closet, Halliday assured me the intern was eighteen. It had all been legal and consensual. No job pressure. Right, George. I can be discrete. Result was an exclusive interview with Senator Cort that kept me in Saul's good graces for a whole week. Ah, the good old days, an entire month ago.

The mood I was in, I would have called the White House, but I knew the President wouldn't give me an appointment. I wasn't totally delusional. George Halliday was the highest-up political person I knew. He socialized with the right people to know all about A United Tomorrow and the real motivations behind the AUT movement. So I dialed a private number on Long Island and assured the screener Mr. Halliday definitely wanted to speak with me.

There was a long pause and George came on the line. He wasn't pleased to hear from me, I was sure of that, but he hid it well. There was a brief negotiation and I caved. Yes, this favor cancelled his debt. My memory of the closet incident was permanently erased after this visit. In return, he'd see me tonight despite a benefit affair at Senator Cort's estate. No, I didn't own an appropriate gown. Twenty-five thousand dollar designer ball gowns were a bit beyond my paycheck. Yeah, I'd enter through the kitchen with the catering staff since I wouldn't be dressed properly. Ouch.

7

I took a train to Long Island that night. When I got off, there was only one taxi waiting for passengers. I got in, gave directions and we drove for ten minutes before turning on a wooded country lane. My taxi followed a wet snake of asphalt, fenced by cypresses dense enough that I couldn't see through the trees. Long expanses of thick brush were interrupted by wrought iron gates, protecting stretched driveways and huge mansions. This definitely wasn't the type of neighborhood where a lowly reporter hangs out. I was in well over my head. I felt it in my tense stomach.

Finally, crowded trees gave way to a long stone wall. After a few minutes of the same wall, I realized Senator Cort's estate was huge and fumbled in my pocket for antacids. There were none. I'd have to live with the acid attack. Maybe I could grab something in the kitchen. Using the catering entrance might have some benefit after all.

Eventually my cab slowed, then wallowed off the road, turning on a cobbled driveway. We hit a security checkpoint and waited for clearance. After that, the road arched over a stone bridge spanning a ribbon of water. The front gardens came into sight and they looked bigger than Manhattan's Central Park. Logic, Drew. The place can't be that size.

The driveway bent around a fountain large enough to fill a street plaza in Rome, then widened into a parking area. We continued past a piano keyboard of black and white limousines, moving toward the lacquered front door of a stately mansion. The house towered above me, illuminated by a flood of lighting washing over a gothic entry and up jutting spires.

The building was created in the early 1900s by a railroad baron and no expense had been spared. Last year's restoration work was publicly disclosed at twenty-five million dollars, funded by one of the Senator's backers. Senator Cort didn't own the estate. He merely rented the place, paying each month about what *The Chronicle* provides me as yearly salary. The Senator's cut-rate rental fee included staff. Power has its perks. I could relate to that. I'm supposed to get a pen and pencil set on my fifth anniversary as a *Chronicle* employee, if I lasted that long.

I got out and the cabby immediately drove off. I didn't blame him. I wasn't comfortable here either. I took a deep breath and headed for the catering entrance, marked by a fleet of delivery vans. A tight knot of chauffeurs in patent leather caps blocked the walkway. They parted long enough for me to slip through and immediately resumed gossiping when I'd passed.

The walkway led me straight to the catering entrance and into the kitchen. Despite ugly looks, I snitched food off trays to quiet the acid attack ravaging my stomach. Pastry puffs stuffed with meats are used at charity functions to keep people half-sober while they guzzle cocktails. The little balls of pie dough are also great for sopping up stomach acid. My belly was finally calm for the first time since I realized the size of Senator Cort's estate, a clear measure of his power.

OK, time to test my cool. I stepped through swinging kitchen doors and walked a short hallway into the brilliant light of diamond necklaces, sequined gowns and starched tuxedo shirts. Chamber music lilted from a string quartet playing before a huge fireplace packed with floral displays.

Smiling until my cheeks ached, I slid along the wall, trying to be invisible. It was impossible to hide when I was wearing a cocktail dress bought at Nordstrom's deep-discount Rack outlet. The sleeveless dress was perfect for a humid summer night. Its empire waist and cleavage-flashing neckline flattered me. But a fifty-dollar fake satin dress doesn't blend into a Long Island charity affair where donations start at the price of a new car.

A couple wearing $10,000 wardrobes giggled past me and went into a guest bathroom. The woman tried to kick the door closed with a spike-heeled shoe and didn't succeed. I saw the guy draw a mirror and a vial of cocaine from his coat pocket – and here I thought they were just going to have sex. How old fashioned of me. I shut the door so they could take their hit in private.

I slipped around a pillar and spotted the grand stairway. George Halliday said he'd wait for me in a library on the second floor. I started upward and a tall man in gray morning coat blocked my progress. A pink tea rose adorned one lapel. Chalk white gloves jutted from his oversized coat sleeves. His arms hung at his sides like a butler. But there was a bulge under one armpit where a gun was slung in a shoulder holster. His eyes were flat as a sidewalk, yet focused on me with laser-like intensity.

I talked like I belonged. "I'm here to see George Halliday, Senator Cort's strategic advisor. I have an appointment."

"You must be Morrissey." There was a strong Jersey accent to his words.

"That's me, Drew Morrissey, *New York Chronicle*." I mocked a curtsey. He didn't get the joke. I smiled instead and it was a complete waste of my tired jaw muscles. He painted me with a look that felt like I was being x-ray scanned at the airport.

"Top of the stairs. I'll escort you. You go first." He unbuttoned the morning coat so I could see his gun.

I shrugged, trying to look unfazed. "Sure," I said. "That way you can keep an eye on me." I softly added, "You can check out the Stairmaster work I do at the gym." I meant he could admire the tight butt I didn't actually have. I assumed he couldn't hear me over the laughter and buzzing voices of the crowd.

My witticism only proved his hearing was excellent. He pointed up the stairway and gave me a sadistic look. "You don't go to the gym. But I do."

"Touché. Point conceded." I did a short bow and ran the stairs to show I was still defiant. We swept up burgundy carpet held on the wide staircase by brass runners. The mandatory brooding oil paintings were hanging on the walls, cracked lacquer glistening in the spotlights.

I was completely winded at the top but Mr. Security was not. He walked at a fast clip along the hallway, teaching me a lesson. I kept pace despite a nearly-desperate lack of breath, determined not to lose face. The hallway paint was an ugly shade of green accented by yellow molding. The color scheme was probably chosen by the trendiest of decorators, but I wouldn't know. My subscription to *Architectural Digest* expired years ago.

At the end of the hall, he stopped and opened a dark walnut door. "You're game, Morrissey, even though you're not in good shape."

"I try hard," I quipped. "It's my mantra. Try-harder Morrissey." I didn't get a smile from him but I did get an amused eyebrow. Shows progress, I told myself.

"I'll be outside, in case Mr. Halliday needs assistance."

"What about me?" I joked.

"You're on your own. Mr. Halliday writes my checks." So much for progress in our relationship.

I wasted another smile and stepped into the room. The library was about the size of a ballroom. It was wallpapered in the spines of leather-bound volumes, except for a Gothic bay window of leaded glass. The elaborate window overlooked a swimming pool where illuminated statues of armless goddesses framed intensely blue waters.

An enormous partner's desk squatted before the bay window. George Halliday sat behind the desk, looking like a sexy grandfather. I could believe the teenage intern was attracted to him. Somehow George managed to radiate vitality and be cuddly at the same time. His shiny bald head reflected chandelier light like a waxed floor. George's black-rimmed glasses were fish bowls sitting over his eyes. Yet there was a lot of energy in his stare.

Halliday got up and exposed his slight frame, extending a polite handshake toward me. George was gracious, even though I was being a pain in his neck. "Drew, how are you? They treating you right at *The Chronicle*?"

"No. I've been there nearly two years and still don't have an office like this."

He laughed. "Give them another six months. Took me thirty years to get this office. So you aren't doing badly. Drink?" He moved to a silver tray holding a crystal decanter.

"I'll pass, George."

He shrugged and poured himself a generous tumbler. Halliday sat in a plush leather chair instead of returning to the power position behind the desk. "What can I do for you, Drew? I've got a drawer full of speeches the Senator's given, if you need a quote."

I perched on an adjacent chair and leaned forward, displaying the pamphlet I'd found in Richie Shaw's apartment. I tapped the brochure. "What do you know about this organization, A United Tomorrow?"

"One word – trouble. Stay away. Write a nice, safe article about the Senator. Talk about all the jobs he's brought to New York state." George sipped from his glass, then put it on an end table. He brought two cigars from his inner pocket. Halliday offered me a cigar. "Smoke?"

"Nah, I get enough soot in Manhattan. But you go ahead. Really, George, I won't mind."

"You sure?"

"Yeah." I owed him a cigar. He was being very nice to me.

He picked up a lighter that looked like a shot-put and probably weighed as much. George lit his cigar and put the lighter down. He looked at me expectantly.

"What kind of trouble is A United Tomorrow?" I asked.

Halliday politely turned his head and blew a puff away from my direction. "You're really stuck on this AUT story."

I nodded. "No choice. Gotta pursue it."

"Leave us out of it. Understood?"

"Scout's honor." I crossed my heart.

"Drew, this is no joke."

"Serious," I assured him and put a stern look on my face.

"You burn Cort and I'll burn you," he warned me. Halliday laughed. "Nobody'd believe a teen intern would bop a guy my age."

"I'm not going to burn you – or the Senator. When I walk out of here, that closet incident is erased." He didn't look convinced. So I added, "In fact, I owe you one. How's that?"

He thought it over. "Deal," he announced. "OK, I'll give you a quick rundown. A United Tomorrow's built connections and influence over two decades. In the last few years, they've really accelerated. I try to steer

Cort away from them, but it's getting harder each month. They've got lobbyists you don't even know are with AUT, pushing on you for a wide range of causes." He really puffed on the cigar now. I was grateful it was aromatic so I didn't gag.

"Lobbying takes money. Where do they get the dollars?"

"It's mostly private money, from a wealthy Southern California industrialist, Jonah Cameron. He got an inheritance from his father, then gambled on futures in the stock market. He turned the gains into ownership of some big companies that are real cash machines. Not even the IRS could tally up his net worth, with all the corporations, trusts and foundations Cameron's got intermeshed. He uses the money to buy influence. A lot of influence. Cameron's got governors, mayors, cops on his payroll."

"All that influence must have a purpose. What's Jonah Cameron want?"

"The White House." George knocked an inch of ash off his cigar.

"How's Cameron going to get there?"

"Fear of terrorism. He wins on terrorism in two ways. First, most of his businesses sell security devices, many of which should be illegal. In my opinion, Cameron and his United Tomorrow don't believe any right to privacy exists. America would be turned into another North Korea, if it were up to them. There'd be electronic bugs in your apartment, your car, hell even up your ass." He gave me an apologetic look. "Sorry, Drew, I got carried away."

I teased him. "Forgot there was a lady present and used a curse word, George?"

He waved the cigar at me. "Hell, I know you're liberated. I offered you a cigar, didn't I?"

"You did indeed," I assured him. "What's the second way Cameron benefits from terrorism?"

"Every time there's a violent crime that might be a terrorist incident, right-wing groups scream the White House is lax on security. They get the terrorist idea in people's minds with headlines and TV stories. The fear sticks even when it's proven afterwards there was no link to foreign terrorists."

"How's that help Cameron?"

"When A United Tomorrow doesn't join the right-wing chorus shouting for tighter controls, it makes them seem less radical and more middle-of-the-road. Looking like a middle-roader broadens AUT's base of support. The strategy's worked. They have triple the membership of the largest pro-gun organization, for example. AUT's giant membership will help Cameron when he runs for President, someday." George Halliday looked at me coyly. "What's your connection to A United Tomorrow?"

"I suspect AUT is involved in these violent attacks on election headquarters, of independents like the Green Party." I folded the pamphlet and slid it in my coat pocket.

George looked shocked at my comments. "Like I said, AUT and Cameron benefit from violence. But you think they're directly tied to the killing?"

I nodded. "I believe AUT sponsors the violence. They hire a pro hit man to do the killings. But they set up some naive kid to take the blame. The last one was Richie Shaw."

"That's white hot, Drew. If you can't handle it, you better drop it." Halliday puffed on the cigar and looked thoughtfully out the window, staring at the pool. A band was setting up electric guitars on a stage at the far end, for those who fell asleep to the chamber music inside. The water was being covered with a dance pavilion.

He talked softly, without looking at me. "You need a direct link, a witness, preferably several witnesses. You better keep them well protected. Cameron and his bunch have the juice to play rough and get away with it. Even *The New York Chronicle* has to cover themselves on something that hot. You're talking criminal charges. You might put Cameron in jail, not just ruin his political ambitions."

"True," I agreed.

The intercom chimed. George picked up the phone and did a series of "uh huhs," then put the receiver down. He looked at me. "You'll have to excuse me for a minute, Drew. The Senator misplaced his after-dinner speech. I'll have my secretary print another copy and be right back." Halliday left with surprising mobility for a man in his sixties.

I wandered restlessly to the bay window. There were dozens of small groups by the pool, each set clustered around a celebrity. Pick your type and they were here at Cort's extravaganza. Love classical musicians? No problem. I recognized three of them. Nearby, the cast of a hit musical were vying for groupies, eyeing each other to see who attracted the most attention. It was proof there are no small egos on Broadway. A TV actress was turning down drinks offered by a dozen horny men. An aging film actor looked dissatisfied at his haul, several menopausal women who normally flirt with the club tennis pro. The actor perked up when approached by a girl who could have been his granddaughter.

Bored with the elite crowd, I turned to look at Halliday's desk. Reporters are born snoops. For some reason, my eyes fixated on some gold-edged paper in the wastebasket. I bent down and picked a linen envelope out of the trash. It was addressed to the Senator in elegant handwriting but there was no return address on the front. I turned the envelope over and looked on the back flap. "Memorial Foundation" was embossed in gold letters but there was no address.

I slid a card out of the envelope. I saw why George Halliday threw this in the trash. It was an invitation to Richie Shaw's funeral. There was a personal note from a Marv Logan scrawled in red pen across the card. Marv Logan wanted to trade Senator Cort's appearance at a "very private and discrete funeral service" for "significant help in the Senator's upcoming re-election campaign." I assumed "The Memorial Foundation" was another disguised piece of A United Tomorrow.

I heard a sound at the door and slipped the envelope in my pocket. I turned around so I'd be gazing thoughtfully out the window when George came inside the library. I heard the door open behind me.

Halliday walked across the room and stood next to me. "Why don't you go out there and mingle? Lots of stories by the pool, Drew. Plus some good drinks, even if you're too late for dinner."

"Thanks, George. But I'll skip it. I appreciate the tips you gave me tonight."

"Wish I could be more help. This AUT thing might be a ticket to the Pulitzer, but it could also destroy your career. Like I say Drew, lots of good stories down by the pool."

"I got the hint, George. Good night. Let me know if anything breaks for the Senator. I'll do my best to get it on the front page." We shook hands.

He moved to the desk and pressed a button. Immediately my security "shadow" appeared in the doorway. "William, call a cab for Ms. Morrissey, will you?"

"Yes, sir."

Half an hour later, I was in the cab, heading for the railway station. I sat in the back seat, playing with the invitation to Shaw's funeral. No press would be allowed at the services, so I couldn't attend as a reporter from *The New York Chronicle*. But I could lie and say I was attending on behalf of Senator Cort.

Was I really crazy enough to walk into the funeral and say I was from Senator Cort's office? Maybe I'd be crazy not to go. I had to get something on A United Tomorrow or I'd be out of a job. At the moment, Saul looked more terrible to me than an irate Senator Cort. I decided to see Richie Shaw one last time.

8

I almost never wear a skirt and high heels. I certainly never wear heels on the subway. But here I was, in my get-a-job suit, wearing toe-crushing stiletto heels and actually carrying a purse. I was surprised people didn't stare in amazement when I rode the subway train to Richie Shaw's funeral. Sitting would have relaxed my feet, but I was afraid of soiling my one-and-only dressy outfit. Its latte-colored fabric was stained by everything I touched. The suit was how Angelina Jolie dressed as a TV news reporter in *Life or Something Like It*. I'd found a gray market knockoff of her designer outfit and snapped it up.

I wanted to wear my best shoes to match the suit, but a heel broke off my pumps that morning and I was forced to borrow a pair from my roommate Carrie. She had toe fungus, so I blasted the insoles with Desenex spray. Worse yet, Carrie's feet were two sizes larger than mine. Despite jamming paper towel in the toes, I wobbled like a penguin whenever I tried to move in her oversized pumps with five-inch heels.

I groaned when the train hit my stop, forcing me to again walk in the high heels. Carefully, I picked my way along the subway car and waddled the corridor to the part I hated most. I sighed in resignation and began three flights of endless stairs. At the top, I felt like a ballerina after an hour of toe dancing. At least Carrie's black Prada pumps looked great. All my roommate's shoes cost over $300 a pair. Carrie never had money for groceries or taxi fare, but she always dressed like a "babe."

At first, I looked like a toddler going up the subway exit stairs, but I finally got the hang of walking in oversized pumps. On the sidewalk, I stopped to orient myself and the unceasing crowd rushed past, knocking repeatedly against the arm I raised to shield my eyes from glaring sunlight. Along Lexington Avenue, a mob was split into bellicose halves, each side using bullhorns to yell slogans. Their amplified shouts were so loud they even drowned out the honking of frustrated drivers. Not surprisingly, Richie Shaw's funeral was a high profile event.

On the far side of the street lay the dome of a funeral parlor, with Micelli and Son chiseled into granite spanning the scrolled tops of fluted columns. To get across Lexington Avenue, I'd have to brave both sets of protestors. So I took a jagged path through stalled traffic toward blue and white police cruisers, monitoring the protests. I pulled Senator Cort's invitation from my purse and showed it to a policeman. I grabbed his elbow and asked him for protection. I pointed to "Senator" on the invitation and shouted in his ear, "I'm Senator Cort's representative. Can you escort me?"

The cop nodded, opened the door to a cruiser and hit the siren. He yelled through a loudspeaker to let me pass. The mob hesitated and he hit the siren again. Then he grabbed my elbow and we pressed into the crowd together. The edge of a protest sign accidentally dug into my head, but I ignored the pain and continued. A woman shouted a slogan in my ear and a man on the other side screamed back, setting off a salvo of bullhorns. Sirens from police cruisers wailed, bringing the decibels past the worst I'd endured at a rock concert, which was pretty bad.

It was disorienting to enter the calm of Micelli and Son's funeral parlor after that noise barrage. I thanked the policeman for his courage and told him I was concerned about his return trip through that mob. He assured me it was no problem. He'd leave through a side entrance and walk a block before crossing Lexington. I'd have done the same if it weren't for the blasted high heels I was wearing.

With protestors outside, I wasn't surprised to see security guards in red blazers flanking a metal detector. I tried to go through, but the alarm brayed. I put my purse on a table and passed through the gate without triggering a response. Instead of looking in my purse for an obvious weapon, a guard emptied my handbag, item by item. He examined my blusher, lipstick, cell phone and Tic Tac breath mints. He seemed particularly interested in the peanut butter and chocolate Luna Bar I'd intended to eat on the subway as breakfast. For a moment, I thought he was going to unwrap the bar and bite off a piece, claiming he was testing it.

But he put the Luna Bar down and removed the rubber band from a jumble of "plastic" – my driver's license, credit card, Blockbuster ID and 24-Hour Fitness membership. Then came a little cash and an item I'd hoped the guard would miss. Of course, he didn't overlook the ancient, unused condom I'd carried since my first year in college, when Mom stuffed the Trojan in my purse and made me promise to use it. All the items were neatly arranged on the table – with the condom in the center, no less – and photographed with a digital camera. I thought about what George Halliday told me, that A United Tomorrow doesn't believe the right to privacy exists. Annoyed, I jammed my belongings in the purse, swallowing my resentment.

They motioned me to the next step in their screening process, a sign-in area where they checked your credentials. A pair of college students sat behind a folding table covered with a sheet skirted in red fringe. The students' cheap perfume and shaving cologne hit me as I bent to sign their guest book.

No press allowed meant I couldn't work for *The Chronicle*, so I signed-in as an editor for a small publishing house that specialized in celebrity bios. That choice was inspired by my roommate, Carrie Bloom, who worked at Wyndham & Dorset. Fortunately, the students didn't want my office phone and e-mail address.

My ears were still ringing from the bullhorns when they asked to see my invitation and I could barely hear the words. I fumbled in my purse and dragged out the now-crumpled paper. The boy flattened the card, then whispered to the girl next to him. She quickly rose and disappeared inside.

The girl returned with a young man wearing a black suit and silver tie. "Ms. Morrissey," the girl intoned. "May I introduce Dr. Mark Humphrey? Dr. Humphrey is president of A United Tomorrow's New York chapter."

Bingo. I had my link between Richie Shaw and AUT. It wasn't enough to bring them down, but it was a start. A shiver of excitement ran down my spine. I looked at Humphrey, sizing him up. He was taller than me by a head, with a tanned face handsome enough he could be a movie actor.

Humphrey squeezed my hand and pumped. "I'm so glad the Senator joined our crusade. Will Senator Cort be with us shortly?" Humphrey peered over my shoulder, hoping to spot the Senator.

"No, Senator Cort sends his apologies. He had to be in Congress for a vote. He hopes you understand."

Disappointment flashed across the beautiful features of Humphrey's face, but he quickly recovered. "Oh, yes, I fully appreciate the needs of the living come before those who've passed to our gentle and compassionate Savior."

Dr. Humphrey offered his arm. "I'll escort you to the front row, where you have a reserved seat with the bereaved family of the late Mr. Shaw." He waited, his elbow askew.

I could hardly refuse him, despite the cold lump growing in my stomach. I wobbled in Carrie's high heels toward the front row, increasingly mindful of how I'd violated last night's promise not to involve Senator Cort. When George Halliday found out, he'd kill me.

Humphrey chattered as we walked. "I'm sorry you had to come through that circus on Lexington Avenue. We would've sent a limousine and brought you to the VIP entrance in the rear of the building, if we'd known you were coming. But no matter. What's done is behind us – and you can ride with me to the internment."

"I, uh . . ." The words died in my confusion. Fortunately, he didn't seem to notice my shocked reaction. Internment? Apparently they expected me at the cemetery, to watch Richie Shaw put in his grave. Saul was right. I never screwed up small.

We stopped at the chapel's front. Humphrey made a slight bow toward the two people sitting closest to the casket. "May I introduce Mr. Andrew Shaw and his daughter, Karen? Andrew and Karen are father and sister of the late Mr. Richard Shaw."

I snapped out of my trance and nodded politely. The father and sister barely noticed me. The old man stared with watery eyes at the coffin. He was burly with rough hands and a soiled collar on his dress shirt. The suit was shiny with wear, its out-of-fashion style dating from twenty years ago. Richie's sister smiled in the plastic look that can only come from a large dose of tranquilizers.

I stood awkwardly for a moment, then moved away, sliding along the front pew. I sat as distant from Richie's family as I dared. Even that far from the casket, an overpowering smell of flowers came to me like a childhood memory of my grandmother's home in New York's Flower District. I flashed on a painful moment at the high school prom, when my date tried to pin a corsage on my dress. Randy stabbed my breast repeatedly. I bled so much one of the chaperones mistook the stain for red embroidery, complementing me on it. After the dance, we made out in his car. My breast was too sore so I let Randy touch me, well, lower for the first time. The rest of that story wasn't appropriate for a funeral, so I refocused on the casket to cool myself off.

The burnished mahogany coffin was embedded in a wall of yellow and white blooms, enough lilies and white dahlias for Easter Sunday at St. Patrick's Cathedral. I stole a glance at Richie Shaw's father, dressed in shabby clothes. He clearly hadn't funded this lavish spectacle. A United Tomorrow was paying for it. I stared at the varnished box with sparkling brass rails, elevated on a red velvet platform. Gradually, I realized a painted portrait of Richie Shaw was buried amid blossoms lining the stage. A United Tomorrow even made an oil painting of Richie's high school graduation picture in gown and mortarboard. I wondered if shooting people was AUT's idea of "graduating?"

The painting was so idealized it didn't look at all like the hopped-up kid I saw leaning on the steering wheel of his UPS truck, shouting into a cell phone. But one thing I knew. The kid in this portrait and the one I'd seen weren't killers. Richie had been a round-faced, big-boned teen with heavy eyebrows and thick lips. His eyes were puppyish. Richie Shaw just wanted to belong, to be a "somebody," making him an easy target for A United Tomorrow.

A thought occurred to me. Most of the people in the chapel were probably AUT members, told to attend so it looked like Richie had many friends. I swiveled my head and saw the stares of people who thought me impolite. I snapped around, struck that they all looked normal, not like people who deliberately hired killers and glorified the results.

Dr. Mark Humphrey walked to the podium and put a positive spin on Richie Shaw's life, talking about what a smart kid Richard had been in grade school. Humphrey described Shaw as a good UPS employee, working unpaid overtime to complete his difficult route in traffic-packed Manhattan. The head of the New York AUT chapter made it sound like Shaw was a good kid who got mixed up by bad ideas. A United Tomorrow just came along too late to straighten him out. That was certainly an ironic piece of propaganda, if I was right that AUT actually sponsored Richie and Elijah to do the murders.

At the moment, there was no concrete link between A United Tomorrow and the killings. Publicly, they were just helping a poor man hold a decent funeral for his son. Richie Shaw was a misguided kid but he was still a member of their organization and they were doing the right thing for his father and sister. Trying to make a scandal of that would just make them seem loving and forgiving to the public. It would also get me fired before Saul's one week deadline elapsed, given AUT's clout.

I wondered how Shaw's father and sister actually felt about Richie joining A United Tomorrow? Maybe going to the internment wasn't a problem but an opportunity. There might be a chance to talk with them for an instant, make a connection I could follow later on.

The New Jersey cemetery was certainly posh. Wooded slopes dipped into neatly mown lawns and every monument stone was decorated with fresh blooms. It was a lovely area, except for where I was standing. In front of me lay a gaping hole, neatly cut into an exact rectangle. The dirt was piled discretely out of sight, masked from view by a nearby tent that also hid the grave-digging machine. Richie's coffin was on sawhorses draped with a black skirt. Security was everywhere, whispering to each other in little mikes on their lapels.

Dr. Humphrey gave each of the Shaws a long-stemmed rose so they could add it to a pile of flowers atop the casket. The tranquilizers were wearing off and Karen looked shocked at the rose. Richie's father led Karen to the casket and helped her drop the flower in the right place. Karen's eyes were more frightened than sad. She acted like she'd been forced into this ritual and was being watched to make sure she did it right. Watched by whom? A United Tomorrow, I assumed.

My chance to talk with Karen hadn't come on the ride out. Dr. Humphrey was seated next to me and I certainly didn't want him overhearing my conversation with Karen. I fell back a little as we walked toward the limo, until I was alongside Karen. I put an arm around her and she finally cracked. Karen put her head on my shoulder and sobbed. We stopped until she was able to go on. I had no chance to say anything. A chauffeur held the limo door open and the Shaws got inside the car, then me. I expected Mark Humphrey to join us, but he was distracted by a pair of security men. They walked away to talk in private.

I asked the driver, "Could you close that door? It's chilly in here." I pointed to Karen, who was shaking a bit. I knew she wasn't shaking from the cold, but it was a good excuse to get a moment alone with Karen and Andrew Shaw.

The chauffeur softly closed the door and I turned to look at Karen. She was large boned, with Richie's wide, puppyish eyes. Her brown hair was pulled back, which made her features seem even more severe. Her looks, like her bones, were exaggerated. With the right makeup, Karen could be a fashion model. Without it, she looked gawky.

I said, "I'm really sorry about your brother. It seems a tragedy he got killed this way."

Karen looked out the window and cold light from the overcast day showed her cheek was streaked by tears. Her eyes hardened with rage. "They did it to him. He wasn't like this before they got to him."

Richie's father, Andrew, shot her a harsh look. Andrew clamped his hand on her arm. "Richie was a hot head. Don't blame them. They treated us good, didn't they? They paid for all this, more than I could have done. Leave them alone, Karen."

"Who are you talking about? A United Tomorrow?" I asked.

Andrew cut me with an icy stare. "It's none of your business."

I shrugged. "Sorry. For a second, I had the feeling you thought they killed Richie."

Karen's face snapped around. She stared at me, her eyes glaring. "Richie'd be alive now if he'd never gone to their meetings. He was such a fool, a damned gullible kid. Why didn't he stay away from them, like I told him? He used to listen to me —"

Andrew cut her off. "That's enough, Karen. You did your best. You were like a mother to him after Lizzy died. It's not your fault. It's not anyone's fault but Richie's. No one could talk sense into him. He was always bragging about the day he'd be a great man. Everyone would look up to him. I was only a dumb janitor. I didn't matter because I paid for things by breaking my ass every week. Richie didn't like work. He said I was a fool for not taking the easy way out."

Karen snapped her arm free of her father's grip. "How would you know? You just took the belt to Richie. You never tried to understand him."

"Have it your way." Andrew crossed his arms, staring out the window. "You're just like him. Neither of you had any gratitude. You've got this big job. You don't need the old man anymore, so dump him."

"You're an ass, papa. I deserve a life. And so did Richie. He trusted people too much. That was his biggest problem."

"Yeah, you should know." Sarcasm dripped off his voice. "You know all about people now they made you the queen bee office manager."

"I've worked at Hermes for ten years, papa. It's about time they gave me something. I been running the place for nine of the ten years, damn you."

Out of the corner of my eye, I saw Mark Humphrey returning. I needed to know where Karen worked, so I could track her down later. I quickly asked, "You work at Hermes Boutique, on Madison near 62nd Street?"

She laughed bitterly. "Yeah, right. I wish. Hermes Messenger Service. I got a great view of the fish market. I open my window and they smell up my office."

I laughed sympathetically and the door opened in a flash of light. Dr. Humphrey sat next to me, jiggling into place with his very calculated mix of proper somberness and uplifting attitude. In its own way, his artificial manner was as gagging as cheap cologne. With Humphrey sitting next to me, all I could do was smile and ride in silence. But now I had a lead with Karen. That had been worth the trip to the cemetery, draining as it was.

9

Stopping at Bleighberg's Grocery on the way home had become a must. I needed to solace myself and the quickest way was a sugar rush. I'd get a pack of tortillas, spread the flat bread with jam, pop it in the microwave and make myself a low class crepe. After eating six of them, I'd feel truly blimped, too lazy to worry about anything.

The name "Bleighberg's Grocery" dignifies a narrow storefront where Mr. Bleighberg actually makes his living by cashing welfare checks for a fee. I was pretty sure the meager profits from everything else went under the betting window at Belmont. Someday, he assured me, I'd see a "permanently closed" sign on the door, when he nailed a hundred-to-one long shot.

Mr. Bleighberg's retirement plan didn't seem crazy to me. We all have our strategy for how we're going to escape. Some buy lottery tickets while others go to Hollywood and park cars, hoping to be "discovered." In my circle of friends, I was one of the few who didn't have a scheme for exiting the system. Not having a way out could be realism or could be a lack of planning. I hadn't decided which it was yet.

I crossed the entry mat and the doorbell chimed. Bleighberg's puffy face dragged up from a tote sheet and I got a nod of recognition, then he resumed analyzing the betting line on each pony. When I checked out, he'd ask me to kiss his betting sheet for good luck. It was our ritual and I always did it for Bleighberg.

Kissing his tote sheet was harmless enough, though I warned him smooching never brought good luck to my doorstep. Every guy I'd dated turned out to be a problem, not a solution. My latest boyfriend, Jamie, was taking the crown as my biggest mistake of all. Bleighberg might be smart in focusing all his passion on horseracing. I could learn something from him.

I squeezed along the store's only aisle, between racks crammed with a motley assortment of cans and bottles. A sink in the back held wilted produce that was examined in detail by flies and gnats. That sink was the only secluded area in the store. Despite the gross buzzing of insects, I used the privacy to hike up my pantyhose. Its elastic was shot.

Normally, I wore knee-highs under my work slacks, so I kept only one set of pantyhose to use at dress occasions. For Jamie, I'd splurged on a garter belt and nylons, but his impatient foreplay wrecked them.

Smoothing the skirt down, I wondered if Bleighberg used a hidden video camera to monitor the sink area. I laughed at the idea of him watching me on a TV screen. Fortunately, I couldn't imagine Mr. Bleighberg getting aroused by anything other than horse track betting.

I went down the aisle and found a tortilla pack, carefully inspecting the flat bread for little green spots. Bleighberg didn't take returns. His margins were too thin. I rejected two packs of tortillas and was on my third when I heard screeching truck brakes echo inside the narrow storefront. I looked up to see boots skipping off the metal diamonds of a truck cab. A Con Ed guy slammed the truck door, walked to Bleighberg and asked, "Where's the gum?"

In that moment, I learned a whole new level of fear. The Con Ed guy was Richie Shaw's accomplice, Elijah, still wearing the stolen uniform. From then on, everything unfolded in freeze-frame.

Bleighberg put down his tote sheet and groped on shelves crammed with booze and cigarettes. He kept a hand on the shelf and pivoted his head. "What kind a gum you want?"

"Spearmint, any brand." Elijah glanced idly around the store. His eyes lingered on the center aisle, where I was standing. I tried to be invisible, shrinking into the darkest area I could find. My heart skipped beats, pumping wildly. I thought I was having a coronary. Finally, Elijah's eyes flitted away. Had he seen me? There was no way of telling.

Bleighberg pulled a calculator from the narrow pocket of his polo shirt and slowly tapped the keys. I silently screamed at Mr. Bleighberg to hurry up. Finally, he slapped a pack of gum on the counter like it was a big transaction and announced the price.

Elijah put down dollar bills. Bleighberg tipped the lid of a cigar box and slid the money inside. Then he squeezed change on a worn green mat. Typical of Bleighberg, the change was a penny short. It was his way of increasing the profit margin.

Elijah ignored the missing penny. He scraped the coins into his hand and buried them in a pants pocket with the gum. Then he glanced down the aisle again. Was that a twisted smile of recognition flashing across Elijah's face? God, I hoped not.

"Thanks," Bleighberg muttered into the tote sheet.

Elijah didn't respond. He faded from the store like he was going for a walk, leaving the Con Ed truck parked in front of the store. Was Elijah hiding around the corner, waiting to shoot me when I left Bleighberg's? There was no exit other than walking straight out the front, where Elijah could be waiting for me.

My mind was broken. I couldn't seem to think. I looked at the tortillas and there was a deep imprint in the pack, filled with sweat where I'd been gripping the flat bread. When I dropped the package on the shelf, my hand ached from tension. I flexed my fingers to get a little circulation going. I pulled my cell phone from the purse to dial 911 and found the battery was still dead from heavy usage in Chinatown. With all the stress, I'd forgotten to recharge. Bleighberg didn't have a payphone in the store and didn't believe in cell phones. "Too expensive," he once told me.

So I got brave and took a step toward the front of the store. A dozen hesitant steps later, I peeked around Bleighberg's steel grating. No sign of Elijah anywhere. Maybe I should go home and call from behind a triple-locked door. But that meant exposing myself to Elijah, if he was nearby.

I didn't know I could walk so fast in heels. I was practically running. Three blocks over and two blocks down I stopped in front of my apartment building. Its once-elegant steps were coated with sticky grime that gripped my shoes as I climbed to the heavy glass door. I looked in my purse and was horrified to see no keys. I'm so used to leaving the keys in my pants that I probably didn't think to transfer them to a seldom-used purse.

Strangely enough, I vividly remembered putting my keys in the handbag. Maybe I'd lost them at the funeral parlor, after they'd searched the purse. In my irritation, I'd done a sloppy job cramming everything inside and the keys fell on the floor. Yeah, that had to be it. I groaned. Another cross-town subway ride to get the keys.

My hand automatically sought a column of buttons next to the thick glass door. I buzzed my own apartment, hoping a roommate would answer. No luck. I ran my fingers down the ivory buttons, jabbing each one.

A familiar voice scratched at me. "Yes?"

I was relieved to hear someone I recognized. "Mrs. Safaeian? It's Drew Morrissey. Can you let me in? I forgot my key."

There was no reply, but the door buzzed with an irritating hum. I jerked the heavy glass open and went inside a small lobby. The entry was lit only by sunlight shining through the door. The floor was a mess of fractured black and white art-deco tiles, their cracks filled with dirt. The scratched elevator doors were hidden by the dusty leaves of an artificial tree. Our lift quit working last year and I complained about the problem every month, when I paid the rent. The owner responded by hiding the elevator behind an artificial tree, to make it seem the lift didn't exist. That was the downside of living in a rent-controlled building. The upside was obvious and greatly out-weighed lugging groceries up several flights of stairs.

I stepped into the dark stairwell and changed my mind about going upstairs by myself. Maybe I ought to ask the building's "super," Sidney Byrne, to come with me. Even a senior citizen in a cardigan was better than no protection at all. Besides, I'd need his master key to get inside the apartment if Donovan wasn't home. Carrie would be at work this time of day.

I softly knocked on the door of Sidney's apartment. The door panel was sandpapered, with long streaks of bare wood showing. Sidney once prepped the door for painting and then forgot to do it. I waited impatiently. There was no response to my hushed tapping, so I did a loud rap. Sidney's parrot screeched, but other than the bird, there was no sound from inside the apartment. I tried the door knob and it was locked. Sidney must have left to run an errand. Maybe it was just as well. There was no reason to get an elderly man shot, in addition to myself. Not exactly positive imaging, Drew. Calm down and think.

I had to call the cops before Elijah drove away in his Con Ed truck and disappeared, lost in a huge city. So I had to use the phone in my apartment. The main stairs curved to my left, a flow of lovely green marble sadly marred by non-skid strips. Amped by an adrenaline rush, I went up the stairs much too fast and was completely out of breath when I got to my floor.

After a momentary rest, I pushed open a metal fire door and started along the dimly lit hallway. My vision hadn't yet adjusted from sunlight and I could barely make out worn doormats in the hazy light of the energy saving bulbs. Despite the wobbly high heels, I walked briskly along the corridor. I reached my door and banged loudly enough to raise the dead. I didn't care if Donovan was sleeping. My need was urgent. I'd explain later. But there wasn't a sound in response, not even a curious neighbor peeking to see who was causing such a racket.

In true New York fashion, there were three deadbolts on the door, all fitting the same key. There was no safe place to hide a spare key, so I'd have to wait for Sidney to get home from his errand. With nothing to lose, I cranked the doorknob and pushed. I nearly fell into the apartment.

None of the deadbolts were locked. Did I leave for Richie Shaw's funeral without securing the door? Was I really that out of it? I cautiously peered into the apartment.

Water dripped into a kitchen sink full of dishes. Muffled traffic noise came from the living room windows. There were the familiar smells of bacon grease and mildew. I moved along the hallway, opening each door, closing it again. A loose floorboard squeaked underfoot and I stopped, listened intently, then continued. The place appeared safe, or would be when I locked the front door.

I leaned into the door and forced the third deadbolt home. Then the phone rang and I jumped. My heart raced like it had in the store when I'd seen Elijah. The phone jangled again and impulsively I snapped up the receiver. Wary, I didn't talk. There was a long pause before a husky male voice spoke. "Drew? Is that you?"

"Yes," I answered, still not sure who was on the other end.

"This is Collie Weiss. I've been leaving messages for you, but you didn't return my calls. I understand if you're upset. Things have changed and —"

"Listen, Collie, this is a bad time for me to talk. I'll call you back tomorrow, OK?" I moved toward the living room, my hand tight as the short cord. Why the hell did I answer the phone? I'd broken up with Collie three months ago. All that remained of our relationship was his sports bag parked under my bed. Was he calling to retrieve his luggage?

"It can't wait until tomorrow. I've been thinking about you all the time. I can't get you out of my mind since we . . . well, since the last time."

"Collie, there's only been one time. We got a little drunk and a lot carried away. I wouldn't make too much of it. I'm not going to tell your wife, if that's what you're worried about." Carrie introduced us at a bar. She worked with Collie, felt sorry for him and thought I'd be good for him. Carrie neglected to mention that Collie Weiss was married. In my book, she owed me a big one for that oversight.

Collie talked smoothly, like a salesman. "Look Drew, I'm getting divorced. I talked to an attorney and he's drawing up all the papers. That's what I called about. Come with me to Connecticut. I've got three nights reserved at a fabulous B&B. That's why I couldn't wait for you to call tomorrow. I had to make sure you were coming with me tonight."

I changed hands on the receiver, confused. Collie Weiss looked so lonely and vulnerable in my bedroom. There was an attractive sadness in his eyes. I remembered how gaunt he was, his body a hanger for dressy clothes. He'd been a marathon runner, with chiseled legs, flat stomach, not much upper body development. But Collie was surprisingly well built where it counted when you were in bed. I remembered the jolt when he'd put himself inside me, then the sense of melting.

"I booked a beautiful suite, with a gorgeous view and a private hot tub. We'll have dinner at a five star place nearby. Great seafood and a fabulous wine cellar."

"I don't have the right clothes for dining in a five star restaurant," I blurted.

"You don't need clothes for the kind of thing I have in mind."

"Well, I, uh, . . ." I muttered. I found myself blushing.

"Look, I came into some money, an inheritance, so I'm spoiling myself a little. I even bought a new Porsche, their latest model, a convertible. They call it a cabriolet. We'll try it out. If I drive too fast, you can take the wheel. How 'bout it?"

The hot car ploy. Did he think I was still in high school? That gaff brought me back to reality. "Collie, I have an urgent call on the other line. It's my boss."

"You work too hard, Drew. Let yourself have a little stress relief. We'll have fun in Connecticut. Unwind. Three days, you'll come back refreshed, ready to take on the world."

"OK, fine. I'll go." I told myself I just wanted him off the line.

"That's great. Listen, could I ask you for a favor? Normally, I'd pick you up, but the Porsche won't be ready until this afternoon. Could you cab to the dealership?"

"Ah, sure. I'll call you back for details." I'd say "no" later, when I could put up with his string of reasons why I was wrong. At the moment, I wasn't sane.

"You bet. If my wife answers, don't worry. We're just sharing the apartment until the lawyers get through with their bullshit. You still got my number?"

I had the feeling I was a pawn in Collie's game. He was using me to stick a knife in his wife's ego – other woman calls and asks for husband so you can appreciate what you're losing, dear. I said, "I'll call your cell phone."

"Ah … well, sure." He sounded disappointed, confirming my "stab wife" theory. I bit my lip. OK, Drew. You'll never again fail to ask if they're married. "Look," I said urgently, "I really, really gotta go. Talk to you soon. Like 'bye." I wagged my hand like I was waving goodbye to my kid on his first day of school.

"Looking forward to it," he said. Finally, there was a click.

I rolled my eyes in exasperation. I'd lost my chance to call the cops. Elijah was long gone by now. Furious with myself for picking up the damn line, I slammed my phone down. There was a rattle when the receiver hit its cradle. I started to walk away, then hesitated. Why a rattle? I picked up the receiver and shook it. Rattle, rattle, rattle. You're going paranoid, Drew. You broke something inside. I picked the phone up and listened to a brassy dial tone. I hadn't broken anything serious. It still worked.

I looked at the mouthpiece and realized it unscrewed. I'd never taken a phone apart. I turned the wrong way and tightened the mouthpiece instead of unscrewing it. I reversed directions and the plastic knob with little holes for talking fell into my hand. Then something else fell out of the phone, a round piece of metal looking like a tiny microphone. On the back was a miniature green circuit board with a watch battery. The bug had been stuck inside my phone with a piece of Spearmint gum. There wasn't time for chewing gum to dry, so it came loose when I slammed the receiver down.

"No," I gasped, when I realized what'd happened. That's why Elijah went in Bleighberg's. He bought gum for sticking electronic surveillance bugs in hiding places all over my apartment. Elijah could be listening to me right now, using the bugs. He could be next door or parked in the alley, for all I knew. Thank God the door was triple locked.

What was I saying? Elijah'd obviously had the key to my place. The security guard for A United Tomorrow must've palmed my keys when he went through my purse. That's how Elijah got inside the apartment. My stomach rolled on top of itself. I felt more nauseous than any flu or food poisoning episode I'd ever experienced. I ran to the kitchen sink and vomited, then splashed water in my mouth.

I looked at myself in a mirror and wiped my face clean. I wondered if I should take that bug with me to show the police? But I didn't want Elijah following me because I was carrying the device. It was possible he could track me with it. Maybe that was beyond what a little eavesdropping bug could do, but I wasn't taking any chances. I replaced the bug, screwed the phone together and put it back on the hook.

I had to think. How else could Elijah have gotten inside my apartment? Maybe he killed Sidney for the master key. That would explain why there was no response when I knocked on Sidney's door. Either way, Elijah would normally re-lock all my deadbolts, leaving things the way he found them, so nobody got suspicious. Were the deadbolts left unclasped because Elijah picked the locks instead of using a key? Maybe he heard me coming upstairs and rushed off, using the fire escape so he wasn't seen in the hallway with a lock pick.

I gave up. I was no good at playing Sherlock Holmes, examining a crime scene and figuring what happened there. Thinking like that hurt my head even when I wasn't insane with panic. The only safe thing was leaving my apartment fast as possible. Where could I stay for a few days?

My friend Sabrina lived in the Village and she was on a cruise with her boyfriend. I could stay there. I knew where she'd hidden a spare key. But what about my roommates? Carrie could stay with her mother. Donovan had a sometime girlfriend who occasionally spent the night with him. Maybe he could sleep with her until the NYPD grabbed Elijah.

What other details did I need to clean up? Anyone eavesdropping thought I was going with Collie Weiss to Connecticut. I'd call him later and warn him it wasn't safe for us to be together. I didn't know how I could make the threat feel real, but that wasn't my worst problem. Getting out of there was more important, at the moment.

In the bedroom, I pulled Collie's duffel from under my bed. I stuffed the bag with clothes, stopping once at a noise. When there was no further sound, I shoved toiletries in the soft-sided bag and zipped it shut. I threw off my dress clothes and pulled on jeans.

On the way out, I impulsively picked up a *New Yorker* magazine with my mail folded inside, apparently left on the entry table by Donovan. Then I took a deep breath and opened my door. There was no one in the hallway. I went out and tried to lock the door behind me before remembering I didn't have the key. I tripped over the magazine stuffed with letters. It had fallen from my hand and I hadn't even noticed. I bent to pick the *New Yorker* up and heard footsteps on the stairs.

The footsteps grew louder. They were slow and methodical. Elijah could be slowly, methodically stalking me. He was a sadistic bastard. I knew that from the election headquarters. Where to hide? Try to get back inside the apartment? No, he had the key and a gun to shoot off locks. The cops would never arrive in time. I ran to the fire exit and pushed on the door. It stuck. I thought my heart was going to explode.

I threw myself at the fire exit. It flew open and I tumbled outside, my mail twirling into space and blowing around. For a moment, I watched the *New Yorker* twist in spirals toward the ground. Focus, Drew. Forget the damn mail. Should you go up the fire escape instead of down, because Elijah won't expect that?

I heard someone talking behind me. The damn fire exit door was still open. Elijah could see me, shoot me.

"Drew?" Sidney asked. "Did you knock earlier? I was asleep."

I slumped in relief against the rusted iron of the fire escape. "Sidney, I've never been so glad to see you in my entire life."

"What'd you need?" he asked, rubbing sleep from his eyes. An iPod headset dangled around his neck, the cord running into his sweater pocket. The iPod was a gift from his grandchildren. They'd taught him to download jazz from the Internet and he loved that idea. No wonder he couldn't hear me knocking on his door. He'd fallen asleep in his recliner, listening to Miles Davis at full volume. Sidney'd forgotten to shut off the iPod and Miles was still wailing his trumpet, exploring the dark night of the soul as only Miles Davis could do. The music was so loud I could hear trumpet and piano on an open fire escape with New York cabs honking in the street below.

"Listen, Sidney. Has anybody unusual been around today, especially anybody who asked about me?" I watched him intently.

The wrinkles of his forehead crinkled deeper as he thought. "No . . . ," he drawled slowly. "Only person around besides the usuals was a Con Ed man readin' meters."

"Of course," I muttered.

"What'd you say?" Sidney asked, finally turning off the iPod.

"Oh, nothing. Look, if this Con Ed guy comes back, would you do me a favor?"

"Sure, Drew." He looked puzzled.

"Call the police."

"Gee, Drew. I don't think I should call the police just because Con Ed's reading the meters." Sidney rubbed his chin thoughtfully.

"Got a point there, Sidney. Just forget it." I needed to get out of there. Elijah might come back any second. I didn't have time to explain. I bent down and grabbed the duffel bag.

I heard Sidney saying, "Well, if you think it's important . . ."

"Nah, not at all. Bye, Sidney." I started down the fire escape.

"Bye, Drew. Something wrong with the stairs?" He looked hurt. Sidney took pride in keeping the building in good shape, despite working for a cheapskate owner.

"No, Sidney," I assured him. "I'm in the mood for some fresh air." I gave him a daughter-like hug and hurried off. At the bottom, I checked the street. No Con Ed truck. I headed for Greenwich Village and Sabrina's apartment, where I had a lot of phone calls to make.

10

A newspaper delivery man slowed his car on Bedford just past Chumley's and tossed *The New York Chronicle* in a graceful arc. This morning's edition cleared a wrought-iron gate and landed on a sunken courtyard tiled with gray flagstones, set a half-story below the sidewalk of Bedford Street. Greenwich Village was graveyard silent at that early hour and the newspaper slapped flagstones like a cannon blast. The sound was loud even through a thick oak door. Behind the arched wooden door, I worked hard at ignoring the thunderclap and continued my sleep.

About three hours later, an old clock sounded its tinny alarm, vibrating against the stone floor. I fumbled with the clock, fighting to stifle its clatter and eventually shut off the alarm. Putting my naked feet on the ice cold floor jolted me awake, dazed but able to realize I was in Sabrina's

Greenwich Village apartment. The icy flagstones paving her studio were a continuation of the miniature courtyard outside.

The tiny apartment didn't have a separate floor because it was built in the 1920s as a storeroom used to hide bootleg gin during Prohibition. The storeroom had originally been paneled in thick planks, so its remodeled interior looked like the captain's cabin on a schooner. The nautical motif was reinforced by a brass porthole serving as the only window. I rose naked and looked out the porthole, where I could see feet scurrying past the courtyard gate. The rush hour crush was beginning, marking the start of another workday in Manhattan.

To move around the room, I was forced to pivot the Murphy bed into the wall. Then I jammed myself into a bathroom the size of a broom closet, where the toilet was actually inside the shower. The toilet worked but not the shower. I cursed my way through a sponge bath at the kitchen basin, a bowl-sized sink next to a hotplate and a micro-refrigerator.

I hung the kitchen towel on its peg and explored the fridge. My luck hadn't changed. There was no food inside the white box, just a small baggie filled with marijuana. Good thing for Sabrina that I'm a *Chronicle* reporter instead of a narc.

I opened a few cabinets buried in the walls and discovered Sabrina had only canned gourmet delicacies, items she'd taken home from her job as a sous chef. I couldn't bring myself to eat salmon eggs or pickled hogs feet for breakfast. A lack of normal food in the apartment made sense. Sabrina ate her one meal a day at the restaurant.

Sometimes she did a takeout binge with Hervé, the Puerto Rican attorney who'd taken Sabrina on a cruise. He'd won a lawsuit for a travel agent and been given a ten day voyage on the ultra-exclusive Seabourn line as his legal fee. While I was dodging Elijah in sweltering heat, Sabrina was sailing from Rio to Chile, drinking champagne chilled with ice from a nearby glacier. Well, there was nothing I could do about it but envy her.

I looked in Collie's duffel bag and confirmed that I'd forgotten to pack nylons, panties or a bra. I'd been so scared to death after seeing Elijah that I'd stuffed winter clothing in the bag instead of underwear. I'd phoned Carrie yesterday at her job and asked her to bring some of my things when she evacuated the apartment, like my toothbrush. I was supposed to meet her at Wyndham & Dorset during her first coffee break and I'd be late if I didn't hurry.

I ran a wet finger over my teeth and fluffed a comb through my disheveled hair. Using Sabrina's spare compact and lipstick, I made an attempt to look better than I usually did. After several tries, I gave up on my looks and opened the massive front door. I bent down and threw *The New York Chronicle* inside where the paper again slapped flagstones. Then I climbed slick steps to the wrought-iron gate and dragged it open with a squeal of protest from its hinges.

My stomach gurgled as I walked to the subway. Fortunately, bagel and cappuccino carts were clustered around the entrance and I bought a garlic bagel and a coffee. Eating on the run meant I'd get to Carrie only a few minutes late. I took one look at the crush of people flooding into the subway and decided to flag a cab. I'd hit Mom for a loan to make up Ulaklowski's dent in my paycheck and my mother had been generous. Touched by my story about the election headquarters shooting, she'd loaned me $750, so I felt rich for a change.

New York's overcast sky released a sliver of lingering sunlight, buttering the hood of my cab when it dragged to a stop at Rockefeller Center. I walked briskly through Channel Gardens toward the golden boy statue and the General Electric Building. The GE skyscraper stood like a huge brown monument etched with thousands of black holes. The "holes" were deeply tinted windows running in columns up the skyscraper's façade. I let the GE Building's revolving door swallow me in its blades. When I came out, the suffocating heat of summer was replaced by a blast of air conditioning.

After a chilling walk to the elevator, I jammed inside the lift with a dozen other people. I fought off the mild attack of claustrophobia that hit me every time I rode an elevator in a high rise building. The problem with having an imagination was that I could envision what it would be like to free-fall umpteen floors in terror, becoming a Jell-O blob at the bottom. I was very grateful when the elevator doors opened at the thirty-first floor.

Jason Phillips greeted me at the maroon U-shaped reception desk, giving me a broad smile. Jason always dressed the same, a calculated Ivy League look, complete with linen suspenders and penny loafers. A cordless headset was looped across his sprayed-in-place JFK haircut. Jason was as much a fixture at Wyndham & Dorset as the publishing house logo embossed on the wall, an 1800s Yankee clipper with its sails cleverly shaped into a "W" and a "D."

I'd boldly asked Jason on a date once and we'd gone out a few times. I had a real crush on him, but at the critical moment in my bedroom, Jason confided he was gay. Well, sometimes he forced himself to be "bi," but really he was gay. After that, Jason just smiled and waved me through whenever I visited Wyndham & Dorset, grateful that I hadn't "outed" him. Keeping silent sometimes pays off for a newspaper reporter.

I wandered among burgundy cubicles until I found Carrie's desk. She was wearing her power suit, pinstripe slacks with a double-breasted jacket over a white blouse. Carrie's hair was swept up and stacked on her head, exposing diamond earrings in her lobes. To warrant all this, she must have been in a meeting with Wyndham, the surviving partner of Wyndham & Dorset. Carrie normally wore Dockers to work.

Despite the power look, Carrie was sucking on a straw jammed in a Red Bull can. She didn't quit sucking, just waved me a greeting. I waited for Carrie's lung power to give out. I knew she'd eventually surface for air. After a long minute, she released the straw from her lips and gasped,

"Don't worry. I remembered your stuff." Carrie reached under her desk and dragged out a plastic garbage bag bulging with my clothing.

I said, "Thanks. I'm sorry for the inconvenience, having to move in with your Mom and all that."

"Are you kidding? My mother thinks it's hot stuff. She wants all the details." Carrie waved a hand in the air, drawing a mock headline. "*Chronicle* reporter stalked by election headquarters killer." She asked eagerly, "Has he tried to shoot you again?"

I deadpanned, "Only shot at me twice today. First slug missed. Other bullet went right through my heart. Actually, I'm a zombie, one of the living dead." I did my Frankenstein imitation, walking stiff legged with my arms in front of me.

My attempts at humor were always lost on Carrie. Once again, she ignored my joking and focused on advancing her personal career. She told me, "Gosh, if this keeps up, I can get you a book contract. We've got a stable of ghost writers who whip out bios over a weekend." Carrie was hoping to impress her boss by signing me for Wyndham & Dorset – on the cheap. I'd heard her brag about doing this to other budding celebrities.

She looked pensive for a moment, then announced, "I should sign you up now, so we can do the bio posthumously if we have to. You know, in case anything happens, like the guy actually does kill you. Don't worry.

Your parents get the royalties, or anybody else you want to put in the contract." Apparently I was worth more to Wyndham & Dorset dead, rather than alive. Carrie probably figured there'd be more publicity if I was popped off by Elijah.

"Thanks, Carrie, but I plan on being around for a while – and I'd like to write my own bio. I am a reporter, you know. I do write prose for a living." I hoisted the plastic bag on my shoulder.

"No insult to your prose style, Drew. It's just pays to be prepared. You never know when something could happen. I mean, look what happened to poor Collie Weiss. You knew Collie, right? I mean you guys were a thing for a while, weren't you?"

I gave her a sarcastic look. "Collie and I were a one-night 'thing.' It was over the next day, when I discovered he was married. You should have told me he had a wife."

Carrie assumed a guilt-look for a moment but quickly changed the subject. "Well, the fact that Collie was married doesn't matter anymore."

"Why not?" I snapped, feeling really irritated. Carrie had more ways of getting under my skin than my brother.

"Collie died last night. I thought you might want to kick in a few bucks. We're taking up a collection to buy flowers for him, and uh, well, his wife."

"She died too?" I was getting a really sick feeling in my guts.

"Yeah. Car accident. They were in his new Porsche and he went too fast around a curve. They skidded through a railing, fell off a cliff."

"Where'd this happen?" I was stunned.

"I dunno. See Joanie, his admin. She made all Collie's travel reservations, even the personal ones."

"Thanks. Oh, here's ten for the flowers." I watched the money disappear inside Carrie's purse and wondered if my ten dollars would ever find its way into lilies and carnations. Well, I tried.

I went a few rows down, found an empty cubicle and sagged into the chair. I saw my reflection in a sliver of window. I was pale and haggard. I looked like I'd slept in the street. That was close to how it felt to sleep in Sabrina's fold-down bed. No wonder she always went to Hervé's for the night. Sabrina bragged how great it was to do it on his waterbed, but I think she stayed overnight at Hervé's to get some rest.

I pulled my reluctant mind back to my real problem. That poor bastard Collie hadn't listened to my warnings. I'd told him our conversation was overheard by a professional hit man and he shouldn't go to Connecticut. But the wandering husband had cozy'd up to his wife when I'd canceled. Her reward for taking Collie back was death. That was supposed to be me in the Porsche with Collie, not his wife.

Elijah didn't waste time, did he? I kept thinking how I was supposed to be dead. The garlic bagel and cappuccino lurched inside me and stomach acid stung my throat. I was the only person in the world who could ID Elijah as the killer. I was also the only person who thought all the election headquarters were hit by the same pro. So I was target number one for Elijah, right in his gun sights.

My only safety lay in finding enough proof so Saul would print an exposé on page one of *The Chronicle*. Then killing me wouldn't help A United Tomorrow. In fact, my death would confirm public suspicion. Elijah might still try for revenge, but I'd have real police protection, not just ten nights in the city jail, sleeping on a bed that made Sabrina's look great.

Electronic surveillance bugs in my apartment would get me some credibility with Saul, but he couldn't run an article based on my being harassed. If I linked Collie's death to his calling me, Saul would become a believer. My other roommate, Donovan, owed me one. I'd trade some rent for using his VW van and drive to the scene of Collie's accident, snoop around and see if there'd been evidence of foul play. I needed to know where Collie had planned to stay the night. I decided to try Joanie, Collie's admin, as Carrie suggested.

I rounded a corner and found Joanie staring at her computer screen. Behind her, I could see into Collie's perfect office. A neat row of *Publishers Weekly* was laid on his credenza. Collie's desk was clean, with only a snakeskin appointment calendar, a blue ribbon bookmarking the date. It looked like he'd walk inside the office any moment and resume work. But I knew that wasn't true, a thought that made me all the sicker.

Pictures of his wife and kids were in gold frames, silhouetted against the beautiful city view of his window. Mrs. Weiss had posed for a soft-focus boudoir photo. I looked a lot like Collie's wife, just younger. The son was in a baseball uniform, wearing a dimpled smile like his father. Collie's daughter was in a formal riding outfit, standing next to her horse and staring at me with the same aloof mask as her mother. What would become of the kids now? Damn. I forced myself to look away at Joanie.

Collie's admin, Joanie, was in her fifties, reed thin with blond hair cut in a pageboy. She wore mauve half-framed glasses that matched her dress color. Carrie once told me that Joanie owned a dozen frames so she could always match her eyeglasses with wardrobe colors. From that fact, I deduced that Joanie'd never had children. Kids and the money to own a dozen designer frames were incompatible. "Joanie," I said quietly.

She hit a key combination to save a spreadsheet, then swiveled her chair around. "Hi, Drew. You heard about Collie?"

"Yeah. I don't know what to say. I'm really sorry."

"Thanks. We'll miss him. You came to contribute to the flowers?" Joanie tapped a pencil on her desk.

"No. Carrie hit me up already. I came to ask a favor. I hate to impose when you're upset, but I have reason to think Collie didn't die accidentally. Do you know where he was going to stay? I want to get all the details before I go to the police."

Joanie looked up the bed and breakfast in her contact file and wrote the address on a Post-It for me.

"Thanks," I said.

"I hope you get whoever did this to him." She crossed her arms. "He was a fine man." Joanie said it with conviction. That was a lot coming from the admin who made reservations for you to cheat on your wife. Well, he was dead, and that washes away many faults.

"I'll sure try to nail them, Joanie. Believe me." Little did Joanie know the depth of my motivation. If I didn't stop Elijah, I was next to die. For a few hours, Elijah thought I was dead, but that would end when the media published it was Nadine Weiss who'd died, not Drew Morrissey. That unfortunate fact could already be on TV and Elijah might be watching, waiting for confirmation of his kill.

I couldn't get access to Donovan's van until tomorrow. He was busy using the VW camper for an escapade in the woods with a kissing cousin. He assured me it wasn't really incest. They'd known each other since she was thirteen and he was eighteen. She'd finally gotten old enough and said yes.

So I headed for Hermes Messenger Service to visit Richie's sister. Karen Shaw almost cracked at the funeral. Maybe she'd crack now, if I pushed a little harder. It was worth a try.

11

Fulton Fish Market isn't home to sardines and crabs so much as it's a home for Yuppies and Dinks. They go there for retail therapy, making Visa and MasterCard happy. Nobody visits the Fulton Market to buy fish anymore. That smelly business is around the corner, discretely conducted in the early morning, when snappers and lobsters arrive in a fleet of trucks, not inside the icy holds of trawlers. By eleven A.M., metal stall doors are pulled down and the fish smell is hosed away. Long before then, delivery vans have taken a "fresh catch of the day" (really yesterday) to gourmet restaurants and grocers across Manhattan. From noon on, the area belongs to tourists. Near sunset, the locals drift home from work and settle into their upscale condos. Taverns and restaurants come alive at night, with jazz riffs lilting into the street until the refrigerated fish trucks arrive again, unloading in the pink light of dawn.

It was afternoon, so I played tourist, which was fair since I wasn't from this area of Manhattan. I was standing with a camera-clicking group on the pier, where people normally admire restored clipper ships docked here. Instead, we were gawking at an amazingly flexible street performer, bending himself into a pretzel. Others were no doubt impressed by his gifted gymnastics. Personally, I was in love with the taut muscles of his Roman stomach and pumped thighs. One of the downsides of breaking up with Jamie was no sex and that was definitely affecting my mental focus. Well, at least my Victoria Secret panties would last longer. He liked to cut them off with scissors.

Just to prove a high sex drive didn't completely dominate my personality, I shifted my gaze and admired the contortionist's plastic box filled with cash donations from bystanders. No federal and state withholding on his weekly stub, just gross pay equals net take-home – provided the city didn't hassle him for a business permit. Then the full bureaucracy would descend, giving his "social" to the IRS, who'd want to know why he didn't file the last ten years and threaten prosecution for tax evasion.

In keeping with that sobering thought, the sidewalk performer struck his set and disappeared immediately after the last dollar bill fell in his collection box. He'd be at another tourist spot tomorrow, selected at random from a city with hundreds of potential venues. Sigh. I'd have to be content with his warm image in bed with me tonight. Well, I told myself, fantasizing about a buffed man is certainly a way of practicing safe sex.

With the main distraction gone, I went back to the business of finding Karen, sister of the late Richie Shaw. I'd searched for Hermes Messenger Service on the Internet and found their web site was "under construction." But they did have a display ad in the Manhattan Yellow Pages, indicating a physical address. In New York, like any big city, nice neighborhoods alternate with seedy ones. When I found Hermes Messenger Service, I was looking at a decrepit warehouse-style building. Its battered exterior was etched in beautiful shadows cast by the fanned cables of the Brooklyn Bridge. The spider web of shadows appealed to the artist in me, provided I screened out the roar of nearby bridge traffic.

Despite its run-down appearance, having an office in that warehouse made sense for Hermes. The building offered close proximity to both Wall Street and courthouses, items of great interest to a messenger service. Brokerages and legal firms always needed papers signed immediately. E-mail didn't work when a legally binding signature was required.

So messenger services were one of the few profitable small businesses in an era where huge firms erased individual competitors everywhere, even in the smallest rural towns. Owning your own business now meant being the manager of a fast-food restaurant in a mall. That job made being a reporter look heavenly.

I went inside the building and its lobby was actually in worse shape than the exterior. Salt water fog had turned mortar to crumbly powder between bricks and left a white crust on everything. Rotting lobby fixtures looked like they could be jerked from mildewed plaster by the soft tug of an infant. I skirted an enormous steam radiator pockmarked with a leprosy of rust, trying hard not to touch the heater. The blistered sores on the radiator made my skin crawl. There was no elevator and I looked at the stairs, wondering if they were safe to use.

I got my answer when a sweating messenger clattered through the doorway, a spare tire slung across his chest. My eyes ran over his foam helmet, purple biking shirt, spandex shorts, muscled legs and plastic shoes. He moved around me like I wasn't there and locked his bike to the radiator I wouldn't have touched to win a thousand dollar bet. With a flip of latches, the front wheel was off the bike and he bounced up the stairs, carrying the bicycle wheel.

The smell of garbage barges followed me up the stairs to the fourth floor, where I paused to get my breath. At the far end of the hallway, a dirty window showed a piece of the huge anchorage for the Brooklyn Bridge's main cable. Sunlight fought through window grit to light the linoleum of the empty hallway. Halfway along the corridor, I pushed a door open and stepped into Hermes Messenger Service.

Survival for a messenger service meant being reliable yet cheap. Cost-consciousness certainly showed in the Hermes office furnishings. The tiny outer office had its window blocked by a filing cabinet with one drawer permanently jammed out. The bicycle messenger was leaning against the stuck drawer, looking cocky and self-assured.

A handsome black man sat on the edge of a battered metal desk, eyeing the messenger with suspicion. "You don't work for me. What do you want?"

"A job," the messenger snorted.

"I'm guessing you just quit somewhere because they didn't pay for a delivery you made. Probably you were late and the customer went ballistic, phoned your boss and raised hell about it. Think I'll pick you up because I'm desperate. Or maybe you think you're hot shit and I'd be lucky to have you." The black man spoke with a slight Jamaican accent to his King's English. A framed degree on the wall indicated he'd graduated from Oxford University with a B.A. in literature.

The messenger grinned. "First time I missed in two years and those bastards stiff me. I was only ten minutes behind on a cross-town shot. Had to take the subway and change lines twice. Wasn't my fault. Trains were running late. So how much you pay?"

The owner picked up a rubber ball and began squishing it for stress relief. "Assuming I try you at all, you'd start at half the going rate."

"That's bullshit," the bicyclist snapped.

"You quit on the other guy. To me, you're a hothead who has to prove himself."

The messenger turned to leave, saw me in the doorway and halted. "Cash," he muttered quietly.

"Sorry, I didn't hear you," the black man said politely.

"You pay in cash and I'll do it for half rate. Once, just to show I'm good."

"Five times and you're paid at the end of the week with a check. You're good or you wouldn't have gotten mad and quit. I need to know you're also dependable."

"When do I get the other half of my check?" A tight smile curled the bicyclist's lip.

The owner sighed. "You don't."

The messenger turned around. I saw the muscles tense in his back. "You really are a bastard."

"That's how I survive. Look, I got a legal firm that wants some docs shuttled this afternoon. A divorce case. Over to the other lawyers and back. I'll count it as two runs. You in or out?"

"I'm in," the bicyclist said with disgust.

"Fine. You know where Broadway and Church is?"

"Yeah. In hell. Church runs parallel to Broadway."

"Good. So go to the corner of Broadway and Fulton instead. My brother-in-law is a lawyer at Samraat, Darbar and Akbed. Ask for Joseph Akbed. He'll give you the details. Come back here with this customer receipt signed and it'll be your first two runs for us." He handed a slip of paper to the messenger.

The bicyclist grabbed the chit and snapped around. He collided with me, pushed off and hurried out the door without even a "sorry." Still, I felt sorry for him. You had to be suicidal to ride a bike in Manhattan traffic, squeezed on your fee just like Hermes was squeezed by their clients.

I asked the owner, "You really go to Oxford?"

He gave me a cynical look. "Sure. Played cricket and punted on the Thames. Rhodes scholar. Gave me all the right connections so I could run a messenger service. Or maybe fifty bucks gives you a parchment from the college of your choice, provided you know the right place in Chinatown. Believe what you want." The owner looked me over. "You're not a client. A friend of Karen?"

I nodded. "I think you did go to Oxford."

His face turned bitter. "Yeah, for all the good it did me." He knocked on the closed door behind him. "Karen?" He talked like her lover, not her boss. He knocked on the door again. "Karen, you've got a visitor."

Karen Shaw's Vee-shaped face poked out of the door. It was a different Karen today. The dowdy black dress was replaced by a blue and white print with a scoop neck. Her hair was curled around her face, softening the harsh angle of her jaw. She had on makeup, not the right stuff, but enough to look a lot better. She took a moment to recognize me, then stepped out, looking skeptical.

I didn't wait to be invited. I shook hands with Karen and pulled her inside, shutting the door. Her small office had a window where a plant struggled for life on a narrow ledge. The window glass was painted over, but the paint was peeling off. In a few years, Karen would have a view office. Her limited personal space was crammed with ledgers, phone books and a little copier that filled the air with ozone.

Her desk was jammed in a corner and a lower drawer was open. Ever curious, I peeked inside the drawer and was startled to see a pair of leather restraints. I glanced at Karen's wrists and ankles. Red marks on her flesh were fading but still visible. Karen pushed the drawer closed with her foot and dumped paper over a used condom in the trash can. A blush crept up her cheeks.

She asked curtly, "Why are you here? I thought you represented Senator Cort. People who work for senators don't drop by my office to chat."

"I need your help." Maybe the honest approach would work.

"My help … for what?" Her eyes flashed. I thought I saw more fear than anger in her eyes.

I pushed on. "Richie didn't die accidentally. He was killed."

"What do you want me to do about it?" She flung her hands wide, a pencil wedged between her fingers.

I took a deep breath. "I want you to help me get his killer."

"You're not from Senator Cort, are you? That was bullshit. You're a cop. Undercover, or what?"

"No. I'm a reporter on *The New York Chronicle*. I was at the election headquarters the day ... well, the day Richie died. A lot of other people also died. Richie didn't kill them. Another man did the shooting. I saw him."

"So go to the police." Karen's shoulders slumped. Her head turned away. She looked hopeless.

"The police won't listen to me. I need help." I moved around the desk so she had to look at me.

Karen turned her back on me and stared at the painted-over window. She fingered wilted leaves on the struggling plant. "I can't help you. I don't know anything."

"You know who recruited Richie. That's a start."

"Look, I don't want any trouble. My brother's dead and there's nothing I can do for him. I have enough problems on my hands."

"Like your married boss." I talked in a whisper so he couldn't hear.

Karen tossed her hair back. She held her chin up high. "He's good to me because I give him what he wants. So what? A lot of guys cheat on their wives."

"I don't judge you – or him. What you do in private is between the two of you and doesn't concern me." Karen didn't respond, but I thought she relaxed a bit. I spoke to her very gently. "Karen, when did Richie join that organization, you know, the one called A United Tomorrow?"

"Last Christmas." She looked out the window through a small oval of peeled paint. Karen wasn't in the room. She was back in time, at a moment when things were better and her brother was alive. "We got together for a holiday dinner and Papa went in the kitchen. Soon as Papa left, Richie told me he'd been accepted into an elite organization. He was bursting with pride. I hadn't seen him that happy since he made the varsity wrestling team in high school." Tears welled in her eyes. "I didn't know who they were then. I thought it was some kind of athletic club, you know, a bunch of jocks."

"What are they instead?" I softly probed. But something about that question broke the spell and Karen hardened.

She glared at me. "You're so smart. You tell me who they are. Look, I got work to do." She sat behind the desk and started playing with files.

I leaned over the desk. "You can make the difference. If we link A United Tomorrow to Richie, I can bring them down."

130

She snapped the pencil in half. "Get out." She said it softly, but she meant it.

I drew a business card out of my wallet and tossed it on the files. "If you change your mind –"

"Get out!" she screamed.

Immediately, the office door opened. The owner glowered at me. He was holding a stun gun. He clicked the trigger and blue lightning crackled across the tips of the gun.

I held up my hands. "OK, OK, I'm leaving." I slid out of the room, past the stun gun. Karen was crying. But she hadn't thrown my card away.

I went down the narrow hallway and my steps echoed along the empty corridor as I walked. When I got to the stairs, he told me, "Best to leave it alone. Life's tough enough without inviting more trouble than you've already got."

"Yeah, sure," I said flatly, with my back to him. Then I turned and looked at him. "There's just one problem."

"Which is?" he asked, looking puzzled.

"Problem is, they won't leave me alone until I'm dead. And I object to that."

His face went hard. "Leave Karen and me out of it. We don't want any part of your problems."

"Can't blame you," I quipped, getting some of my spunk back. "I don't want any part of my problems either."

He softened. "Good luck."

I waved a flippant goodbye and headed down the stairs. It seemed Mr. Hermes Messenger Service had a heart after all. Maybe the leather restraints were Karen's idea. Who knows? Well, this much I knew for certain. I had to find a better lead than Karen Shaw. I couldn't sit around waiting for her to call me. By then I could be dead.

I walked a few blocks to a tavern that was once Meyer's Hotel, the last residence of cowgirl and sharpshooter Annie Oakley. I hoped her ghost would inspire me. To that end, I bought a drink named in her honor and saluted her indomitable personality. Too bad I didn't have her for a bodyguard.

After the drink, I used my recharged cell phone to call Donovan. He assured me the tryst was everything he'd dreamed. I told him I was happy his libido got release. But was his van available? Thankfully, the answer was yes. My credit cards were maxed, so I couldn't rent a car from Hertz or Avis, and I needed transportation out of the city to track other leads.

I'd done my homework in the morgue of *The New York Chronicle*, where they keep dead editions, not dead bodies. From that research, I had a list of all the hits on election headquarters. There'd been a killing in Albany, the state capital. Long as I had Donovan's van, I'd go to Albany after I visited the site where Collie Weiss died.

It was a long subway ride to Queens, where Donovan kept his VW van in the garage of his parents' house. Then, it was an even longer drive to Connecticut. I wasn't going to get any sleep that night if I wanted to be in Connecticut the next morning. Well, look on the bright side, Drew. The way you're moving around, Elijah will have a heck of a time tracking you down. With that encouraging thought, I paid my bar tab and left.

12

Dawn's shadows combed their long fingers across the VW van when I puttered into Ralph's Bait 'N Fill Shop in Glassberry, Connecticut. The gravel apron curled around a patchy lawn and led to a pair of red pumps from a bygone era. Hidden behind the antiques was a modern gas pump, camouflaged by an old-fashioned Coca-Cola dispenser and stacks of wooden bottle crates.

A teenager scuttled toward my van with a spray bottle dangling from the hammer loop on his bib overalls. He stopped in front of the rainbow-painted van and ran his eyes over all the peace symbols and flowers decorating the vehicle. My roommate Donovan was a 1960s hippie at heart, despite being born in 1982. Donovan even kept a complete collection of Led Zeppelin in the van.

The teenager stared in amazement at pink sunglasses and love beads dangling from the windshield mirror. "Wow, I bet you were at that Woodstock thing, where everybody took their clothes off."

I laughed. "Woodstock was before my time. And with my body, I'd better keep my clothes on." I started to get out, so I could pump the gas.

He put a hand up to stop me. "We're full serve." He beamed with pride. "Last in the country, except an Arco in Texas that does full serve at Christmas."

I knew better. I'd done an article on the resurgence of independent gas stations trying full service as a gimmick to attract customers. But I didn't want to hurt his feelings by contradicting him. So I just shrugged and got behind the steering wheel again. "Um, go at it, then."

"What grade you take?" he asked.

"Cheapest you got. This thing runs on anything you can light with a match." My humor got a smile from him, but he was generous with his smiles. I watched in the van's passenger-side mirror as the teen inserted a gas nozzle and started the pump. His red cap and faded overalls returned to the windshield and a spray of glass cleaner blocked my view. While he smeared bugs across my windshield, I glanced out the side at a rusted Model T truck that was supposed to add charm to the place. After the windows, he checked my oil level and tire inflation.

The pump clicked off and I was again confronted by the teenager's eager face. "That'll be twenty-four dollars and fifty-one cents. Owner said I don't have to collect the penny if people are nice. You've been nice. Forget the penny."

I handed him a fifty and waited for change. He refused the two dollar tip I offered. I groped on the seat to find the Post-It from Joanie with the name of the place where Collie Weiss was going when he died. "Isn't there a B&B near here?"

"You mean a campground, right?" He lifted the baseball cap by its folded brim. The teen smoothed his thick hair with a freckled hand.

"No, I was looking for a bed and breakfast. It's an expensive place." Blast me for losing that Post-It. I put Donovan's CD holder on the floor, careful not to damage his precious Led Zeppelin albums. I still didn't find anything on the seat.

The teen scratched his head and looked skeptically at the VW van. "You sure you don't want a campground? State park's nearby. Only five dollars a night to stay there."

"Positive," I muttered. I opened my duffel bag and started rummaging.

"Well, the place for you might be Warden's Motel, 'bout ten miles up the road." He pointed down the highway.

"Oh, I see. You think I mean to stay at this B&B. No, I'm just going to ask them a few questions. You judged me correctly. I don't have the kind of money it takes to rent a room in this place I'm looking for. It's a really high-end bed and breakfast."

"No insult meant, miss."

"No insult taken."

His face relaxed. "You must be looking for Charter House. It's mighty expensive."

"That's the place." I sighed in relief. There was an auto club road atlas on the dashboard, opened to a map of the area. I held the book where he could point at the map. "Where's Charter House located?"

He ignored the road atlas and gave me directions. "Get back on the road, the way you was goin' and keep on about a mile. You'll see a sign for Charter House, just before a steep driveway. Can't miss it. None of my business, but if'n you only want to ask questions, why not just call 'em? Pay phone's over there." He pointed at a booth near a patio with tables and metal umbrellas.

"Thanks, but I'll have to drive there. My questions are a bit complicated. I want to make sure they understand, so I get the right answers. Say, those picnic tables remind me how hungry I am. You serve any food this early?"

"Hope you don't want something cooked. Ralph does the cooking, not me, and he's gone today." The teen frowned.

"No problem. Need to lose some weight anyway. Thanks."

He shrugged and walked away, looking happy and carefree.

I certainly envied him. I put the van in gear and idled toward the highway, gravel crunching lightly under the tires. Dew misted off the lawn as the sun hit the grass. A dog on the porch barked at me. I glanced down the two lane strip and there was no one else on the road, so I accelerated and the van bounced onto the highway. Trees lined the highway and their branches rippled in the wind of a coming storm, but the sky was clear for the moment.

A mile later, I saw the sign for Charter House, right where the teen said it would be. I raced the VW's overburdened engine to climb their steep driveway. Foliage and vines hung down stone walls on both sides of me as the van swung up the curved ascent. At the top, the driveway fanned into a cobbled motor court with a fountain in the center, where a gardener was planting yellow and blue pansies. Charter House sat across the far end, bordered by ivy covered cottages. The main structure was a two-story building made of the same stones lining the driveway. Tree roses fanned on both sides of the lacquered front door. A large brass knocker hung in the center of the door, gleaming in the bright sunlight.

I parked and walked a short flagstone path lined with yet more flowers to a side entrance. The door was ajar, so I stepped inside and was halted by a pile of laundry in the hallway. I gingerly stepped over the jumbled sheets and stole a glance into a room. The place was idyllic, to say the least.

A floral print on the canopy of a four poster bed matched a goose down comforter tossed in a heap on the thick carpet. Canopy and comforter were complemented by a floral pattern on the drapes. The curtains were parted to let sunlight filter through sheers and caress a massive sea chest with brass hinges and lock. I could smell sandalwood potpourri, in ceramic bowls on the tops of antique dressers. Well, Collie Weiss had class, asking me to a place like this. A wave of guilt hit me and I shook it off, telling myself I hadn't killed him. Elijah had done it.

I went into the parlor, looking for the innkeeper. There was a loveseat in front of a bay window with a gorgeous view. A massive hearth held burned logs from last night's romantic fire. A nearby table offered sherry in a crystal decanter. I kept going until I hit the check-in area, but there was no innkeeper behind the desk. I saw the red and black checks of a flannel shirt through the bay window, so I went out the front door and found I'd looped back to where I'd begun my walking tour, only a few steps from Donovan's VW.

The flannel shirt was bent over, rolling up a hose. He looked very L.L. Bean in his check shirt, twill pants and rubber boots. Trying not to startle him, I gently said, "Good morning. I'm looking for the innkeeper."

I didn't get an answer right away. He finished rolling the hose on an ornate cast-iron wheel. Then he stayed bent over and began pulling weeds. He talked into the flower bed. "That'd be me. I'm the innkeeper."

I guess he reserved his charm for paying guests. "Some friends of mine were supposed to stay with you this weekend. Collie Weiss and his wife. As you may know, they died on the way here."

"Not hard to know. Made the front page of our paper." He looked at me. There were no emotions showing in his wrinkled face.

I exhaled. My breath fogged in the damp morning air. "Well, you see, I think they didn't die by accident." I let that one hang, to see where it would get me. It didn't take me very far.

He just said, "Oh?"

"Did you by any chance see a short man, built like a jockey, last night? With curly hair?"

The innkeeper scratched his chin thoughtfully. But I had the feeling he was just going through the motions.

I prompted him. "You might have seen this jockey in the parking lot, maybe after dark."

"Nope. We go to bed early, so we can get up early." He picked two leaves off the gravel path and dropped them on the pile of weeds.

"Well, if you remember something, give me a call, OK?" I handed him my business card, figuring I had nothing to lose.

He looked at my card like it was a court summons. I knew it was going into the compost pile with the leaves, after I left.

I shuffled a bit. "Where's the local police station?"

Finally, he showed some enthusiasm. He was getting rid of me. He pointed down the hill. "Go back the way you came. Make a right out of the driveway. Keep on for five miles. State troopers are on the left. You won't have any trouble recognizing their place."

"Thanks," I muttered. I stepped over a meowing black cat and wondered if that was an omen. I got in Donovan's VW and put-putted off to see the cops. The innkeeper was actually understated in describing the state trooper headquarters as unmistakable. The low stucco building bristled with a nest of antennas. Cop cars were parked at one end of the sterile building. The patrol cars were lined up exactly parallel, in precise law-and-order fashion.

Inside, I was hit by an overpowering odor of disinfectant and urine from holding cells in the back. I heard someone in a holding cell cough, then flush a toilet. The narrow visitor entrance was blocked by a counter where a binder of incident reports was opened to today. I rang a bell and peeked around the corner, putting my best smile on my face.

A tall, lean sergeant put down his coffee cup. He was a wiry gym rat, pumped arms and thin body. His thick black hair was slicked back, exposing his tan forehead. He managed to be rugged and masculine without being good looking. Immune to my charming smile, he asked flatly, "You need something?"

"Well, yeah. I need to talk to someone about that accident where a Porsche went off the road and two people were killed." I put my elbows on the counter and rocked on my toes. I wasn't sure where this would go, but I was hoping it went farther than my chats with Karen Shaw and the innkeeper.

"You a witness or a relative?" His eyes were tired, but his movements were quick and alert. His nameplate read "J. Doherty."

"A friend." I waited until Doherty came closer. He stood in front of me, hands on his equipment belt, head slightly cocked. I took that as a question mark and continued, "I have reason to think it was a killing, not an accident." I saw his eyes widen.

Doherty turned and pulled a folder from the holder on a desk. He opened the folder and read a few lines. "The Porsche was probably going ninety when it hit the railing and flipped into a ravine. Why do you think it was a killing, not someone being stupid or drunk?"

"For a lot of reasons." I produced my card and gave it to him. As he eyed it, I said, "I believe it enough to drive all the way from Manhattan. Was there any evidence that the car was tampered with?"

He flipped my card between his thumb and forefinger. "Truth is, Ms. Morrissey, we didn't look. It seemed like reckless driving. There'd been a rock slide and he lost control on the gravel, spun into the rail and flipped."

"Call me Drew. Any chance I could go there and look around? I'd welcome your help, if you'd like to go too." I realized he was alone in the desk area. "That is, if someone can cover for you, Sergeant."

"Yeah, I can get somebody in here. Wait a minute and we'll go out there in my car. It isn't far. We can be there in a few minutes." He donned his Smokey-the-Bear hat and disappeared into the holding cell area. When he returned, Doherty was wearing his leather jacket and twirling a key ring. "Come on, let's go." He flipped the counter up and walked through. "And you can call me Jay."

We drove for about ten miles alongside the surging waters of the Housatonic River as it cut a gorge through surrounding mountains. I was wedged between a shotgun, a computer terminal, a portable radio and a first-aid kit. Now I knew why they reduced the qualifying height for police officers. It had nothing to do with giving women equal opportunity. They allowed shorter police officers because every team needed a midget to fit in the passenger seat. I wouldn't have minded riding in the back, since none of my friends would see me in the cage.

Jay gave me a compassionate look. "It's not much farther."

"How do you stand this for hours at a time?" I massaged a leg cramp.

He laughed. "Luckily, state police seldom ride in pairs. When we do, I pull the shotgun out and put it in the trunk."

"Don't let me stop you."

"Have no fear. I'll remove the shotgun before we start back." He pointed ahead, where the road lifted and ran straight along a ridge, then took a sharp turn. At the bend was an overlook, bordered by a guard rail. "That's where the accident happened." Jay stopped at the overlook and talked into his lapel mike, giving his location.

I got out and stretched, rubbing a knee that had forgotten it was attached to me. I squinted at the hillside across the highway. Along the hill's base was a jumble of rocks the size of golf balls. They'd been swept there recently. There were streaks of red dust on the road from the cleanup effort. "That where the slide occurred?"

"Yeah. We've never had rocks come loose there before. I wrote it off as a deer running up the hill, kicking a boulder loose and starting a little avalanche. But you think this was a killing. Seems we ought to give that hillside a closer inspection."

We scampered across the highway and climbed, slipping on loose shale, until we reached the top. From the crest, I had a view of the straight-away approaching the overlook. Elijah could easily spot Collie's Porsche coming into the turn. I looked down. There were a series of holes evenly spaced across the hillside.

Jay came alongside me. He looked at the holes and said, "Yeah, it does seem someone planted charges, doesn't it?"

"Can you tell anything from soil samples? Would an explosive leave traces?"

"Dunno. I can try." He took a plastic baggie from his coat pocket. I helped him fill the bag with a soil sample from each hole. Our path took us down the hillside, toward the road. Halfway, I paused to look at the twisted guardrail on the other side. There were black tire marks leading to a bent section, where silver car paint was streaked along the Armco barrier.

Finished with the soil samples, we walked to the guardrail. I leaned over and looked down. In the gorge below, Mrs. Collie Weiss' brightly colored scarf was streaming in the wind, caught on a jagged piece of door. The Porsche was shattered into pieces no larger than a fender.

Doherty remarked, "Weiss must have been going at the Porsche's top speed, about 180 miles per hour, when he flew off the road. The guardrail barely slowed the car down. That's why the scene looks more like a jet crash than a car accident. The car parts are scattered over quite an area since the impact was so large. But we can still walk through it. It's quite a hike down there and back. You game for it?"

"No," I said, laughing. "But I'll do it anyway."

My frayed Nikes didn't have much grip in the sandy dirt, so I slid more than walked down. I was wondering the whole time how I'd get back up. Then I saw a trail that wound to the top in switchbacks, about a hundred yards from where we were. I was relieved Doherty wouldn't have to helicopter me out. Once I got to the bottom, I realized I didn't know what to look for and my eyes just skittered across debris without a focus.

Fortunately, Jay had training in these things. He donned latex gloves and picked up a twisted wheel attached to a rod. "Drew, I think you're right."

He offered me a better look at the metal bar, but I declined. I hadn't any idea why he thought I was right. But it was nice by comparison with Saul's opinions of me lately.

"Don't know what this is?" Jay asked.

"No. Truth is, I don't know much about cars, except how to drive one."

"You're not alone. Most of the world couldn't identify this part. It's the steering rack. Few cars in the world use rack and pinion steering today, but Porsche does. See here?" He pointed to the jagged edge.

"Yeah?" I started to touch it, then realized he was wearing gloves to protect any fingerprints on the bar.

"This jagged tear is where the steering rack was blown apart. It didn't break from the crash. The rack is tempered steel. It would have bent, maybe even snapped. But it wouldn't have shattered like this. I'll bet my badge the lab will find traces of explosive on the metal rod."

"Great," I said, then regretted my words. It wasn't great that Collie Weiss and his wife had been killed. "Jay, how long will it take before you know for sure?"

"I'll put a rush on it. Forty-eight hours max. I'll call you when I get the results. Your cell phone's on the business card, right?"

"Yeah. I'm going to Albany next, to see the Coroner there."

"This pro stage another accident in Albany?" He pushed his hat back in astonishment.

"Not an accident. I believe he walked into an election headquarters in Albany and gunned down a bunch of people." I kicked a rock with my toe and sent it scuttling into the river.

"Last year? I thought that was a kooky kid, went nuts."

"Everyone does. That's why I have to go to Albany. I think I know who sponsors this guy. Thanks Jay, you've been a big help."

"Sure. Good luck."

"I don't need luck," I joked. "I need that shotgun moved to the trunk on the ride back."

"That you've got. Race me to the top? Loser buys a cola?"

"I concede. You win. I'm taking that switchback path, the easy trail for out-of-shape tourists like me."

He smiled. "I'll keep you company. I'm in no hurry to ride in a patrol car. I do that enough hours a day."

By the time we got to his patrol car, I was thinking about breaking my rule against dating a cop. Then I remembered how far from Manhattan he lived. Nah, it couldn't possibly work out. He was older, wouldn't have the same values as my generation. It'd only be a physical relationship, based on his hard body.

Jay pulled the shotgun out and put it in the trunk. When he got in the car, his leg brushed mine and I felt a tingle of man-woman electricity. Think about the coroner's office in Albany, Drew. That's where you're going next. Keep your focus on cold bodies in a morgue – not the warm hunk sitting next to you in the car. But my restraint didn't last.

"Um, Jay," I said coyly, "I might need your home number." He cocked an eyebrow. I knew he'd see through my ruse but I kept going anyway. "In case I need to ask an urgent question and you aren't at work …"

13

The Albany Coroner's office was in a neatly restored turn-of-the-century building, located in the old downtown area of the city. A small tower on the building's front corner held a clock with black hands marking the time on Roman numerals. The tower clock looked like a giant's pocket watch. The clock's minute hand hung straight down, pointing at me, when I bounded up salt and pepper granite steps and swung through a heavy beveled glass door.

I kept trying to convince myself that all this running around was leading somewhere. It had, after all, led to Jay Doherty and potential evidence Collie Weiss was murdered. But that evidence certainly didn't implicate A United Tomorrow or Elijah, at this point. I had to keep probing and hope something else turned up.

It was cold inside the building and the air was heavy with pungent chemicals. Light from a distant window carried along the shiny black stone floor, showing me a series of doors along a hallway. Heavy brass knobs jutted in procession along the corridor. The doors had frosted glass windows with gilt lettering defining the occupants.

It might have been an office building filled with tax accountants, except that I was standing near an industrial refrigerator door, the kind used in supermarkets. Milk wasn't kept behind that stainless steel door. This was where the coroner kept dead bodies, and the smells were from chemicals used during autopsies. It was eerie to be alone in the lobby with no one around but corpses.

A porcelain bowl lamp hung on chains above the first step of a staircase, flooding the building directory with light. White push-in letters were laid neatly in the black furrows of the directory, showing that the Head Coroner's office was on the second floor. So I went up the green marble staircase with an ornate railing, my steps echoing off a copper ceiling.

At the top, I found a row of office doors identical to the ones below. The door at the very end was labeled "Head Coroner." A typewriter chattered away inside, the only sign of life I'd heard in the building. I knocked lightly on the rippled glass.

"Come in," came the masculine reply.

I opened the door, expecting an old man in suspenders at an antique Remington, the kind with round keys and a gleaming ebony case. I found a college-age boy hitting the keys of a gray plastic typewriter. His name plate read "Michael Devon." Michael's reddish-blonde hair was cut high-and-tight. The crew-cut sides of his beefy head led to a thick neck bulging in a shirt collar. The knot of his tie bobbed as talked. "How can I help you?"

"I have an appointment with the Head Coroner. My name is Drew Morrissey. I'm a reporter with *The New York Chronicle*."

"I'll tell Dr. Horning you're here. There was an emergency about an hour ago. A guy was found dead by the interstate and they brought the body here for autopsy. Have a seat." Michael pointed to a wooden bench pushed between oak filing cabinets. The opposite wall was lined with bookshelves, their glass faces pulled down to keep out dust. Devon left and I heard his shoes tapping the black stone corridor as he briskly strode away.

I sat on the bench for only a moment. Waiting was not my forte. I got up and peered out the window. A few seconds of examining the parking lot were all I could handle and then I began inspecting bookcases. I discovered there was one vinyl three-ring binder for each calendar year, starting with 1972. The binders were followed by cardboard holders packed with medical journals. I tried looking at one of the journals and was grossed-out by interior shots of a man's colon during advancing stages of cancer.

Ugly photos don't stop an inquiring reporter or a bored Drew Morrissey. I squatted on my haunches to see what was on the lowest rows of the bookshelves. Same thing, just older journals with less vivid but still disturbing pictures, black and white shots of gall bladder surgery. I popped up and moved to the filing cabinets. Each drawer was labeled with a range of letters in the alphabet. I tried "H" for Hinkle, the name of the fall guy for the Albany election headquarters killings, but it was locked. In frustration, I tried every drawer and found them all locked.

I gave up being a snoop and let the rigid wood of the bench crease my jeans. In moments, I was restless again, went to the restroom, splashed water on my face and bought breath mints from the vending machine. I didn't buy the Butterfinger bar that was winking at me. In case anything developed with State Trooper Jay Doherty, I needed to lose the seven pounds I'd recently gained. My new lover since Jamie left was Haagen-Daz. We went to bed together and watched Jay Leno while I drained the pint of Vanilla Swiss Almond down to wet cardboard. The breath mint was sugar free and as poor a substitute for Haagen-Daz as ice cream was for sex.

But chewing two breath mints gave me a bright idea. I tried picking the lock on the "H" drawer with a bent paper clip. I almost made the lock when I heard two sets of shoes coming toward me. There was the unmistakable slap of Michael Devon's brogues and a pair of soft rubber shoes, so light in their step they were almost inaudible. I threw the bent paper clip in the trash and rushed to the bench, trying to look like a sweet, innocent girl who'd never even think of examining the coroner's files without authorization.

The door opened and Michael stepped inside. Then the coroner came through the doorway, his hair under a gauze cap, a surgical mask draped on his chest. A blue surgical gown covered his business clothes and his shoes were wrapped in latex booties, which accounted for the soft footsteps.

The coroner had an elongated face, made even longer by elegant sideburns turning gray at the tips. I wondered if he'd groomed those sideburns for a role in a local play or was an amateur musician. His eyes, though, were intense and went with a lumpy nose broken a few times in football or boxing. Long hairs flared from his thick eyebrows. He seemed part mad scientist, part street-smart fighter.

He moved over to me and introduced himself in a cold, professional voice. "I'm Martin Horning. Sorry you were kept waiting. Michael explained why."

"Yes, he did." I rose and shook Dr. Horning's hand. He indicated I should follow him to his private office.

Horning disposed of the surgical garments, then sat behind his desk in a wooden swivel chair. He folded his hands on a green felt blotter with leather edges. The desk was piled with manila folders and his in-basket was clogged. "What can I do for you, Ms. Morrissey?"

"I was hoping you could shed some light on killings at an election headquarters in Albany last year. I think they may be related to murders that happened last week in midtown Manhattan."

"The police caught the Albany killer and he's been convicted. That case is closed."

"Yes, but maybe they only caught one of the killers – or maybe they got the wrong man." I realized too late that Dr. Horning probably had a major role in convicting Hinkle and resented my implication there'd been errors in the case.

"You're entitled to your theories, but Tom Hinkle confessed, did he not?"

"Yes, I understand Hinkle confessed to doing the murders."

Horning's face was expressionless, except for an irritable droop of his mouth. "Hinkle knew details that only the killer could have known, Ms. Morrissey."

I suggested, "Hinkle could have been there but done no killing. Or Hinkle could have been briefed by the real killer."

"So you theorize that Tom Hinkle voluntarily let himself be sentenced to life imprisonment for a crime he didn't commit? Why in the world would someone do that?"

"Fame," I answered. "A desperate need to be somebody. Or paid a lot of money. Maybe he didn't know what he was getting into. Maybe he was fanatically loyal. There are lots of reasons, Dr. Horning, that people do crazy things. Some people blow up a federal courthouse in Oklahoma City. Others spray a Tokyo subway with nerve gas. It's a sick world and we're living in the nation with the highest concentration of disturbed people in the world, with the possible exception of the Middle East." I wasn't going to back down.

Horning softened a little, but not much. He rocked in his chair, took off his glasses and wiped them. "Let's take your theory one step farther. Suppose Hinkle was motivated by one of the reasons you hypothesize. What do you have as evidence of a conspiracy? That Hinkle had a good legal defense, so there must be money behind the killings here in Albany?"

"That's a piece of the puzzle, yes. The rest of the puzzle is this – I think Hinkle was a well planned fall guy like Richie Shaw was in Manhattan. I happened to be inside the Manhattan election headquarters when the killings took place. I escaped by a miracle. I won't go into the details. Afterwards, I went through the election headquarters with the police. I saw every victim had been systematically killed. They were disabled by a messy shot, if necessary, but then they were double-tapped in the head as a coup de grace. That's not the technique of a hopped-up fanatic."

"You were surprisingly observant for someone who was excited and stressed." Horning still looked skeptical.

"I'm paid to be observant, Dr. Horning. I'm a reporter."

"Touché," he conceded.

"I add this fact – the weapon used in Manhattan was a submachine gun, but there were no bullets sprayed around. A pro would use a submachine gun in just that manner. The high-firepower weapon was a safety factor in case cops showed up unexpectedly. But the gun was fired like a sporting pistol, single shots, deadly accurate."

"That's it? I could explain the accurate shots as the result of training, perhaps in the military. If there was no military record for the assailant, then he was a covert member of a paramilitary organization. There are thousands of them around the country. Query the Internet and you're drowned in web sites for them."

"Fine, Dr. Horning, but why weren't Richie Shaw's fingerprints in the election headquarters? Why bother hiding your prints if you intend to confess? Plus, I saw Richie Shaw, the fall guy in New York City, sitting in his UPS truck while the murders were happening. Shaw was talking to Howard Stern as the shooting went on. Shaw identified himself on the air. He wanted the world to think he did it. Does any of this sound like the Hinkle case?"

Horning cleared his throat. "This is an election year for me, Ms. Morrissey. I have to be careful what I say to a reporter. May I call you Drew?"

I nodded. He could call me Miss Piggy as long as he gave me some data. Oink.

Horning got up and paced in front of his window. "This is strictly off the record. You are not authorized to quote me or allude to this meeting, is that understood?"

"Sure. I just need data to convince my editor. What do you know that I can't print?"

"I won't show you any crime scene photos or autopsy reports. Hinkle has an appeal pending and the court sealed all evidence." Dr. Horning leaned on his window sill and looked into the parking lot.

"So what can you do?"

"I can tell you that Hinkle had no military record, no obvious paramilitary associations, no record of police training. Yet the wounds in Albany were just as you described for New York. They were fatal shots, reinforced in a calculated manner by a second shot. I performed a frontal craniotomy on each victim and pulled two slugs out of their brains. Double-tapped, as you call it. Ballistics ID'd the bullets as NATO-style ammunition consistent with a submachine gun."

"Did the police ever find the gun?" I asked.

"No. Hinkle claimed he dumped it in a garbage truck. They tore up the local landfill without success, which makes me thinks Hinkle was lying.

They sifted through ten days of garbage collection by hand and found every burger wrapper, but no gun. Metal detectors were used and all the garbage workers voluntarily took lie detector tests to prove they didn't find the weapon and keep it themselves. I tried to get the police to look at a second man scenario, but they had their case wrapped up and weren't interested."

"No spray of bullets, like an enraged co-worker or drugged killer?"

"Not a wasted shot. From a clinical perspective, it was eerie." He stared vacantly out the window, as though recalling from memory the actual bodies and sifting for a contradiction to his statement. He came back from the trance and reaffirmed, "No extra shots at all. Cool, calculated execution."

"A pro."

"Definitely. But who would sponsor such a thing?"

"Off the record? Please don't quote me on this." I grinned.

Horning smiled back, appreciating the humor in this change of roles. "Certainly, as you insist."

"A well-organized movement called A United Tomorrow. I think they arrange it, finance it, want it."

"But why? A United Tomorrow has plenty of power without these killings. They seem to have another senator in their pocket every week."

"That's the sick part. They hire the killings done to make themselves look more moderate so they can attract mainstream voters. 'Terrible, this persecution of people who disagree with us,' they say."

"That is sick." Horning sat again in his swivel chair and tapped a pen on his blotter. "I hope you get them, Drew, but please be careful. If they did hire a pro, he won't hesitate to kill you."

"I know. That's why I'm here. He's already made a second attempt on my life."

Dr. Horning winced. "Glad he missed."

"Missed me, but killed two innocent people."

"Damn. That's terrible." Horning's fighting instincts came out. "Hinkle is in Attica. You could interview him. Prison changes people. He might be willing to talk."

I shrugged. "Sure. I'll see him."

"Good luck, Drew. He's a real case. I don't think he's lived in reality since early childhood. Both parents were druggies."

"I'll keep that in mind." We shook hands and I left. I walked past the refrigerator with its body bags and stood on the granite steps for a moment, breathing fresh air into my lungs to purge the formaldehyde.

Maybe I was making progress after all. Jay Doherty thought the Porsche was ambushed and Dr. Horning's opinions confirmed mine. Yeah, he was off the record, but combine that with bugs in my apartment and seeing Elijah at Bleighberg's Grocery. Then even cynical Saul Morgenthal might think I was right about the killings. I decided to leave Saul a message telling him I was going to Attica. I called Saul on my cell phone and he wasn't available. What else is new? I left him a voicemail updating him on my progress.

Then I looked at Donovan's road atlas and mapped a route to Attica. I'd never been to a maximum security prison. I wondered what it would feel like?

14

Attica State Prison was a giant of unbending steel and stone, glowering at me with an intimidating stare as I stood in its guardhouse. Somehow the prison felt run-down without being derelict in the slightest. Actually, the place was immaculate, scrubbed clean like a military barracks, yet the sterility was terribly depressing. The prison was like the clipboard held by the guard, an unattractive but functional artifact, something no one would want if they were given a choice. The clipboard's hard back was scrubbed of any shine, its metal clip dulled by the press of hundreds of thumbs. The guard flipped pages and found "Morrissey, D." on the last sheet.

"Are you here for a tour?" the guard asked politely.

"No, an interview with Tom Hinkle, an inmate. I'm with *The New York Chronicle*," I explained.

"Follow the signs. You can't get lost." He pressed the release button and a heavy lock on the exit gate buzzed irritably.

"Thanks." I turned up the collar of my jacket and went through the metal barrier. Wind kicked a gust of rain into my face as I stepped outside. Icy water stung my hands and cheeks, so I ran, dodging potholes filled with water. My hair was soaked by the time I reached a metal door and pressed it open.

It was oppressively hot inside the prison building. I pulled off my jacket and folded it over my arm. Then I shook my hair and water pelted off. I'd really gotten drenched. I discovered my choices for where I could go were limited, to say the least. I could walk five steps, visit employment and apply for a job – or I could follow a line painted on the floor, to the visiting area. I opted for the dotted red line, which took me to a coat check alcove.

A young woman in a guard's uniform was sitting behind the chipped Formica counter of the coat room. "Want to check your jacket?" she asked. Behind her was a wall of pigeonholes, some filled by purses and bags.

"Ah, sure," I answered, laying my jacket on the counter. "Just let me get my pen and pad out."

She pushed a numbered token at me. "Don't lose this. I can't give anything back without a token."

I winced. A prison's institutional mentality affected even their coat checking.

She caught my reaction and explained, "Families of inmates are poor. They can't afford to lose anything. Tokens prevent someone from taking a purse that doesn't belong to them. You have a good jacket. You don't want me handing your coat to someone else, do you?

"No," I agreed. It wouldn't have been hard for her to remember me and return the jacket without a token. But I didn't argue with her. She was doing her job the way they taught her to do it, by the prison's long list of rules. Hell, as the ultimate prison, must have an even larger set of regulations. In keeping with prison rules, I signed the visitor roster and filled out a request card for seeing Hinkle. At that point, there was nothing I could do but wait. I was hoping Tom Hinkle was in the mood to see me. Months of isolation should make him eager to talk with another human being.

I looked around the waiting room. The area had a dull, two-tone paint job that made the place seem even more desolate than its audience. A small group of what politicians call the "underclass" were sitting on metal folding chairs arranged in rows. At the far end were cubicles where prisoners talked to visitors through microphones, separated by thick glass. Did they record everything, I wondered? Probably. I could hardly wait to get out of there. I couldn't imagine Hinkle trading the rest of his life in Attica for a fleeting moment of fame. I was having difficulty with visiting for a few minutes.

There was a middle-aged guard with her arms folded, eyes glazed from boredom. I walked to her and asked, "Is there any way to check on my request to see Tom Hinkle? I'm not a friend. I'm here to interview him for *The New York Chronicle*. I made an appointment through the warden's office yesterday."

"Sure. It'll give me something to do. Have a seat. It'll be a few minutes. It's a long walk to Hinkle's area from here." She gestured at the metal chairs, then swiped her ID card and vanished through a door.

I fidgeted for about thirty minutes before the door opened again. The female guard was there with a male companion, an Hispanic man in dress trousers and sports coat. His tie had a stain and his shirt collar was frayed, like the man's expression. "Ms. Morrissey?" he asked, scanning the room.

I stood up and crossed to him, holding out my hand.

He shook my hand without enthusiasm. "I'm Jorge Garcia, an associate warden here at Attica. You came to see Tom Hinkle?"

"Yes." I looked at the cubicles, but I didn't see Hinkle's face. "Is he here?"

"No, Ms. Morrissey." Garcia coughed. He fingered his coat pocket for a lozenge and popped one in his mouth. "Regrettably, Tom Hinkle is dead. I'm sorry your trip was in vain."

I was stunned, to say the least. "Why didn't somebody tell me this before I drove here?"

"We called your cell phone this morning and left a message." He couldn't look at me when he said the words. He was bluffing.

I dug my hands into my pockets in frustration. "When did this happen? I mean, Hinkle dying."

"Just before you arrived."

"How did he die?" I stared intently at Associate Warden Garcia. My stomach was tight as a fist.

"Hinkle was killed in the exercise yard by another life-termer. The man who murdered Tom Hinkle is an expert with the knife. He knew exactly where to stab so Hinkle died before we could rush him to our hospital. The life-term cell block is on lock-down and we're searching to make sure there're no more hidden weapons. It appears the "knife" was fabricated in our maintenance area by another prisoner. Probably the crude blade was hidden in the exercise yard at a pre-arranged "drop." We're reviewing security video to see if we can spot the drop and the pickup. To answer your next question, Ms. Morrissey, I'm sorry, but you can't interview Hinkle's killer. Later, perhaps, after our investigation is concluded. Then, he'll be arraigned for yet another murder, although it's a crime few care about."

"I care about it. Hinkle was an important link to a string of politically motivated homicides. He was probably murdered to keep me from talking to him."

Garcia nodded. "Makes sense. Killing by a lifer is always paid on the outside. I'm convinced of it, even though we've never cracked a single case. When they do a hit inside, it's to make sure their family gets money. They get nothing from it themselves. In fact, they lose a lot. Lifers cherish the few privileges they earn. Do a hit, they're gone for good. You're in chains. His defense will say the killing was racial. The killer was black. Hinkle was white. But Hinkle was a mouse. He never said an ugly word to anyone. He was too scared to pick a fight."

"How many people at Attica knew I was visiting Hinkle?"

Garcia didn't answer. He scowled at me. "Attica is maximum security. That means we run extended background investigations on our employees, even the cleaning crews. Plus, our guards are randomly sampled for drugs and submit to lie-detector tests. You do that at *The Chronicle*, Ms. Morrissey? How many people at *The Chronicle* knew you were visiting Hinkle?"

"We have a drug-free workplace," I said lamely.

"It's not the same and you know it. Besides, nobody who works here wants to be inside a prison. They see everyday how bad it is. You can imagine what happens if a guard goes to prison, how they get treated."

I gave up. This was a useless fight. "OK, the leak probably wasn't here. You satisfied?"

Jorge looked at his watch. "Anything else I can do for you, Ms. Morrissey? May I offer you a tour of the prison as long as you're here? We try very hard to cooperate with the press."

"I'll pass on the tour. I've got the flavor of the place. Look, forget my questioning your integrity. I apologize. Will you do this for me? If something breaks and you find a link does exist in Hinkle's murder, will you call me?"

"Of course. But don't hold your breath. It would be the first time ever."

"Well, there's a first time for everything. I've had a lot of unpleasant firsts lately. I'm overdue for something good to happen."

"Hope it does." Garcia shook my hand, just as limply as he did the first time. Then he swiped his badge and disappeared inside the prison, doing a job I couldn't be forced into for even an hour, much less until retirement.

I returned to the chipped counter, plucked the token from my jeans pocket and spun it on the Formica. The girl already had my jacket waiting, even before she saw the token. I put the jacket on and went outside. It was still pouring and I was soaked again by the time I made the guard shack. The guard opened the door for me and yawned, revealing a depressing amount of dental work.

"What a lousy day," I sighed.

"Supposed to rain tomorrow, also." He thought I meant the weather. I wished I only had the weather to worry about.

He said enviously, "It must be great being a reporter and traveling around. Me, I just sit here."

"No," I warned him, "being a reporter isn't fun. Being a reporter is like all the other jobs in this crazy world, hard work with little reward." I wagged a hand in a goodbye gesture and sprinted through the rain toward Donovan's van.

I had a long drive ahead of me. I didn't trust phones anymore. After the shock of finding Hinkle dead, I decided to catch Saul at the pressroom when he put tonight's edition to bed. He was such a workaholic that Saul watched them roll the presses at midnight, printing the last sections of the paper. Even A United Tomorrow couldn't hear me talking to Saul over the thunder of those printing presses.

15

A block-long concrete slab vibrated under my feet when I walked into the printing plant at College Point, Queens. The four-story-tall presses of *The New York Chronicle* were rolling paper and ink into the next edition. I climbed stairs to the second level and walked alongside a torrent flowing at 50,000 newspapers an hour. Nearby, press operators wore ear protectors as they casually moved along the metal catwalk, oblivious to the frightening prospect of being crushed between rollers that laid ink on paper. It was one o'clock in the morning and I teetered from exhaustion on the catwalk, grabbing the handrail tightly to make sure I didn't fall in the machinery. My nostrils burned from fixer spray used to quickly dry the ink.

I spotted Saul Morgenthal in a glass booth they call the Master Work Station. Saul was joking with the foreman, inspecting a huge sheet of newsprint containing uncut pages. I waved to Morgenthal and he twisted his face, hunching his posture. I could see that talking to him was going to be so much fun.

Saul left the control booth and came toward me, swinging his bulk gracefully under a railing and descending a ladder. The editor scowled at me as we approached. When we met, I tried shouting at Saul, but he just frowned and gestured toward the break area. It was impossible to hear any conversation over the thunder of the press line.

Morgenthal put his beefy hand on the break room's door and swung it open. The racket followed us inside, then ceased to a hum when the door shut. Inside the break area were round tables with plastic chairs and a wall of vending machines. Saul ignored me and put change in the coffee dispenser.

I went for the sodas. No sleep the night before meant I needed a real jolt to keep going. Mere coffee wasn't going to cut it. A dollar poorer, I slumped in an orange scoop chair and sipped an icy cola.

Saul patiently waited for instant brew to fill a paper cup, holding his thumb insistently on the extra-cream button. The editor dragged a chair across the linoleum with a screech and sat down, toying with the hot cup. He risked a sip and winced in pain. Saul had remained calm while the cup was filling, yet it drove him nuts waiting for the coffee to cool so he could drink. This was one of the many contradictions I termed "Saul-isms."

Morgenthal eyed me suspiciously over his steaming coffee. "OK, hot shot, what've you got for me? It must be good for you to drive here at one in the morning."

"We needed to talk outside your office. It's safer."

"Safer? It can't be safer. I'm here, Morrissey, waiting to fire your ass."

"Safer from electronic surveillance bugs. Listen, Saul —"

"Bugs!" Morgenthal laughed, spitting out a sip of coffee. "You're losing it, Drew. Nobody bugs *The New York Chronicle*."

"I called yesterday and left a message saying I was heading for Attica Prison to interview Tom Hinkle. He's the kid who took the rap for a hit in Albany last year. Guess what Saul?"

He wrinkled his eyebrows. "OK, what?"

"Hinkle was dead when I arrived at the prison. He was stabbed just before I got to Attica. Another inmate serving a life term, an expert at killing with a knife, did the job. An associate warden, Jorge Garcia, thinks somebody on the outside paid for this kill. Hinkle was murdered to keep him from talking to me."

Saul blew across his coffee and shrugged. "OK, that's a point on your scorecard. I'll tell security to sweep for bugs. They do it annually. I'll tell 'em to do it tomorrow." Saul tried another sip. "What else you got, besides paranoia? By the way, you on coke? They say the last stage of cocaine addiction is paranoia."

"Pepsi only," I joked, waving my soda can.

"OK, Pepsi girl, where's the front page article in this one?"

I flashed the brochure about A United Tomorrow on the table and tapped it with a forefinger. "Your remember this flyer I found in Richie Shaw's apartment?"

Morgenthal shrugged, like it was no big deal.

"I went out to Long Island and chatted with George Halliday. You remember him?"

Saul adjusted his bulk in the little plastic scoop. "Vaguely. New York's a big town, Drew. Refresh my memory."

"We interviewed George when Senator Cort got some pork-barrel legislation passed, brought a bunch of jobs to New York State for a change, instead of Texas. Halliday is Senator Cort's old friend and key advisor."

Morgenthal turned his coffee cup slowly. "Yeah, I place him now."

"George told me A United Tomorrow is run by Jonah Cameron, a rich wonder kid from California. Cameron wants to be President, and he's setting that up. A United Tomorrow is his cult following, recruiting members, coercing others, lobbying. Halliday agrees that A United Tomorrow may be sponsoring these election headquarters hits to make themselves look moderate by comparison with extremists."

"So you guys like each other's opinions. There's no story in that. Look, Drew. A United Tomorrow is no small time enemy. I need facts to take them on. Opinions won't cut it." He glugged half his coffee.

"I pulled an invitation out of Halliday's trash can and –"

Saul muttered, "I didn't hear that."

I persisted. "The invitation was to Richie Shaw's funeral. The card had a handwritten note from someone named Marv Logan. I checked. Logan is an executive VP of A United Tomorrow."

Saul put out his hand. "You got the invitation?"

My face sagged. "No, they took it from me at Richie Shaw's funeral."

He looked shocked. "You attended Shaw's funeral?"

"Yeah, I had to do something." At least I'd gotten his attention.

"Guts you got, Drew. Brains – I don't know." Morgenthal shook his head.

"Thanks, Saul, I think. My point is that A United Tomorrow sponsored a lavish funeral for a killer. Isn't that an article?"

"No. Too bad you didn't keep the invitation. That little scrap of paper, especially with Logan's signature, was worth something. Probably they confiscated your invitation for that very reason. A United Tomorrow isn't dumb. Nasty, yes. Dumb, no." He finished his coffee and tossed the cup at a wastebasket. It bounced off and scattered across the linoleum, dribbling a brown leak. Morgenthal cleaned up the mess and bought himself another cup. He turned toward me, keeping his thumb on the extra cream button. "That all you got?"

"No. My apartment was bugged and Collie Weiss lost his life for calling me there."

Morgenthal looked shocked by what I'd said. He recoiled, then machine-gunned questions at me. "You sure? Can you prove it? How'd it happen?" He juggled the hot coffee cup between his hands and sat down again.

I felt a lot better. Saul never got excited like this. "After Shaw's funeral, I stopped at Bleighberg's Grocery, around the corner from my apartment. I was in Bleighberg's when a guy wandered into the store, wearing a Con Ed uniform. But he wasn't a Con Ed employee. The guy in a Con Ed uniform was Elijah, the pro hit man I saw at the election headquarters. After he shoved a gun in my face, I'd know him anywhere. You remember me saying a Con Ed guy was in Shaw's apartment before he died? You didn't believe me then, huh?"

"Not sure I believe you now," Saul hedged. But I knew he was hooked.

"OK, Elijah buys a pack of gum at Bleighberg's. I go home and find a bug in my phone, attached by a fresh wad of gum."

Saul leaned his elbows on the table and it tilted, spilling his coffee a little. He blotted the coffee. "Thrilling, Morrissey, but a gummy spy bug doesn't get you an 'A' head on my front page. How did having your phone bugged cause your friend to die?"

"I'm getting to that. Collie Weiss invited me to go with him to a bed and breakfast in Connecticut. I agreed just to get him off the phone. I called him later from a safe phone and turned him off, but he went to Connecticut anyway."

"Wow, that is news. I didn't think you had a sex life, Drew."

I ignored his sarcasm and continued. "A new Porsche driven by Collie Weiss was found in a ravine, with Weiss dead. State Troopers thought it was an accident. But I got a trooper to look around. He discovered that a piece of the Porsche's steering had been shattered by an explosion. Also, there was a rock slide on the highway. It appears the rocks were blown there by explosives. Sergeant Jay Doherty is going to call me with lab results. After that, I went to Albany."

"On my expense account, huh?" But Morgenthal's eyes were alive with interest.

"You bet. I kept the receipts, including one for $500 that got me this pamphlet."

Saul rolled his eyes.

"The Coroner in Albany, Dr. Martin Horning, thinks last year's hits at an election headquarters were also done by a pro. It was the same style of shooting, double tapping the victims."

"Can you quote Horning?" Saul asked. He'd forgotten his coffee.

"No. Horning's up for re-election and insisted it was all off the record."

Saul moaned, then drank his second coffee in one gulp. He crushed the empty paper cup and threw it again at the wastebasket. The results were identical to his skill with the first cup. Saul grunted as he picked the cup off the floor. "I don't suppose you had a wire on you. Didn't record Horning, by any chance, did you?"

"Yes," I beamed. I pulled out my cellular. "I set my phone to record Horning's conversation as a message to myself." I tried to replay the message. At first, there was nothing but static. For a moment I panicked, then Martin Horning's voice came through the tiny speaker.

After he'd listened to the Albany Coroner, Morgenthal chortled. "Well, well, Morrissey. That's a start. But not a finish, by any means." He got up to leave.

I nearly had a heart attack. I raced to say, "What about Hinkle? That can't be coincidence, can it?"

Saul leaned on the back of his chair. The plastic scoop sagged under his weight. "Regrettably, Hinkle isn't useful. No link to anyone outside the prison, even though I grant you Hinkle dying the moment you want to interview him is mighty suspicious. I'll do this for you Drew. You can run with this story for two more weeks – and I'll start prepping our lawyers. I don't want them having a heart attack if I come to them with an article about A United Tomorrow. I can't print anything about an outfit that powerful, Drew, unless we hold all the cards. *The Chronicle* has to protect itself."

Two more weeks felt good. I pressed my luck. "What about my expenses, including Ulaklowski?"

He sighed in disgust. "OK, Drew, I give in. I'll sign the reimbursement chit for Ulaklowski – and your trips. Get your conversation with Dr. Horning transcribed. Have an audio copy made of the recording, as well. Tell Archives to put both the audio and the transcription in their safe."

"Thanks, Saul." I beamed a smile and that was, of course, a mistake.

"You know, Ms. Paranoia, there is a fast way to prove this whole thing."

"What's that, Saul?" I foolishly asked.

"Get yourself killed by this Elijah."

I looked into my soda can, anger and hurt swelling inside me. Finally, I brought my head up and caught Morgenthal's eyes. "I'm right, Saul. And I don't need to die to prove it. I need to live."

For once, my editor was apologetic. Saul patted me on the back. "I was kidding. Bad taste in jokes."

"You're tired, Saul. Get some rest."

"Yeah, I am," he admitted. "You're not sleeping at home tonight, are you? You can't stay in that apartment anymore. It isn't safe."

"No. I'm at a friend's place in the Village. She's on a cruise with her lover."

"You didn't tell anyone where you're staying? No phone messages about it, like the one you left me?"

"None," I reassured him.

"Good." Morgenthal nodded. Then he opened the break room door and disappeared. I was in shock. Maybe Saul Morgenthal cared about me after all. That was news.

16

The next morning, I looked on the Internet for transcription services that could turn my conversation with Dr. Horning into a Word "doc." I picked a service in SoHo, directly across the street from a gourmet market I loved. While they transcribed, I'd splurge on lunch. I thought of my food binge as playing the futures market. After all, I was spending the $500 reimbursement Saul authorized last night, but it'd be two weeks before I saw the money. I was just buying a ham sandwich in SoHo instead of leveraging pork bellies on the Chicago Exchange.

I left my cell phone at the transcription service and jaywalked across Broadway, stopping in front of the deli. I spent a few moments enjoying Vivaldi's *Four Seasons*, played by a Julliard student. In gratitude for her skill, I dropped my pocket change in her violin case. She nodded and continued playing while I checked out bobble-head dolls offered on a folding table by a rapster in dreadlocks. I was torn between a butterfly, which I wished I were at the moment so I could fly away, and an armadillo whose thick skin seemed very practical. I bought the armadillo as an aid in protecting myself from Saul's wisecracks. Protection from Elijah required an armored truck and the rapster wasn't selling one of those at three dollars. Too bad. I'd have bought it.

Empowered by that dose of whimsy, I slid under the deli's green awnings and through its glass doors. I ignored anything that might be good for my body, like the summer fruit heaped in wicker baskets. I wove through the islands of healthy food and headed for the desserts. In the back, I found what I wanted, a display case with cheesecakes and specialty tarts. I went for a strawberry cloud cheesecake topped in a quartet of blueberries, with a thin crust of crushed pecans. Guilt from buying the dessert forced me to order something relatively healthy. So I bought a sandwich of black forest ham, gruyere cheese, alfalfa sprouts, Dijon mustard and baby lettuce on a Kaiser roll.

I needed a wheelbarrow to carry the mountain of food to a stand-up eating area at the front. After a few bites of ham sandwich, I put the rest in a plastic carton as rations for tomorrow. Having paid modest attention to my body's physical needs, I binged on the cheesecake. Oink, Drew. I wasn't alone in my indulgence. A couple at the same bench were eating comparable health-hazards, while stressing themselves with cell phone conversations. Influenced by their bad example, I felt naked without my phone, orphaned across the street at the transcription service.

Not to worry. If anyone knows how to stress themselves, it's Drew Morrissey. There was a pay phone in the back of the deli, not far from a bread island with spinach and cheddar muffins, almond brioches and worst of all, loaves of Valrhona chocolate bread. Fortunately, I was too blimped by the dessert to cave and buy chocolate.

I used a calling card and dialed my voicemail at work. I had only two messages, one from my mother wondering if I was alive, and the other from Joanie at Wyndham & Dorset. Someone named Truitt Hastings from A United Tomorrow had called, thinking I worked at the publishing house. When Hastings told the switchboard I edited celebrity bios, they transferred him to Joanie. Made sense, since Joanie was the admin for Collie Weiss, who actually did edit celebrity bios. Lucky for me, Joanie was fast on her feet and played along with everything.

I called Joanie and said, "Hi, this is Drew. Thanks for the quick thinking."

Joanie replied, "Oh sure. You mean that man Hastings, from A United Tomorrow. I figured you were using us as a cover for checking into Collie's death. You want this Truitt Hastings' number?"

"Sure." I had nothing to lose, even if I didn't think I'd ever talk to someone from A United Tomorrow outside a law court. I wrote down the number and asked, "Truitt Hastings say anything else?"

"Yeah, Drew, but I got a call on the other line. Can you hold?"

"For you, anytime." I waited, passing the time by flirting with the buffalo head on the wall behind the butcher case. He exuded strong, masculine appeal but had kind eyes.

"Drew?" she asked.

"Yeah, I'm still here. Whatcha got for me?"

"Hastings left his home phone too. He was really eager to talk with you. Apparently you went to Richie Shaw's funeral and said you do volunteer work for Senator Cort."

"True," I admitted. "I couldn't very well say I worked for *The Chronicle* and was trying to bring them down."

Joanie laughed. "I'm glad it's you and not me that Senator Cort is going to roast when he finds out."

"Maybe he'll never find out," I said hopefully.

"Perhaps with your luck, Drew, but definitely not with mine. You want the home phone for this Hastings guy?"`

"Might as well have it." The prefix mapped to an exclusive neighborhood on the west side of Central Park. Money, power, politics all go together.

Joanie's voice turned sad. "Drew, you find out anything about Collie and his wife, like how they died?"

"Yeah, I did. I drove to Connecticut and went with a state trooper to the crime scene. It seems a pro did a hit on Collie and staged it to look like an accident."

"Damn, poor Collie and Nadine. They didn't deserve that. Drew, you're gonna get whoever did this, right?" Joanie's voice sounded tight.

"I'm sure working on it. I'll let you know if anything breaks."

"Please do. I'll keep answering the phone for you in case anyone else calls from this A United Tomorrow organization. Anything else you need?"

"Not yet. I'll let you know if I do."

"OK, bye."

"Bye, Joanie – and thanks." I hung up. Talking about Connecticut reminded me I should call Jay Doherty about the lab results. I found Jay's card in my pocket and dialed him up.

"Connecticut State Troopers, Glassberry office," was the answer.

"Jay Doherty, please." I got put on hold and waited several minutes.

"Hello?" Doherty asked.

"Hi, Jay. This is Drew." I waited, hoping for a warm greeting. The longer I waited, the more foolish I felt. Was all that flirting between us just my imagination? Then again, maybe Jay was uncomfortable in phone conversations with girls. I'd gotten pretty serious with a guy like that in college, almost engaged. He'd pet like a pro, leave me all steamy and call the next day sounding like we were exchanging chem lab notes. The only way to relate on the phone with him was talking shop.

So I tried that with Doherty. "I was curious if you got any lab results yet, on that steering piece you salvaged from the Porsche wreck. It's my excuse for calling you."

"Uh, yeah, they finished analyzing the metal." He stopped like that was the end of our conversation.

"So, what'd they come up with?" This was like playing tennis with a wet sheet. I hit the ball and it gets swallowed, not returned.

"Inconclusive," was his simple reply.

Was Jay Doherty running out of lung power to speak or what? This wasn't the same guy I'd been with in Connecticut. That Jay Doherty was fired up to bring justice into this crazy world.

I pushed him, "What do you mean, inconclusive? You said the steering rack definitely looked shattered from an explosion."

"Well, I'm no expert."

"Can you send me the report?" I was exasperated.

"No. You'll have to file a Freedom of Information Act request. You can fill out a form on the web site for the State of Connecticut."

My new armadillo hide wasn't thick enough for this. I felt really hurt, on both a personal and professional level. "What about the soil samples? From the hillside, remember?"

"Nothing. Plain old dirt."

"How about sending me the samples and the Porsche part? So I can have an independent lab test them."

"They're being held as evidence. I can't do that."

"You said there was no evidence on the dirt samples. So why are they being held?"

"Got a call on the other line, Drew. Please hold." The line buzzed in my ear, then clicked dead.

I tried redialing, but it was busy. When I finally got through, they told me Sergeant Doherty was out. Great. The only concrete evidence I had just evaporated. It sounded like A United Tomorrow had gotten to Doherty. The idea made me sick.

I didn't want anyone else to wind up dead because they called my apartment. I dialed my home voicemail, worried somebody else left a message for me and was overheard by Elijah.

There were the same five messages I'd reviewed before, blinking at me when I'd watched Lindquist on TV a million years ago as this whole thing began. Then I discovered there was one more message. I was stunned to find it was from Karen Shaw. Why in the world had she called me at home, instead of at *The Chronicle*? Blast. I'd written my home number on the back of my business card out of habit. I had to call Karen and warn her about Elijah.

I phoned Hermes. The seconds passed with agonizing slowness. I watched a wall clock tick, tick, tick – like a leaky faucet dripping. I thought maybe Karen wouldn't talk to me. Then I heard Karen's nasal accent.

"Hi, it's Drew. You called me, remember?"

"Oh, yeah. Look Drew, I changed my mind, OK? Just leave me alone."

"You can't change your mind. It's too late for that now."

"I made a mistake calling you. Forget I called, OK?"

"You called me at home, Karen."

"So what?"

"My home line is tapped. The pro hit man that killed Richie tapped the line. Now Elijah knows you wanted to talk with me. You're in danger. He may try to kill you."

"Kill me? What'da you mean?" Karen couldn't accept the truth of her situation.

I tried to explain. "Elijah is the pro hit man who murdered your brother. He'll want to kill you, Karen, before you can talk to me. Elijah is afraid you know something that can implicate him. He's better off with you dead."

"What the hell'd you do to me? You crazy bastard reporters."

"I didn't do anything to you, Karen. Elijah did it to us. You're not safe now. The only way out is to tell me what you know, so we can catch Elijah."

"Oh, swell." Her angry breathing came through the phone. She was really upset.

"You alone at Hermes?" I asked. I imagined Karen sitting alone with her dying plant, looking through a dust-streaked window at a Brooklyn Bridge pillar.

"We can't talk here. The owner already told me he'd fire me if I talk to you. I never seen him so scared. His pants smelled."

"I understand what it's like to be that scared. I'm sorry. Give me a moment. I'll think of somewhere else we can meet." Sabrina was coming home tonight from South America. I needed to clear out of her apartment. Might as well have Karen meet me nearby. "I know a quiet place we can talk. Maybe you've heard of Chumley's, in Greenwich Village?"

"No. I eat off the carts." Now she sounded despondent instead of angry.

"Take a taxi. The driver will know Chumley's. It's at 86 Bedford. You got that?"

"Yeah. I got it." She was really depressed. "When?"

"Half an hour. I'll buy you lunch. I had mine already."

"I don't want lunch."

There was a long pause. I didn't know what else to say. Finally, I urged her, "Don't stand me up, Karen."

She didn't answer me. Instead, the line went dead.

I tapped on the payphone, wondering why the line suddenly went dead. Maybe Karen's boss walked inside her office. My mouth went dry when I realized Elijah might have walked into Karen's office, instead. If Elijah overheard our call, he'd be at Chumley's.

Meeting Karen Shaw could prove a very unhealthy thing to do. But I had no evidence and she was my only lead in the case. State Trooper Jay Doherty vanished on me only moments ago. I'd recorded Dr. Horning, but he was just spouting opinions. I had no facts.

So I was going to Chumley's. Maybe Karen Shaw would show up. If Elijah came instead, it was collision time. Was the pen mightier than the sword? Maybe, but Elijah was carrying a gun, not a dagger.

17

I sat in the darkest corner of Chumley's, sipping Widmer's cider, poured from a tap behind the bar. A youthful couple kept me company, looking down from their portrait on the wall. In that photograph, F. Scott Fitzgerald and his wife Zelda were baby-faced young, not a wrinkle on their smiling cheeks. They hadn't aged since Chumley's opened in 1928 as an illegal speakeasy, selling bootleg liquor. The place was frequented in its early days by poor authors using Greenwich Village as a cheap place to live while they agonized over their prose.

The emotional support they got from hanging out together worked. Many of the speakeasy's early clientele made it big and dust jackets from their books lined the walls. The list of "nobody types" haunting Chumley's in the 1930s included William Faulkner, John Steinbeck, Edna St. Vincent Millay, Eugene O'Neill and Willa Cather. A longer list of alumni filled a plaque over the fireplace, but I was too intimidated to read it. Me, I'm still trying to write the outline for my epic novel, forget the prose.

Twenty feet from me, the bartender wiped smudges off glasses with a soft cloth, his head bent to the task. The shined glasses were stacked around a heavy brass bulldog squatting on the bar, seemingly restrained by a motorcycle chain with an enormous case-hardened lock. No one seemed to know how or when the bulldog came to ornament Chumley's bar. But it was nice to have him there for protection, under my current circumstances.`

Every time the front door opened, I tensed, concerned who might be coming inside. The next time the door opened, the light silhouetted a bulky, middle-aged man in a rumpled suit, his tie pulled loose. He walked up to the bar and put a foot on the boot rail. Judging from the bartender's reaction, the newcomer wasn't a regular. He ordered a boilermaker and swallowed his bourbon in one gulp, then drained the beer as chaser.

He saw me in the dim corner, determined that I was of the opposite sex and blurted, "Hi doll, come over and I'll buy you a drink."

Normally, I would have written this guy off as a loser, fired from his job and drowning his bitterness. Today, I was worried the guy was a setup, sent by Elijah, another hit man, trying to get close enough to kill me. Chumley's was empty in mid-day. I was alone with just the bartender to protect me. "Sorry," I said, "I'm expecting someone. He'll be joining me shortly."

He said loudly, "Your boyfriend's not coming, doll. I can help you with whatever you want."

"Sorry, you're not my type." I got up and edged toward the back door.

He staggered in my direction. "Try me."

The bartender grabbed the man's arm. "The lady prefers to wait alone. Let me buy you a shot on the house."

"Well, OK," the pudgy man groused. "I didn't mean any harm." He returned to the bar.

I gave the bartender a wave of gratitude and retreated to my corner table. I wasn't the least bit hungry after binging at the gourmet market in SoHo. So I sat for half an hour, sipping my non-alcoholic cider. I couldn't indulge in anything stronger when Elijah might come through the door instead of Karen Shaw. I gave Karen an hour more and then concluded she'd either flaked out or was dead.

The drunk had left and I was free to visit the bar and settle my bill. I gave the bartender a generous tip for helping me earlier. I started to leave the back way, when the front door opened with a burst of light. A foursome came inside, waved to the bartender, and took their normal table. Then my brain did a flip of amazement. Karen Shaw, the woman I'd thought dead, entered right after the foursome.

She was wearing a paisley print dress that looked as wilted as Karen's face. She stood in the doorway, silhouetted by sunlight. I waved and she dully made out the motion, then shuffled listlessly toward me. When she sat at my table, I could make out the tight, angry lines around her mouth. We sat there and stared at each other.

Finally, I said, "Thanks for coming. It took guts. I'm proud of you."

"I don't know what I'm doing here. I must be crazy." Her eyes were glazed like they'd been at the funeral. Karen had done a major hit on tranquilizers again. Would that work for me or against me, I wondered?

I guessed I had to be blunt to burn through her fog. I cut the small talk and went right for what I wanted to know. "How did Richie come to join A United Tomorrow?"

"He told me they came to his door. Some girl, pretty. He liked her a lot so he went with her to a meeting. They announced his name and everybody applauded. My brother was a sucker for that kind of gimmick."

"Did they recruit anybody else in Richie's building? I mean, were they going door-to-door, like evangelists?"

"He never mentioned it, if they did."

I wondered if they had been targeting UPS drivers. Maybe there was a pattern to their recruitment. "Richie know of any other UPS driver who joined A United Tomorrow?"

"Yeah, a few. He did think that was strange. There were a lot of delivery people there, UPS, Fed Ex, DHL, Airborne. I just assumed they were looking for people in that age bracket. Lugging boxes is for kids. I'd warned Richie he needed to plan more, figure out what he was going to do when his back gave out."

I nodded. "You were a good sister to Richie."

"Yeah." Karen put her head down on her hands, like she was going to fall asleep on me.

I gently nudged her and she sat up. "Richie ever act strange after the meetings?" I asked.

"Yeah. About a month ago, he said they helped him buy a gun and taught him how to use it. I asked Richie what he was going to use the gun on. I was frightened he would shoot Papa when they argued. They were always shouting at each other. Then I got scared Richie was going to kill people at work, like his supervisor. So I pressed my brother what he was going to do with the gun."

"What'd he say?" I leaned over eagerly.

"He just smiled. He wouldn't tell me anything. I told him he was just making it up about the gun, taunting him so he'd have to tell me what he really was going to do. But he just got quiet and looked smug. I'd never seen him that way before. It really frightened me."

"Did Richie ever show you the gun or say how he got it?"

"Richie never showed it to me, but he did say someone he'd met at one of the meetings sold it to him. This guy also showed him how to load the gun and fire it."

"Who sold Richie the gun? Was his name Elijah?"

"I don't remember. I don't know much. Coming here was a big mistake. I can't help you." Karen pushed her chair back.

I grabbed her wrist. "You are helping me. You know Richie belonged to A United Tomorrow and can say that in court. That's a big help. We've got to stop them before they kill more people."

"I think you're makin' this up, Drew, to get a story for your paper. I was stupid to listen to you. I shouldn't have come here. I gotta go." She pulled her wrist away.

A flash of bright light hit my eyes. I looked at the front door. It was being held open by a man in a business suit. Two young women went through it, then he followed. As the door started to close, I flinched. There was someone standing across the street, watching Chumley's.

"Excuse me a second," I told Karen, then wove my way to the door. I didn't open it, just cracked the speakeasy panel and stood where the sunlight wouldn't show my face.

"Oh, God," I gasped. I slammed the panel shut and sagged against the door. I felt Karen pressing into me.

"I wanna go," she whimpered, almost crying.

"You can't go out this way," I warned her.

"Why not?" she asked defiantly.

"Elijah's right outside the door, across the street. He's waiting to kill you – and me."

Her eyes flashed at me. "I don't believe you. You're makin' this up."

"You said the owner told you never to talk to me again and his pants smelled, like he was very frightened. Just before then, he had a visitor, someone you've never seen before. Am I right?"

"Yeah, a guy that said he wanted to be a new messenger. We get 'em all the time. One business gets a lull, they jump to the next guy. Some messengers are hustling for three or four services."

"Karen, I want you to go to the door and open just the speakeasy panel, not the door itself. You'll see a guy across the street in a khaki Army jacket. Short, curly hair, looks like a jockey. Tell me if that's the new messenger you've been talking about."

She gave me a queer look, but did what I'd asked. Before Karen opened the peep hatch, I drew the black curtain behind us so we wouldn't be noticeable. Karen became agitated and slapped the hatch close. She whispered, "Yeah, that's him."

"I wasn't kidding you, was I?"

"No," she said meekly. "Is that really Elijah, the man who killed my brother?"

I nodded.

"I'm calling the police." Karen looked vengeful enough to try capturing Elijah herself. "Let me use your cell phone. I was rattled when I left Hermes. My cell's on my desk at the messenger service."

I shook my head. "Calling the cops from here isn't a good idea."

"Why not?" she demanded.

"Elijah's a pro. He has an escape route planned. From his position, he can see cops driving down the street, so it's doubtful they'd grab him. Worse yet, his escape path might be running into Chumley's and out the side door. He could shoot us on his way through."

"But there'd be witnesses," she protested.

"Karen, you're naïve. Elijah's wearing an army jacket with pockets big enough for a Halloween mask. He could don the mask before entering Chumley's. Even if he doesn't hide his face, eyewitnesses are notoriously unreliable in a violent situation. Everyone's ducking for cover. Nobody wants to get involved. Elijah knows that."

"What should we do?" she asked limply.

"Leave through the side door. We'll find a safe place to hide and then we'll get help from the police. Come on." I pulled on Karen's arm. "This way."

We stepped through an arched door into a little courtyard lined with colorfully painted flagstones. The courtyard gate led to a beautiful, tree-lined lane, where brick homes were an oasis of calm inside the chaos of Manhattan. At least, it should have been a calm place. Halfway along the street, Elijah spotted us. He tried to cross Bedford and was thwarted by traffic. But our luck wouldn't hold forever. Soon it would be a test of his speed versus ours. I doubted we could simply outrace him, but we had to try.

"Run," I hissed, tugging on Karen. She jerked her head around to see why I was fleeing. My eyes instinctively followed and I saw that Elijah was already in the middle of Bedford street, dodging bumpers.

It seemed a thousand steps to the angled corner with Seventh Avenue. Then we jogged along crowded sidewalks, my lungs burning, my legs heavy. There must be somewhere to hide, yet a good spot eluded me. The open glass front of a Thai restaurant was followed by the huge window of an Indian place. Neither would screen us from view. Maybe it was time for a reading from Zena the Clairvoyant Psychic. A sign on the door gave her cell phone for making appointments. No time for that. The Actor's Playhouse was closed until tonight's performance. A Euro-style café had only outdoor tables. There's no room to hide anyone inside Village Cigars unless they could fit in a humidor.

I was getting desperate enough to scramble on the roof of the Jekyll and Hyde Social Club for Mad Scientists and Explorers, see if I could blend with the four skeletons wearing safari outfits and pith helmets. Karen had a better idea. She dragged me toward a gray-green railing and down a subway entrance.

I fed my metro card into a turnstile, saw the neon "go" and lurched through. Karen was stuck on the other side. "How can you live in Manhattan and not have a metro card?" I fumed.

She looked at me apologetically. "I never take the subway."

I was stunned by her response. "How'd you get to Chumley's from the Fulton Market area?"

"I walked." Well, that explained why she was so late in meeting me. It also explained why Elijah'd easily tailed her to the rendezvous. Karen fumbled cash into a ticket machine. Finally, she ripped a card from the ticket machine and slid the pass into a turnstile.

When she got through the barrier, I grabbed Karen's hand. We raced toward the station platform, feeding on each other's anxiety. A graffiti-splattered train roared out of the tunnel and screeched to a stop. Air whooshed and its doors opened. A thin crowd spattered past Karen and me as we forced our way inside. We waited an eternity for the train doors to close, watching anxiously for Elijah. When the doors shut and the train jerked forward, I sighed in relief.

I glanced at Karen, wrapped around a pole like I was. We hadn't bothered to find a seat, though the car was almost empty. I reached out, patting a seat near me. "Might as well be comfortable," I joked. Karen peeled herself off the metal pole and sat in a plastic scoop near mine. I was facing the doors and Karen was looking along the car.

"Where are we going?" she asked.

"Uptown, I think." My breathing was returning to normal. Blast, I'd forgotten about Sabrina's. I had to get Collie's duffel bag, with all my belongings. "I need to get off and reverse directions. I've been staying at a friend's apartment and she's due back tonight. We could phone the police from there."

"Sure," Karen answered dully. I stole a glance at her. She was tapping her fingers together and rocking in her seat. Karen looked disoriented.

The train slowed and we popped into the bright light of a station. I instinctively rose, bracing myself against a pole near the doors. I turned my head without thinking, a woman's instinctive response when she feels a man staring at her. I froze. Elijah was two cars away. He jumped away from the glass window in a connecting door, but I'd caught a flash of him. "Elijah's here," I yelled.

Karen looked around, confused. "What can we do?"

"Let's try to fake him out." The car's pneumatic doors shot open. "Come on," I said. We stepped on the platform and halted, looking down the train toward Elijah. My heart stopped when he stepped out. Elijah calmly turned toward us, wearing his icy smile. One hand was in a bulging jacket pocket, cradling his gun.

Elijah moved toward us. There was no one else on the platform. He was only fifteen feet away. Karen looked hypnotized, terrified into paralysis. Elijah grinned sadistically and slid his gun out.

A warning chime sounded. The train doors were closing. I threw myself at the subway car, dragging Karen along. She collided with me, forcing us hard into rubber padding at the edge of the doors. The closing doors squeezed me so tightly that my breath shot out. Then the doors released and we tumbled into the train.

I fought for balance and lost, skidding across the charcoal linoleum of the train's floor. I felt a jolt of pain as my knee hit a pole. Then Karen fell on me, driving my head into hard seat plastic. Bolts of light jarred my vision.

Karen rolled off when the train jerked forward. "Sorry," she muttered, pulling herself up. She grabbed my arm and helped me to my feet.

My head and knee throbbed, but I forced myself to look for Elijah. He was in the next car, wrapped around a pole as the train accelerated with surprising force. He caught me looking at him and smiled again. There was no one else in the subway cars.

I grabbed Karen's dress and pulled hard. The dress tore, but Karen didn't budge. "Come on," I urged her. "We've got to move. We need witnesses to make him cautious." Finally, I ignored her and flung myself forward, slapping against benches and poles. At the end, I opened the inter-car door. I jabbed the release handle and pushed through the doorway.

Loud rumbling and ugly smells hit me. I was on a little platform, covered with a leaky rubber shroud. I skidded across an open metal grate and entered another car. Suddenly I realized someone was right behind me and turned in horror, thinking it must be Elijah. It was only a sheepish Karen. But behind her, I could see Elijah moving quickly toward us.

I moved recklessly forward, careening off plastic scoops and poles like a pinball. When I collided with the next door, it flung open. I shot across to the other car. There were three people in this car, spaced around it. I grabbed Karen's hand and pulled her to the far end. That door was padlocked. We flew under a maintenance light in the tunnel and I caught a glimpse of rails flashing beneath the door window. There was nowhere else to run.

I turned around and saw Elijah enter the car. I felt myself pressed backward. The train was decelerating, slowing for another stop. How long would it take before the doors opened, giving us a chance to live?

Elijah stood at the far end, bracing himself with his legs, surveying the car. There was a litter of newspapers on the floor. One section of light bulbs flickered. A woman with sagging nylons and thick shoes was huddled near me, but she was staring out the windows, not seeing anyone else. Behind her, a teenager with a spiked hair-do was lost in *Heavy Metal*.

Nearest Elijah was a man in a sports coat, his legs crossed, exposing white socks that ended in penny-loafers. He had a crew cut and a serious expression on his face. He was studying Karen and me carefully, unaware of Elijah. The man started to get up and the train jerked, throwing the man upright. Elijah slid into the man and they apologized, then came apart. They both started toward us.

I felt faint and forced myself to breathe. Light hit me in a burst and brakes shrieked in my ears. The train slowed abruptly. I pushed Karen and she resisted, understandably reluctant to move toward Elijah. Then Karen realized that Elijah was cutting off our escape, trapping us against the end of the car. The exit doors were in the middle and we had to get there first. We made a run for the exit.

The train jerked to a stop and its doors hissed open. Elijah squeezed past the man in front of him. The man was thrown against a seat and Elijah tripped on the guy's outstretched leg, buying us time to reach the exit doors.

I cleared the train and Karen was almost outside when I saw Elijah bring his gun out. I heard glass shatter behind me. I dove forward and tumbled on a crowded platform. People surged past me into the car, unaware gunshots were being fired. Karen and I pushed until we cleared the dense crowd. Ahead of us lay several flights of stairs.

I turned around and saw Elijah forcing his way out of the car against a tidal flow of people. I locked eyes with Elijah and felt a jolt of adrenaline. I ran up stairs, Karen doing her best to keep pace. The flights of stairs were endless. By the top of the last flight, my knees buckled and I had to stop. Karen was bent over, trying to catch her breath. She couldn't go on.

I heard footsteps behind us. Elijah was running up the stairs two at a time, unstoppable. "Damn him," I muttered. I yanked Karen's arm. "Come on!" I shouted.

We made the last steps and wove into street traffic. A cab swerved to avoid us. I deliberately ran in front of the taxi to stop him. The cabby slammed his brakes and I bounced hard against the hood.

"You crazy idiot!" the cab driver shrieked. He threw his door open. Horns bellowed around us. He calmed down and asked, "You all right?"

"Yeah," I said, holding my ribs. "Sorry, but I'm desperate for a cab." I opened the back door and pushed Karen inside. I saw Elijah clear the subway and try for the street. A bus cut him off and I smiled for the first time in hours.

The cabby got in the driver's seat. "You guys are crazy," he said through a well-chewed but unlit cigar, "You could've gotten killed out there."

"You don't know the half of it," I said, clutching my ribs.

The cabby flashed a puzzled look. He gave up trying to understand and asked, "So where to?"

"Federal Plaza."

"OK." The cabby checked his mirrors. He swerved around the bus as it pulled away from the curb.

Despite the pain, I twisted to catch a glimpse of Elijah, standing with hands on his hips in a posture of frustration. I rolled my window down and flipped him the bird. God, that felt good.

"Why are we going to Federal Plaza?" Karen asked. "I thought people only went there to get a passport."

"I know the guy who runs FBI's New York office, Jake Balducci. I once interviewed him for a story on the FBI's anti-terrorist efforts."

"Are you sure he'll help?" Karen's hands were clenched tightly on her knees.

"Sure." I said it with more conviction than I felt. I remembered how Jay Doherty wanted to help and faded away. My encounter with Detective Lieutenant Lindquist of the NYPD had also gone badly. So I was going to the FBI.

Originally, I didn't wanted to involve the FBI until I had more proof, concrete evidence that A United Tomorrow was backing Elijah. Now I had no choice. What kind of twist the FBI would put on my life, I didn't know. But I got out of the cab anyway when it stopped at Federal Plaza, home to the New York office of the Federal Bureau of Investigation. I had nowhere else to turn.

18

Quick safety faded to slow misery as I sat in the FBI's waiting area with an ice bag taped to my knee and a cold pack wedged between my aching ribs and the chair. The cut over my eye was closed with butterfly bandages but it throbbed like a car drumming rap music at full volume. Karen chafed in a seat across from me, poking at magazines on the metal coffee table and rejecting them over and over again.

A cheerful FBI agent came into the reception area, wearing a pinstripe three-piece suit. He waited until I was ready, then handed me a small metal travel-tin of aspirin and a cup of water. I was grateful for the FBI's help with my medical needs, but what I really craved was a stiff drink and a calm night's sleep in my own bed.

Nonetheless, I struggled to look appreciative and muttered, "thanks." I pinched a corner of the tin and popped four aspirin into my mouth.

Gulping water from a foam coffee cup caused an aspirin pill to stick in my throat. My face puckered from the bitter taste and a bolt of pain hit my temple above the cut eyebrow. I put down the water cup and wearily looked up to see another agent standing over me.

"Special Agent Balducci can see you now. Will you come with me?"

I shrugged and went down an antiseptic hallway with industrial art on the walls, led by the agent. He walked with a bouncy step that got under my skin. I felt anything but perky. We reached a corner office and halted. The agent announced in a hushed, confidential tone, "Special Agent Balducci is in charge of the entire New York Office."

I was supposed to be impressed, but I was tired and hurting so it was hard to look awestruck, especially when I'd already met Jake Balducci and knew about him. I managed a nod and an appreciative smile. We stood in the doorway and waited for Balducci to finish a phone call.

The phone was put down and Jake Balducci rose behind the desk. He swept a basketball player sized hand toward a set of leather chairs. "Come in."

Jake Balducci was lean, in his late forties. His pale face was framed by dark hair combed straight back, leaving a V peak at the front. There was a heavy shadow on his cheeks and tufts of hair stuck from his nose. Balducci appeared more a Mafia Don than an FBI agent. But his attire was formal FBI – dark navy suit, white shirt, button-down collar, silver tie with flecks of red, wingtip shoes.

Balducci closed the door to his office and sat with us in a chair, not behind his desk. He read from a paper he'd taken off the desk. "You're in danger of being killed by the assassin who hit an election headquarters in midtown Manhattan. You believe the same man has been responsible for the deaths at other election headquarters, across the country. Does that sum it up?"

"Well, that's the essence of it," I replied. "You left out that he just tried to kill us on the subway." I looked at Karen for support, but she wilted into her chair and plucked at her skirt, pretending not to be here.

Balducci nodded. "Is there anything that corroborates your story about Elijah?"

"There's a bullet hole in a subway car," I snorted. "There's my knee and ribs, unless you think I was playing football at the 14th Street station before I came here."

"I'm not saying that I doubt your story, Drew. But you want protection, is that correct?" Balducci put the paper down.

"Yes, of course. I'm not able to go home, my career is a wreck, my lead at Attica, Tom Hinkle, was killed the day I was supposed to interview him. This bastard Elijah is running around loose, trying to kill Karen and me, and he's probably going to hit more election headquarters before all this is finished – if you don't catch him."

"Right." Balducci tapped the chair arms lightly with his long fingers. "The problem is, we're stretched very thin, Drew. So we have to prioritize what we do, just as *The New York Chronicle* can't investigate every lead that comes along. The more you give me, the more protection I can give you."

I shifted uneasily in my chair and was reminded of the damage to my rib cage. "Elijah killed a former boyfriend of mine, Collie Weiss, thinking I was in Collie's Porsche. Can you get some evidence that Sergeant Jay Doherty of the Connecticut State Troopers found and have it analyzed?"

Balducci twisted his long torso around and dragged a legal pad off the corner of his desk. He plucked a Cross pencil from his inner coat pocket and twisted it to advance the lead. "When did this Porsche accident happen? And where?"

"A few days ago, in Connecticut. I went to the crime scene with Doherty and he was convinced explosives were used. But A United Tomorrow got to Doherty somehow and he changed his story." I watched Balducci carefully when I said "A United Tomorrow," but there was no change of expression.

"I'll check that, thanks. It will help if we find something was done to the car, but that'll take a few days. Anything else?"

Karen and I exchanged blank stares. "I can't think of anything . . . well, someone from A United Tomorrow called me. I think they wanted to recruit me. Maybe that was some kind of setup for this Elijah."

Balducci sat up in his chair and leaned over. He asked in amazement, "They wanted you to join them? Who called?"

"Someone named Truitt Hastings. I have his home and work numbers." I reached for the little notepad I carry and flipped it open. I showed Balducci the page where I'd written Joanie's message.

Balducci copied the data, muttering, "Yes . . ."

While he was writing, I said, "Look, Jake, they killed that kid Hinkle in Attica when I was supposed to talk to him. Is that a lead you can pursue?"

Balducci shook his head. "We'll never pin that on anyone outside the prison, Drew. It's hopeless. I've tried chasing that kind of thing before. The leads just evaporate." Balducci put his pencil down.

"Well, there was one other thing. I found a bug in my home phone by unscrewing the mouthpiece. My landlord said a Con Ed man was in the apartment house that day." I pointed at Karen seated next to me. "The landlord for Karen's brother told me a Con Ed guy was in Richie Shaw's apartment the day he died. I checked with Con Ed. Richie's block wasn't scheduled for meter reading and no repair work was being done anywhere around there."

"Do I have permission to search your apartment for bugs, Drew?" Balducci stared at me.

"Of course," I shot back. Somehow the whole episode was beginning to feel surreal.

"My admin will give you a release to sign. Do you have the keys to the apartment with you? That will facilitate our entry."

I dragged out my keys and tried peeling off the front door keys, gave up and threw the lot on Balducci's desk. "I want them back," I said, returning his stare. "Uncopied," I added.

"Of course," Balducci replied smoothly. "I have a number of phone calls to make to set everything up. I have artists ready to work with each of you on a composite sketch of Elijah." Jake Balducci rose in a fluid, athletic motion and escorted us from his office. "I'll see you again in four hours, right here."

19

Jake Balducci's office door was set in a bronze-anodized frame and covered with fake rosewood veneer. I had every chip in the frame and every ripple in the veneer memorized. Karen was slumped in a chair next to me, her boots crossed on a messy stack of magazines atop the coffee table. Her head was tilted back and Karen was snoring. I thought about waking her, but we'd exhausted all conversation hours ago, after the sketch artists were through with us.

Two differing but similar versions of Elijah were on the coffee table just beyond Karen's lace-up granny boots. Sketches of Elijah didn't satisfy me. I wanted the real person locked in a maximum security prison like Attica, with no parole.

Balducci's door opened. His coat was off and his tie pulled down. He waved at me, undulating the shovel of his hand. He looked away, like something was eating at him.

I jiggled Karen's foot. She snorted and pulled her head erect, rubbing her eyes. "What time is it?" she asked.

"Time to see Jake," I said, picking up the sketches and moving toward his doorway. I deliberately took a different chair this time, one where the glare from fluorescents wouldn't hide so much of Balducci's facial expression. My keys were on a corner of the desk. I gave the FBI agent a questioning look and he nodded, returning the keys to me. "Not duplicated," Jake Balducci said. A smile played on his lips.

"Thanks," I replied softly, putting the keys back in my pockets. I found the courage to ask, "Did they find more bugs?"

"Your apartment was loaded with them. Every room, even the toilet. Someone wants to listen to you very badly. Short range devices. We don't know where the listening post is yet. If it's been torn down, we'll never know. I have surveillance on the apartment house for the next forty-eight hours." Balducci picked up a letter opener and tapped it on his blotter.

I sighed in relief, thinking this confirmed everything. But it didn't.

"Bugging is common in industrial espionage," Balducci said flatly, like it happened every day.

My heart skipped a beat, then pounded in my ears. "What do you mean?" I stammered.

"A rival newspaper, a divorce, a jealous boyfriend. There are lots of reasons for bugging somebody besides wanting to kill them." Balducci studied the blinds on his office windows, leaning back in his chair.

"But the bullet hole . . . I was shot at."

Balducci shrugged. "Maintenance crews won't have a chance to check out trains until third shift, after midnight. Until then, I have to take everything at face value." He played some more with the letter opener.

"What does that mean?" I put my head in my hands and rubbed my temples.

"In terms of what?" the FBI agent asked.

"Protection. I want some protection. I want to sleep at night and go to work and feel safe." I felt a hot flush rise in my face.

Balducci put the letter opener down and turned to face me. "You can go home. I have agents watching the building."

"From the outside?" I scoffed. "What good is that?"

"Better than you had before."

"Isn't there anything else you can do?" I pleaded. "Until he's caught?" My voice broke and I hated that. I looked at Karen Shaw. Why didn't she say something?

Karen returned my glance, then looked at the far wall.

"Are there other options?" I asked in a distracted voice.

"Well . . ." Balducci flipped over a piece of paper on his desk. "Ms. Morrissey –"

"Oh, stop the formality and call me Drew."

"OK, Drew. I spoke to the Director himself. Cooperate with the FBI and I can offer you protection while we explore whether these killings involve a conspiracy. If they do, the Director will invoke the witness identity plan on your behalf."

I groaned. "I am cooperating with the FBI."

"What I mean, Drew, is that we want you to join A United Tomorrow and work with Truitt Hastings."

They weren't going to protect me. They were just going to use me as bait. "Maybe joining A United Tomorrow is what Elijah wants. It makes me easy to kill. I attend one of their meetings and he knows where I am. Afterwards, I'm dead."

"I don't think so, Drew. They don't want you killed on their doorstep because that smears dirt on them. The bugs are probably from Truitt Hastings' people, not Elijah. His presence near your apartment was just coincidence. They're a well financed, sophisticated and paranoid bunch. Bugging potential members is their style."

"Great. So I walk into their sophisticated, well-equipped and paranoid trap. What do I get for this sacrifice?"

"You stay at a safe house. You get transported by the FBI. If and when there is a trial, you get anonymity – as much as possible. Then, if the threat is still there, we give you a whole new life. New ID, new job, new location. Plastic surgery even, if you want that."

"What I want is Elijah sent to prison. Why don't you catch him instead of using me as bait to probe A United Tomorrow?"

Balducci slid open a door in the credenza behind him. He pulled out stack after stack and tossed them on his desk. He tilted one of the flyers up so I could see it. "These are people wanted by the FBI. Just the current stack. After a year, we keep the data in computers but don't circulate flyers. There are more than a thousand people here. We can't find them and they aren't hardened pros like Elijah, who is used to life on the run."

I sagged against the chair. My eyes lost focus.

Balducci really laid it on me. "Will it end, Drew, when Elijah gets caught? Even in prison, he has money offshore. He can easily buy a hit on you."

"This isn't about Elijah, is it?" I asked angrily. "He isn't enough, is he?"

"No," Balducci replied honestly. "He isn't."

I snorted. "So the FBI Director wants a big attaboy. He gets it when the President rids himself of Jonah Cameron as a political threat. For that, I link A United Tomorrow to the killings. In return, I get to spend the rest of my life in hiding."

"You're overreacting, Drew. Chances are good that once the trial is over, you'll have your freedom. Your career will get an enormous boost from the stories you run in *The Chronicle* – and media attention at the trial. Plus you may get a book deal out of it."

"What makes you think I'll live that long? Why don't you think Truitt Hastings is working with Elijah?"

Balducci got up and wandered in front of his desk. He put a massive hand on a globe, spinning the earth like a basketball. "Let's assume Elijah is being run by someone at A United Tomorrow. Elijah's connection would be known to only one or two people. Probably Elijah is run by Jonah Cameron or the head of Cameron's personal security squad. Truitt Hastings wouldn't know Elijah exists. Hastings recruits well-connected people to expand the organization's influence. He personally handles only top people. He's got a huge staff for all the others."

"Then why is Hastings calling me? I'm a nobody." I shifted irritably in my chair. I knew the FBI would do something screwy, but I didn't think it would be this bad.

"That one is easy. You signed at Richie Shaw's funeral as working for Wyndham & Dorset. Hastings thinks you're an editor in a publishing house, which your friend Joanie confirmed for you." He twirled the globe and let me digest his words.

"How do you know that?" I asked skeptically.

"We've been busy, Drew." He stopped the globe at Africa and traced a mountain chain with his forefinger.

"You've been busy snooping around me, instead of finding Elijah," I snapped.

He sighed. "Look, we happen to know that Jonah Cameron covertly heads A United Tomorrow and –"

"Yeah," I interrupted, "I know that too. So what?"

"Cameron wants a ghost writer to do a bio on him, praising him as the next George Washington, the man who's going to reinvent this country."

"Oh, puke," I commented.

"Well, to each their own political beliefs." He laughed and went behind his desk again. He sat down and swiveled toward me.

"All right," I said dejectedly. "Lay it on me. Why me – and why Wyndham & Dorset?"

"They're one of the few small, independent publishing houses left. Cameron can buy them, if he needs to, and make the bio come out the way he wants. That's his style."

"So how do I fit in this scheme?" I put my head on one hand and stared idly out Balducci's windows at the night lights of New York.

"You got lucky," he laughed again. "When Truitt called Wyndham & Dorset, Joanie made up your title as senior editor. When Truitt pushed for what you did, Joanie said celebrity bios, because that's what Collie Weiss used to do at the house."

"Oh, great," I said, feeling more trapped than ever.

"Cheer up, Drew. We both win. I've been wanting to get inside A United Tomorrow for a long time. You scoop the entire media with your exclusive, insider story. It's a great opportunity. Maybe you'll even win a Pulitzer."

"Maybe I'll win a bullet courtesy of Elijah," I sulked.

"No. I'll put people on you like I pour syrup on my pancakes," Balducci promised. "Elijah won't get within a thousand miles of you."

"Thanks. I always wanted to be smothered by the FBI. It's been my dream since kindergarten."

"So you'll do it?" Balducci asked.

"Do I get a choice?"

"Good. I'll call the Director in the morning. In the meantime, we'll move you to a safe house in New Jersey. Around the clock protection, two agents plus surveillance, bullet-proof transportation, a crash team ready to go if there's trouble." He picked up the phone and Karen interrupted.

She whined, "What about me? It took nine years to get my job as office manager and now my boss is gonna fire me."

Balducci put his phone down. "Where did you say you worked?"

"Hermes Messenger Service." Karen announced it proudly, like she was at IBM.

"I think we can take care of your boss," Balducci assured her. "He won't fire you, unless he wants his taxes audited for the last thirty years. In the meantime, you can stay at the safe house with Drew. I'll list you as a material witness. Maybe there's something you know that will help tie Elijah to A United Tomorrow." He buzzed the intercom.

While Balducci gave instructions, I studied the skyline through his windows. It felt like I was being pushed into a trap so I could be eliminated, safe house or no. But the safe house was better than my apartment. I could always bow out if it looked dangerous, couldn't I?

No, was the answer. But I didn't know that yet – and when I did, it would be too late.

20

The thin drapes on a small window were pulled back, providing me a view of ugly fence boards with rounded tops. Beyond the fence, I watched a rusted child's swing creak back and forth in a patch of moonlight. I'd opened the screened window to exchange humid outside air for stale inside air. It was demoralizing to be in an FBI safe house, unpacking my clothes. I was even more disgusted that I couldn't think of a better alternative.

The New Jersey safe house felt to me like a rat cage, an impression reinforced by its decor. The faded red window drapes matched a shabby bedspread with tasseled edges. The bedspread's knobby texture had been laundered threadbare in spots, turning the fabric into a desert-like scrub brush landscape. The covering hung over the sagging bed until it touched a shag carpet running from one beige wall to another.

Against the far wall was a scarred dresser that was yard-sale-chic in 1960. A portable TV with bent rabbit ears owned one end of the cigarette-burned dresser top. The drawers were pulled out and my clothes peeped from every drawer in disorganized piles. The room's only touch of class, a cheap motel-quality seascape, hung over the bed's headboard, tilted of course.

In the center of the bed's red desert landscape were the muted browns of a new suitcase. Resale tags were still on the luggage, bought that day by the FBI. I pulled a stack of underwear from the suitcase and followed with toiletries in a Ziploc bag. The last item in the suitcase was a jacket I'd worn to the election headquarters. The garment was still flecked with tile chips and coated in dust. I sighed and put the jacket aside to be dry cleaned. The FBI ought to be good for that bill, I thought.

There was no room for luggage in the cramped closet. I was pushing the suitcase under the bed when there was a light knock at my door. I was surprised to see Karen Shaw in the doorway, looking sheepish and needy. Karen was dressed in pink Big Dog sweats with booties, like she was going to a pre-teen slumber party. But her face showed extreme anxiety. I straightened to watch her anxious expression in the dresser mirror, my right hand involuntarily clinging to my jacket.

Karen talked with forced perkiness. "Getting settled in, I see."

I moved to the foot of my bed and looked at the TV for a second, then back at Karen. I suggested, "You're probably tense about being here.

Can't sleep, huh? Me too. I got an idea. Let's watch Jay Leno. He's a riot." I yanked the power knob and the little screen blossomed. I spun the dial until I saw Leno's jutting chin. Then I turned up the volume to an annoying level.

Karen winced. She complained, "Hey, Drew, how 'bout turning it down?"

I whispered in her ear. "The room is probably bugged. If you want to talk, we have to keep our voices down."

Karen looked shocked. I patted the mottled bedspread, suggesting that she sit next to me, as though watching the show.

The bed jiggled as Karen sat down. Leno was making funny faces at a girl, then a commercial shot on the screen with disorienting kinetics and deafening sound. I reduced the TV's sound level a bit, but it was still very loud.

I faced Karen. "What's up?"

"I don't feel right here." She plucked at her pants leg like a little girl.

"What do you mean?" I peered around her to make sure the door was closed. It was open slightly, so I got up and closed it.

"The FBI won't let me call work. I don't know if I still have my job. I can't even call a neighbor to feed my cat." She looked at me despairingly. "I mean, you got me into this. Can't you do something about it?"

"Karen, I'm trapped like you are. If you ask to leave, they'll let you go. But Elijah knows where you work, so he knows where he can kill you. He saw us together at Chumley's, then he tried to kill us in the subway. Elijah must believe you revealed something important to me, something Richie once told you. Did your brother ever say that A United Tomorrow was involved in planning the hit on the election head —" I stopped at a sudden creaking of hallway boards outside the door.

An FBI agent poked his head in the room. "Uh, could you guys turn down that TV? We have some calls to make."

I said, "Sure." What else could I say? I reached for the volume control. Sound trickled from the little TV. "OK?"

"Thanks." The Fibbie closed the door.

I flipped the bird at the closed door and turned up the volume enough to cover our voices, if we whispered. "So, did Richie tell you anything?"

"Yeah," Karen said dejectedly, eyes on the worn carpet.

"What?" I pressed.

"He thought he'd been chosen by A United Tomorrow because the election headquarters was on his route at UPS. Richie figured they wanted him because he could get close to the security guard without suspicion."

"That's great," I said a little too loud. I toned my voice down. "Have you got anything else?"

"Well, I have a reimbursement chit for Richie's membership in a New Jersey gun club. He gave it to me as proof they thought he was important. It's a check from A United Tomorrow that Richie never cashed."

I whispered, "Where's the check?"

"In a safe deposit box."

"Karen, you're smarter than you let on. When did you put the receipt in a safe deposit box?"

"Yesterday, before coming to see you. I also put in a letter written me by Richie. It came in the mail a few days ago." Her eyes watered. "He wrote me a good-bye."

"I'm sorry." I patted her knee.

She nodded. "He sent a photograph with the letter. It showed him with Elijah and the gun. They were dressed in hunting clothes, you know the kind with all those dark splotches."

"Yeah, camo gear. That helps. Anything else? Like something directly linking Elijah to A United Tomorrow?" I was hoping to get out of my undercover gig. Maybe I wouldn't have to play biographer to the great Jonah Cameron.

"No . . ." Her voice trailed off.

"Well, look, I'm going to sneak out of here tonight. I won't be gone long. I'm going to call my editor. I'll tell him what you've got. In case anything happens to us, he can follow up."

"Happens to us? Like what?" she hissed.

"Like getting killed."

"How can we get killed? An FBI guy stands outside the bathroom when I pee." Her fists were tight balls now, pressed against her knees.

"Oh, Karen, the FBI is good, but it isn't perfect. If Balducci is bought or blackmailed, he'll set up a lapse in the security and –"

"No," she said firmly, "I refuse to believe that."

"Well, suit yourself. Me, I'm going to watch my backside, as best I can. Thanks for the info on the receipt and the picture. Which bank has your safe deposit box?"

"Citibank, on Fulton at Water. I brought the key with me."

"Good. Let me have the key and I'll mail it to Saul Morgenthal, my editor."

"Why?"

"So the Fibbies don't get it. I don't trust them. I can't put my finger on it, but something isn't quite right. "

"Oh, God, what have I been dragged into?" She despondently put the safe deposit key in my hand and rose. "I'm going to bed."

I turned off the little TV. It crackled with static as the image shrank to a white point.

I decided to join the Fibbie guards in a game of cards, something to kill the time until everyone went to sleep. Then I'd slip out and call Saul Morgenthal. I trusted Saul even when I didn't trust anyone else. He was too abrasive to be a liar. Sneaky just wasn't in Saul's personality.

21

I watched the FBI agent draw from the deck centered on the dinette table. He slid a card in place among a fistful of playing cards and gleefully announced, "Gin." The agent scraped away the pile of matchsticks representing the current pot. "How about another round?"

"Not my game. Not my night for it, anyway." I got up to stretch. A streetlight glared in the kitchen window, painting yellow halogen glow on a porcelain sink. I opened the hot water tap, letting it run. The kitchen window showed a row of tract homes with garbage cans stacked in front for morning pickup. I tested the water, mixed in some cold, and filled my hands. Warm water on my face was soothing but it didn't quell my restlessness. Staying in this safe house, for even a few days, was going to drive me nuts.

"I think I'll catch some winks," the agent told me, stretching his arms toward the yellow kitchen ceiling. A shoulder holster bobbed against the man's chest.

"I'm too wired to sleep. I'll play solitaire for a while," I said. I watched the agent leave the kitchen through an archway, then slid a green vinyl chair across the linoleum floor and sat backwards in the chair. I could see another agent in the front room, sitting on the sofa, staring out the front window. There were two more agents in a car across the street. I quickly dealt myself a hand of solitaire. I found an ace and put it up, so I could play on it.

Two hands later, the agent on the sofa stretched out comfortably. With enough cheating, I finally played a hand to completion. There was gentle snoring coming from the couch, so I looked through the archway and out the living room window. Heads were nodding in the car, too. I rose carefully and checked for sounds of life. The refrigerator buzzed in a low whirring. The stove clock ticked. But nobody moved into the kitchen to check on me.

I walked like a cat toward the back door, avoiding a squeaky floorboard I'd discovered earlier. Very slowly, I turned the doorknob, pulling up as I opened, to reduce the squeak. Behind was an old screen door with a pneumatic return. These screen door closers invariably made a racket and this one looked to be no exception. Still, it was worth a try. I'd tell them I was going into the backyard for a smoke if they discovered me. I pressed gently but insistently on the screen door.

I almost got it open far enough to leave when the closing mechanism made a scraping noise. I twisted around to see if anyone noticed. The agent on the couch rolled over, but didn't wake up. The pair in the car seemed even more out of it than before, but I really couldn't tell. I risked pushing harder. The screen door quietly gave way and I eased out. I fixed the closing mechanism so the screen wouldn't return, slamming against the door.

Outside, damp earth smell met me. I moved across isolated clumps of brown grass. Everything looked yellow in the glow of the streetlights. There was a low fence separating this yard from a house on the next street. I put my palms on the fence, then awkwardly pushed myself up, my Nikes making a scraping noise on the wood. The fence wavered as I spent a tiny moment balancing on top. Then I was over, letting the fall carry my body into a crouch. I stayed in that low squat as I went under the neighbor's windows.

I was grateful to find no dog in their yard. I made a mental note of the house number when I moved to the street. Then made a note of the street name as I came to the corner. I didn't think I'd get lost, but calling Balducci for a ride wouldn't be funny. Cold pressed into my light T-shirt as I walked, making me wish for a jacket. But that couldn't be helped. Bringing a jacket into the kitchen would have made the Fibbies suspicious.

My cell phone was still in SoHo, at the transcription service. I'd rushed to Chumley's so I could meet Karen, not realizing she'd be an hour late for our appointment. I hadn't a chance since then to retrieve my cellular. Pay phones are hard to find, so I was forced to explore quite a bit. Several blocks from the FBI safe house, I found a grammar school. I heard a window broken and a pair of boys with broad grins ran across the school yard and scaled the chain link fence. They briefly glared at me and then ran off.

I kept going, past a section where there was no sidewalk, just long stretches of ivy creeping into the street, reaching for my feet. I could see the neon lights of a main avenue ahead. I went towards it like a beacon, despite worrying that everything would be closed. But it wasn't. A donut shop was open.

I went inside, found some loose bills in a pocket and got myself a gooey donut and a small cup of black acid they said was coffee. A plastic table beckoned to me, but that didn't last. The night clerk slopped a mop across the checkerboard floor, slapping dirty water on my shoes as an invitation for me to leave. I accepted his invitation and went outside, standing in the bright glow of neon and streetlights.

Bingo. There was a pay phone at the car wash across the street. With no traffic, I sauntered across, taking a bite from the donut and trying a swig of coffee. The coffee was too hot and I spat it out, leaving a dark stain on the asphalt. I got to the pay phone and balanced the donut atop the phone, on a palm-sized napkin. I put the coffee on the ground by my foot. Kicking it over would be no great loss.

Amazingly, the phone actually had a dial tone. Most pay phones in New Jersey were dead, cut off by local businessmen and homeowners to stop drug traffickers from using their area as a hangout. I dialed "0" and waited.

"May I help you?" the operator asked.

"Yes. I'd like to make a collect call. It's to *The New York Chronicle* press room. Make that person-to-person, for a Mr. Saul Morgenthal." I gave her the unlisted number and leaned against the scant phone booth for support.

Eventually, I heard Morgenthal accept the call. Then he said, "Morrissey, you run out of money already?"

"And good morning to you, too. I have some news for you, but not printable just yet."

"Wait a minute. I'll get a recorder hooked to the phone." There was a loud clunk as he set the receiver down.

I bent over and tried the coffee again. It hadn't improved. I tossed the acid brew at the street. Then I aimed the paper container at a trash can but the cup drifted off course. I'd pick it up when I was through, true ecologist that I was.

Saul fumbled around, nearly breaking my eardrum a couple of times. Then he came back on the line with more eagerness than I'd ever seen in Saul Morgenthal. "Shoot, Morrissey."

"You remember Richie Shaw?"

"Yeah, Mr. Killer who got killed. Let me guess. There was a miracle and you resurrected him from the dead. It'll make page one."

"Not quite. I stuck to the living. I got his sister, Karen, to meet me at Chumley's."

"And you want me to pay the bar tab, right?" he asked sarcastically.

"No. Elijah followed Karen, chased us on the subway and took a shot at me."

"You all right?"

This was more concern from Saul Morgenthal than I thought possible. I nearly fainted. "Yeah, I made it to a cab with only bruised ribs and a minor concussion. I went to the FBI for protection. I figured I wasn't going to live long enough to give you a story if I didn't."

"You calling from the Federal Building?"

"No. I'm at a pay phone in Jersey. They put Karen and me in a safe house. They won't let us make calls, so I sneaked out."

He snorted. "How're you going to get me a story when you're locked in a safe house?"

"That's so like you Saul – always concerned about the safety of your reporters. Actually, Mr. Morgenthal, you're going to like what the FBI has in mind. They want me to join A United Tomorrow." I waited for a response. For once, Saul Morgenthal was speechless.

Finally, he said, "Go on."

"Remember how I went to Shaw's funeral?"

"Vividly. I got a call this morning from George Halliday. You are now persona non grata with Senator Cort. Halliday isn't going to bother with a lawsuit. He's going to personally strangle you. I explained to Halliday that you were crazy, not malicious. For some reason he bought it."

"So he covered for me with A United Tomorrow, right?"

"You lead a charmed life, Morrissey. Yes, Halliday covered for you."

"Good, because the head of recruiting for A United Tomorrow has invited me to lunch at Daniel."

Saul was astonished. "Daniel? Home of the ninety-nine dollar hamburger? How'd you arrange this?"

"At the funeral, it said no press allowed, so I put down my roommate's profession – editor at Wyndham & Dorset. It turns out Jonah Cameron is hot to have a bio done on him. He thinks Wyndham & Dorset is a good choice because if he doesn't like the book, he'll buy the place, fire me, and have his bio re-written. Soft management touch, don't you think Saul? You and Jonah Cameron have a lot in common."

"Har, har, Morrissey. How is the FBI going to carry off this farce? I mean, besides the fact that you can barely read, much less write, how are you going to pose as an editor?"

I could hear Saul chortling at his own sarcasm. Well, I had taken the first swipe by comparing him to Jonah Cameron. What did I expect?

I shrugged it off. "Joanie, Collie Weiss' secretary, is covering for me. Wyndham approved it. He's madder than hell about Collie's murder. A United Tomorrow already faxed a form to Wyndham & Dorset and they filled it out, with the FBI's help. The FBI set up college references and stuff, so I'll pass when A United Tomorrow checks me out."

"Great. When do you file the story?"

"When the FBI clears it for publication."

"Hell, they never clear anything. They don't want a newspaper story prejudicing the jury pool."

"Well, it may not go to trial. We just need a story our lawyers say will stand up to Cameron's influence and legal staff. Then, I'm free of Elijah, pretty much. After that story breaks, there's no point in killing me. Elijah will just disappear with his money. The problem is linking A United Tomorrow to the election headquarters murders, but I got a break tonight."

"Good. What is it?" The presses started in the background, probably running cleaner fluid to remove ink left by today's edition. It was about 3:00 A.M. and they were done with this morning's paper.

I shouted in the hope Saul could hear me over the presses. "Richie's sister kept a photo of Richie and Elijah with the gun, target shooting — and she's got a receipt showing A United Tomorrow reimbursed her brother for joining a gun club. I'm mailing you the key to her safe deposit box, where she put this receipt and photo."

Saul screamed into the phone so he could be heard over the machinery behind him. "That stuff is good, but it's not enough. It still doesn't tie Elijah to A United Tomorrow. They can claim they were just sponsoring private ownership of assault weapons, something they publicly advocate."

"I know that, Saul. That's why I'm going to meet this Truitt Hastings. I'll call you again, as soon as I can sneak away."

"OK Drew. And stay alive, will you?"

"Yeah, but that's not up to me. It's up to the FBI. By the way, do you know anything about Jake Balducci, who heads the New York FBI office?"

"No, but I can check him out. Call me when you can."

"OK, Saul. Bye."

Well, that was certainly an improvement over my call from Ulaklowski's apartment. I hung up and started off, then remembered my civic duty and threw the coffee cup away. I wondered what I'd get to eat at the lunch with Truitt Hastings – or if I'd have any appetite once I got there.

22

Winning through intimidation is a corporate style that pre-dates Genghis Khan. I had no doubt inviting me to lunch at Daniel was an act of pure intimidation and I was determined it wouldn't work. I took a deep breath and pressed on the gold cummerbund of a revolving door, stepping into another world.

This wasn't a Princess cruise. It was the Queen's yacht. From around the globe, power and wealth come to Daniel so they can play the connections game in a lavish setting, totally pampered and indulged. To look like you belong here, you have to act self-assured. So I approached the reservation desk and confidently announced myself. "Drew Morrissey. I'm having lunch with Truitt Hastings."

The maitre d' gave me a pleasant smile and ran a pen across an entry in his appointment book. "This way," he said and led me toward the main dining salon.

I went past a gold-leaf bar and cherry wood paneled lounge. Walking down a few steps took me into a Venetian palace sent via time machine to modern New York from the Italian Renaissance. Medici nobles would have been at home here, practicing the intrigues Machiavelli advocated in *The Prince*, a bestseller among power brokers in all centuries.

Even with warning bells ringing in my mind, I couldn't help admiring the restaurant's beauty. The warm bisque shade of a coffered ceiling complemented salmon-colored Bernardaud china on the tables. Silk curtains were tied back to frame arched colonnades that gave the salon depth and spatial balance under its eighteen foot ceilings. Fine art was hidden in niches sprinkled throughout the room, illuminated by sconces.

The maitre d' led me to a private table, hidden by curtains at the perimeter of the room. A very pretty man in his late twenties rose to greet me. Truitt Hastings was handsome enough to be a model showing off designer fashions for men. He was dressed to make the cover of *GQ*, wearing a Brioni three button pinstripe suit with a waistcoat-style vest, straight off the runways of Milan. A silk handkerchief, folded in triple peaks, was stuffed in his breast pocket and matched his tie. Including handmade shoes, Hasting's clothes rang the cash register higher than my gross monthly salary.

I could only hold my own against Truitt's elegant attire because the FBI had sprung for a backless DKNY emerald chiffon and lace dress. My necklace and earrings were borrowed from Cartier's. Balducci claimed he'd pledged his 401K as collateral for the gems. The dress and jewelry made it clear Balducci had more at stake than a casual investigation. His desire to get something on A United Tomorrow seemed personal and imperative. It made me wonder if AUT had something on Balducci and he was fighting back. At the moment, it didn't matter why Jake Balducci was sponsoring me with such gusto. I was just grateful for the help, especially at a power lunch like this.

"Drew, thank you for coming. It's a pleasure to meet you," Truitt said with a wide smile.

"Thanks." I shook Truitt's hand, a formality that felt more like NFL teams meeting center-field for the coin toss than striking up a new friendship.

"Do you come here often? It's my favorite spot for a quick lunch."

"Off and on," I hedged. "Mostly I catch lunch in the square outside the GE Building. In winter, I do a little skating on the ice. I'd guess you're pretty athletic yourself. Tennis?"

"Yes. I play as often as my busy schedule permits. How about you? Doubles or singles player?" Truitt was looking directly at me now, radiating warmth. He had being charming down to a science.

"Neither. I leave tennis to my boss." I couldn't imagine Saul in shorts, but I knew Wyndham, the surviving partner of Wyndham & Dorset, was a tennis nut.

"Mr. Wyndham?" Truitt asked, appearing to read the menu, but I had a sense of being closely watched.

"Yes, I work directly for Mr. Wyndham. He's difficult, but I try hard to please him." I hoped I sounded convincing.

"Oh, you please him. Mr. Wyndham spoke very highly of you."

A subwaiter wearing a black silk vest brought me an assortment of breads in a wicker tray. I pointed to an olive-rosemary roll and he gently placed it on my bread plate using silver tongs. Hastings chose a slice of walnut bread. I tried the olive-rosemary roll and it was exquisite, with a nutty flavor and salty kalamata olives, spiced by fresh sprigs of dry rosemary.

The headwaiter appeared at the table to take our order. He'd been at the FBI briefing before I left for the restaurant. I felt both calm and irritated at the FBI's efficiency. Before I could open the menu, the headwaiter courteously asked, "Will it be your usual lunch, Ms. Morrissey?"

"Yes, I'll have my old standard," I said, enjoying the idea of being someone who frequented Daniel, though it wasn't close to the truth. My normal lunch was taken off a hot dog cart. But the ruse worked. I looked at Truitt Hastings and saw there was genuine respect in his eyes.

"I'll have your vegetarian sampler," Truitt announced, folding the menu and handing it to the waiter. Hastings turned to me and asked, "Are there any questions I could answer for you while we're waiting?"

"Well, for starters, what assignment did you have in mind for me at A United Tomorrow? Editing promotional brochures and the like?"

"Oh, heavens, no," Truitt exclaimed. "No, I wasn't thinking you'd come to work for us just yet. You certainly want to stay at Wyndham & Dorset for a while, don't you? I mean, you said Wyndham was difficult, but it must be a very rewarding career. Isn't it?"

"Yes . . . Then what did you have in mind?"

"Let me begin at the end and work backwards, Drew. Eventually, I would like you to work for us. What I have in mind for you is a plum job, media director of A United Tomorrow, New York Operations. We're very well funded, so there'd be a substantial increase in your salary and bonuses."

"Hmm," I said noncommittally.

Truitt leaned over and talked in a confidential manner. "You'll meet the most influential people in the world. I spent half an hour today with Senator Noland, the man certain to be majority leader this year. This afternoon, I'll meet Gunther Moss, CEO of MicroCom. That's why I joined, Drew. No one can possibly get to the top on just talent. It's who you know that matters. Life's a connection sport. You know what I mean?"

I nodded and his face brightened.

"So, Drew, you probably want to know what the price is for this plum job, right?" Truitt's face was alive with energy now.

"Yes, I certainly want to know that," I replied, with more honesty than Truitt Hastings could possibly imagine. White medical tape pulled against my skin as I adjusted my chair. A microphone was taped to my rib cage, just below the neckline of the dress. The FBI told me it was only a precaution. The table itself was bugged.

"Well —" Truitt stopped talking because a waiter appeared with his first course. It was a delicate bird's nest of butter lettuce and arugula, topped with onion skin-thin chips of radish, beet and taro. There were baby mushrooms stuck in the salad like tuxedo shirt pins.

The waiter nodded at me. "Your hamburger will be ready shortly, Ms. Morrissey."

I smiled. Saul wasn't kidding when he said Daniel was the home of the ninety-nine dollar burger. It seemed I was going to experience one and I was certain it would prove quite a contrast to my usual Big Mac.

Hastings took a bite of his salad.

When Truitt finished, I hinted, "You were about to say . . ."

"Oh, yes. The price of glory, so to speak. Well, let's be candid, shall we Drew?" Truitt waited patiently, staring at me.

"Sure," I replied warily.

Hastings again talked in a hushed, confidential tone that I found particularly ironic considering how many FBI agents were eavesdropping on us. Truitt whispered, "I happen to know that the sponsor for A United Tomorrow wants to do a bio of himself and his life goals." He folded his arms and looked smugly at me. "Enter Drew Morrissey, editor for celebrity bios!"

"It's certainly possible that we could do the trade you propose. I'd have to know more about your sponsor before I could sell the project to Mr. Wyndham. Who is this person?"

"Well, that's a secret," Truitt said, pressing a fork into his salad. He tore off half the bird's nest, cut it in pieces and began wolfing the fragments.

"Well," I laughed, "It's not possible to get a bio published about a person without knowing who they are."

"True," Hastings conceded.

"I have to talk to 'him.' Do you expect me to work with him blindfolded?" I asked facetiously.

Truitt nodded. "You'll meet him. First there's a preliminary interview with Marv Logan, head of New York Operations. He's on the west coast right now, so it'll be done by video teleconferencing."

I flashed on the signature scrawled across Senator Cort's invitation to Richie Shaw's funeral – Marv Logan.

Truitt put down his fork and smiled proudly. "If Marv likes you, you'll be flown to California and work with our leader in person. I've met our leader once, but of course, I wasn't told who he really was, just that he was visiting, you know."

"Your leader?" I pried gently.

Hastings stared across the room. Suddenly, his gaze came back to me and we locked eyes. "OK. I'll let you in on a secret. His name is Jonah Cameron."

"Really." I tried to look super impressed. "When do you think I'll meet him?"

"You'll talk with Marv Logan first. Tomorrow, at our headquarters in the Chrysler building. We have a whole floor there. I'm sure Marv will like you. Then we'll fly you out so you can meet Jonah. Cameron Industries has their own jet."

At that point, Truitt's second course arrived, a fricassee of summer vegetables, along with my "burger." I looked at the awesome stack of gourmet ingredients comprising my hamburger and verified they did include a bun and ground sirloin steak. Of course, there were also fresh black truffles and a dozen other goodies not normally found on a hamburger. Although it seemed a shame to destroy such a beautiful creation, I immediately began eating. I was starved.

Between bites, I talked on autopilot. "Impressive that Cameron has his own jet. How did he make his money?"

"Stock market futures, investing his inheritance. He only started with twenty million."

Only twenty million, I thought. Gee, I wish I'd had only twenty million to start with. I wonder what that would've been like? As much as I like Donovan as a person, I probably wouldn't have him for a roommate, if I had twenty million in the bank. That train of thought suggested a question to me. "Where does Mr. Cameron live?" I asked.

"He has a compound on the ocean, at the outskirts of Malibu. A lot of movie stars live nearby."

"Interesting," I said, again trying to look impressed. Actually I was impressed, not with the Hollywood glamour angle, just with the money. That's Drew Morrissey, always going for the basics. How many bucks do you have? Sure. That's why I'd never dated a rich guy in my entire life. However, twenty million calories later, I finished ninety-eight of the ninety-nine dollars worth of hamburger.

The headwaiter stepped to our table and inquired, "Would either of you care for dessert? An after-lunch drink? Coffee?"

I wagged my head. "Not for me. Truitt?"

"No, just the check." He slipped a credit card in the thin leather Daniel folder without looking at the bill. Hastings told me, "I'll call you this afternoon to finalize the time for the video-teleconference."

"I'll be in an acquisitions meeting with our sales director. Why don't you send me an e-mail instead? I'm certain I can break your time slot loose. Tomorrow's schedule is pretty flexible."

"Sure." He nodded and signed the credit card receipt. I walked with Hastings through the revolving doors, thanked him for lunch and waved good-bye as he left in a cab. When Truitt was out of sight, I turned and went toward a white Suburban parked a block away.

I walked past a homeless man, clinging to a bottle in a paper bag, his fingertips twitching in frayed gloves with their ends cut off. I quickened my pace. A gust of wind blew a plastic shopping bag against my legs. I reached down and pulled it off my shins, dropping the bag in a wire trash basket. When I brought my hand out of the crumpled mesh frame, I instinctively felt myself being watched and turned around. The destitute man was behind me, babbling incoherent phrases. I peered into his eyes and he turned his face away.

The Suburban rolled alongside, a door flew open and a young Fibbie got out. She grabbed my arm and urged me inside. I let myself be pushed in the back seat and immediately felt safer behind the Suburban's bullet-proof glass. Then it hit me. Could that homeless man have been Elijah, heavily made up so I didn't recognize him? I was grateful when the Suburban roared into traffic, jerked forward by its huge engine.

Jake Balducci turned in the front passenger seat so he could face me. "How'd it go?" he asked.

I shrugged. "You tell me, Jake. You had the place bugged."

"I think you're in," he said, giving me a thumbs up.

"Great," I muttered. Everything was going according to plan, so I should feel good. There was, however, a reason I didn't feel good. It wasn't my plan, so I didn't know where this roadmap was taking me. Plus, I'd passed some odd signposts today and they worried me. That homeless man was one of the unusual signposts. The other warning sign was my lunch with Truitt Hastings. It had gone way too smoothly. Something was wrong. But what? I had no answer to that question.

I just knew I felt like a pawn in everybody else's game. Jake Balducci was moving me around on his chess board. Truitt Hastings knew what I was going to do for him. Maybe even Elijah wanted me alive now and was tracking me instead of trying to kill me. All three men seemed to have one goal in common. They were using me as bait to get at Jonah Cameron.

My father took me fishing only one time when I was a little girl. I remembered what happened to the bait. It got eaten. Yet tomorrow, I was going to walk into A United Tomorrow and smile. Think happy bait, Drew. After all, you also want to get at Jonah Cameron.

23

I walked briskly across the lobby of the Chrysler building, my patent-leather pumps clicking on the stone floor. I was dressed in a black suit with a starched banded-collar blouse and ebony studs accenting the tuxedo cut of my wardrobe. Fortunately, the outfit hadn't gone on my Visa card. The FBI purchased my clothes at Bloomingdale's, along with $600 an ounce perfume. I was walking into the grip of powerbrokers without a conscience. All they understood was money and prestige, so I had to look like I belonged in their world.

I stopped at the elevator bank for the upper floors and waited impatiently, clasping my hands, then releasing them. I stared unseeing at the vast painted ceiling, covered with Edward Trumball's scenes of transportation in the 1920s. Finally, I heard the elevator doors hiss and their elaborate cascade of art-deco fans separated. Humanity packed into the elevator pushed out, flowing around me. Despite that exiting crowd, I was alone when I stepped inside and had a solitary ride to the 72nd floor.

When I got out, I found myself in a small metal anteroom. It felt like being inside a garbage can and that didn't help my anxious mood. There were only two ways to leave the chamber, the elevator behind me or a thick metal door ahead. A security camera whirred as its lens focused on me and a disembodied voice asked, "May I help you?"

"I'm here to see Truitt Hastings."

"Your name?"

"Drew Morrissey. We had an appointment for 2 P.M."

"One moment, please. We'll contact Mr. Hastings for you."

I shrugged and lifted a platinum earring that pulled on my lobe like a piece of lead pipe. The jewelry looked great with my outfit, but the earrings were killing me and I hadn't worn them for half an hour. I pulled the latest copy of *Elle* off a chrome coffee table and picked idly at glossy pages. After a few minutes, I got tired of standing and sank into the buffalo leather of a Roche-Bobois chair.

The door clicked and Truitt Hastings stood looking at me. "Welcome, Drew. Come on in."

I dropped the magazine on the coffee table and coasted by Truitt holding the door open. He joined me on the other side and we went in tandem across a snowscape of albino carpet, past islands of rosewood desks, walking toward huge windows. Outside the glass, the beak of a steel gargoyle hung like a vicious hawk, perched over a view of the Ford Foundation, three blocks away.

"This is the area where staff members make calls during elections. A United Tomorrow, as you know, is working hard to bring voters to the polls. We want them to express their opinions about where America should be going."

"Impressive," I said, but it actually felt oppressive. I longed for the Poland Spring cooler and my chipped desk. Even Muzak was better than this atmosphere of sterile perfection. The only thing relaxing me was Truitt Hastings working so hard to impress me. Hastings, at least, was convinced he needed me.

"Why don't we take the private escalator to our upper floor, so you can see the conference facility better? The auditorium would be of great use to you in a future position as our media director. We bring a lot of influential people here to give them an orientation to A United Tomorrow and its goals."

"I'm sure I'll find that very informative." I pasted a smile on my face and glided up an escalator with a massive tiered chandelier hanging above the automated stairway. Apparently AUT leased both the 72nd floor and the one above. It was a testimonial to their lush funding level. I was impressed again when I went through theater-style doors at balcony level of their conference center.

Below me lay the grand conference room for A United Tomorrow's New York Operations. The room was basically a lecture hall, complete with amphitheater seating cascading from where I stood to one story below. Between the audience gallery and the speaker's podium was a massive conference table, floating like an aircraft carrier on a froth of white carpeting.

"Come on. I'll take you for a ride." He said it with boyish enthusiasm, which surprised me in the formal surroundings.

We sat together on a personal elevator, the kind used in wealthy homes to move invalids between floors. The seat was mounted on a railing that swept us downward in a smooth glide. At the bottom, we got off and walked to a conference table that loomed even larger now that I was close to it. Despite the table's size, I could see it could be retracted into the floor.

Hastings stood by the conference table and pushed on a trapdoor panel I saw replicated at every position around the table. A monitor popped up. "These are connected to a computer for showing charts, graphs, spreadsheets and PowerPoints. You can bring your own notebook and feed data into the display network."

I pointed at a circuit of black dots running around the table. "Microphones?"

"Yes." Truitt poked one of the dots and it popped up. He pulled the microphone out and twisted the stem toward me. Hastings pointed upward. "In the ceiling are spotlights that shine on each individual's face. TV cameras with zoom lenses controlled from the operator's balcony." He pointed to a crow's nest hung over the back of the audience gallery.

"Are there conference rooms like this in every city?"

"No, just the major ones. We link everybody together twice a year, with the hub being here in New York. Marv's been in charge of giving those shows for the last two years." Truitt stepped on a little platform with a podium. "Behind this speaker's podium are back-projection screens and white boards that can transmit hand-drawn images to our other offices." He waved a hand at a bank of electronics. "You name it, we've got it — computers to project animations, THX sound, everything."

"How long does it take to learn?" I asked, playing with one of the chairs.

"Oh, it's like having a big screen TV where you decide what programming to watch. You personally don't have to worry about details. Technicians operate the equipment, and we hire ad firms to build the presentations. You just approve them. It took me a while to get comfortable with it, but once you see your ideas come to life, you'll be very excited."

I nodded in appreciation. "Where do I sit for the interview with Mr. Logan?"

"Call him Marv. We all do. Marv's just an easy-going professor. You'll see. Try that chair," Truitt said, offering me the closest one. "The tech upstairs will focus the camera and adjust the sound. You just relax. I'll be right back. I have to give the tech some cues and we'll get started."

I rolled out one of the fifty tall-backed executive chairs pushed against the massive conference table. As I got comfortable in the chair, Truitt wound along the topmost seats until he found the technician in his perch. Hastings chatted with him briefly, then took the elevator-chair down to the conference table.

Even as Truitt slid downward, huge screens on the wall began changing. One displayed a video panorama of Cameron's Malibu compound, shot from a helicopter overhead. Another screen zoomed across the Malibu waves at the main structure with its block-long series of blue-tinted windows. At the last moment, when a collision seemed inevitable, the screen dissolved into a pan of the conference room at Malibu where Marv Logan would be talking to me.

Truitt claimed a chair at the conference table, near me. He folded his hands, and watched a clock superimposed on a static shot of the Malibu conference room. The clock hand rotated toward a noon position and when it hit, the time disappeared and the Malibu conference table jittered slightly. We were now watching live video.

Marv Logan walked to the center of the conference table and sat down. The image zoomed, showing an immaculately groomed face, with small eyeglasses and a polka-dot bow tie. Close-cropped iron gray hair ran over Logan's head like beard stubble. He struck me as a conservative law professor who'd gone commercial, trading academic ideals for a very comfortable lifestyle.

Truitt reached over and hit a key in front of me. The monitor showed a picture of me, apparently what Marv Logan was seeing in Malibu. I looked my usual self, except with professional makeup and a blow-dried haircut. Cosmetics applied by a TV news makeup artist did wonders for my looks. I couldn't help feeling pleased at the makeover. I looked at Hastings and he started the dialogue.

Truitt asked, "Good morning, Marv. How's Malibu treating you?"

"Same old stuff. I see you've got a guest. Why don't you introduce us?"

"Sure," Hastings replied. "This is Drew Morrissey, senior editor of celebrity bios at Wyndham & Dorset."

I smiled and waved a bit with my right hand. "Hi, Marv. Pleased to meet you." Now I was a pro at video teleconferencing. That was why my mouth was so dry.

"Pleased to meet you, Drew. How'd you like to work on the bio of the man I consider the most important influence on our country since George Washington?" He actually said it with a straight face.

I tried to answer with a straight face, nervously sneaking a peek at myself in the monitor. "Sure, how can I pass that one up? But you know, editors just fix bent prose. We need a ghostwriter, don't we?"

"Got a staff of 'em. A first draft is ready for you to look at when you visit us in Malibu and meet Jonah."

This was way too slick. I should have had to sell myself to Marv. In preparation for this interview, I'd been force-fed a list of all the bios Wyndham & Dorset ever published, complete with ghostwriters and agents. I was ready to spout for an hour, like an oral exam, and none of it was necessary. I improvised a decent, if not great recovery. "You're really prepared, aren't you?"

"That's how we win, Drew, by being so prepared. When can you fly to the coast? Truitt'll escort you on the jet. We'd like to get going. Jonah has a slot open . . ." He looked at an appointment book, "In three days. Can you clear that with Wyndham? Want me to call him?"

"No, that won't be necessary. I briefed him yesterday and he authorized the project and this trip to Malibu. Mr. Wyndham wants me to go over your draft and then he'll be sending your agent a contract. Who'd you get to represent Jonah?"

"We have an entertainment attorney locally that goes over the fine print. This trip is mostly to get acquainted. We'll put you up at the Hotel Bel-

Air and our limo will take you to Jonah's compound. I'm looking forward to meeting you."

"Great," I said, feeling queasy.

The screens went blank and the lights came on. Truitt pushed his chair back and stood. He put a hand on my shoulder and said: "See, that wasn't so bad, was it?"

"No," I lied.

"No," is what I should have said to Balducci when he first proposed this undercover assignment. Now it was too late.

Any doubts I was being rammed into a setup vanished with this "interview." Marv Logan had already made up his mind before he talked to me. I could have worn a sweatshirt with love beads, been stoned, and Logan would have invited me to Malibu. Just what was waiting for me when I got on their corporate jet? I hated to think about it.

24

Naturally, Cameron Industries didn't own a mere two-engine Learjet for executive transportation. They owned an Airbus A380 capable of flying to Europe or Australia. The Airbus was larger and more luxurious than a Boeing 747. Stepping inside the jet, I realized its first class cabin had been replaced by a designer foyer. If I had to categorize the décor, I'd call it art deco, modified to suit FAA safety regulations. Everything glowed with a lacquered shine, even in the plane's subdued nightclub lighting. An ebony table held silk flowers in a black trophy vase. In the plane's muted illumination, the dark vase vanished, leaving the flowers to float on a beam of light from the ceiling. It was a clever optical illusion and highlighted the silk flowers beautifully.

The foyer had ribbed gray carpet edged in black and white stripes, with walls echoing that linear design. All the lines flowed naturally into the spiral of a staircase leading to the upper cabin. The staircase railing was a faux walnut banister, tracked by a parallel set of brushed metal ribs. At the top of the spiral staircase, a pair of tasseled spectator shoes descended, flashing their brown and white leather.

Following the shoes were cream pants and a navy blazer with a very white handkerchief folded in the breast pocket. Jutting from the blazer sleeves were French cuffs with gold cufflinks. Tanned hands tracked the banister downward until a Gatsby ascot appeared, followed by Truitt Hastings' bronzed face. His thick blond hair was swept back and slicked down.

"Hello again, Drew." Truitt put out a hand.

I shook the hand, feeling completely out of place in such lavish settings. Expecting a normal jet, I'd dressed casually, in slacks, a silk shirt and suede boots. To break the awkward silence, I said, "This is quite a plane."

Hastings smoothly replied, "Yes, isn't it. May I show you around? You can leave your attaché and suitcase here, if you like. It'll make it easier to move through the plane." Truitt smiled and the ceiling lights gleamed on his actor-perfect teeth.

I put my suitcase on the carpet, but kept my attaché. There wasn't anything inside the thin briefcase I didn't want them to find. It just didn't feel right to leave it there somehow.

Truitt startled me with a very practiced glide across the foyer. I twisted to follow, confused that we weren't going toward the rear of the plane. He touched a lighted switch and a panel slid back with a whisper of rushing air. It felt like I was in a Star Trek episode, though I didn't have a transporter beam so I could leave whenever I wanted. Karen Shaw and the Fibbies were following on a government Learjet, but that wouldn't do me any good. If there was any trouble on this flight, I was on my own.

Hastings announced, "This is the master suite. It's used by Mr. Cameron himself on overseas trips. In case you'd like to nap during the flight, Mr. Cameron's personal suite has been reserved for you."

I was flattered, but I assumed the room was wired and had hidden cameras. I followed Truitt through the doorway. Cameron's bedroom was decorated in black and a muted yellow, not my colors but still very tasteful. There was a pearlescent bowl with a spray of yellow flowers on a dresser. Alabaster and bronze sconces sprayed light on the ceiling. A satin comforter swathed the bed.

Hastings moved around the bed and tapped another lighted switch. "In here's the bath. If you'd like to freshen up before landing, there's a shower module that can be used as a steam bath or sauna. If you need help, a stewardess will explain the controls."

I glanced inside the tub. There was a complex of brass nozzles jutting from green tiles. Over the sink, round mirrors had frames shimmering like the inside of polished seashells. It was all very luxurious. A United Tomorrow was trying to impress me and they were succeeding.

Were they also trying to undress me so they could see if I was wired? If so, they weren't going to find anything on me. The FBI told me I couldn't wear a micro-recorder here the way I did at Daniel. Jake Balducci said A United Tomorrow would have detectors that can pick up the equipment. They might also have the type of x-ray gear used at some airports to look through people's clothing.

When Balducci told me I couldn't be wired, I argued with Jake. There had to be some technology that could avoid detection. I lost the argument. Still, I believed the FBI should have found a way to monitor me when I was on the Cameron jet and inside the Malibu compound. I came back to reality and nodded admiringly at all the gadgets Truitt was pointing out to me.

Truitt continued with his tour, not seeming to notice my indifference. Eventually, Hastings returned me to the foyer and pointed at a door leading toward the rear of the plane. "We have an office set aside for you in the aft spaces. It has all the amenities, both a PC and a Mac, fax and copying machines, dictating equipment and hi-resolution color printers. Would you like to use any of it?"

I smiled at that idea. "No, I'll take a short vacation from the office on the flight out. This is quite a treat."

"You have the right idea. They'll have you going full time when you get to Malibu. Let's go upstairs to the lounge. I was there when you arrived. There's a full bar. I'll bet you're ready for a drink after that drive from Manhattan." He said it with polish, like it had been used a hundred times before.

Drinking was in the finest tradition of *New York Chronicle* reporting. But that was when they were covering a story, not being the story. My article might be printed in the obituary column. I wasn't going to reduce my chances of living by touching alcohol. "I'll have a Coca Cola with lime."

I followed Truitt toward the staircase leading to the upper deck. I noticed my suitcase was missing from the foyer. Were they searching my bag?

Hastings saw my concerned look. "Don't worry about your suitcase. It's been stored for takeoff, but it'll be in the bedroom once we're airborne."

"Nice," I muttered. Available after takeoff? No doubt my suitcase contents would be re-assembled by then. Or were they just x-raying my bag? I followed Hastings upstairs, carefully watching each tread in my suede boots. At the top, I poked my head into the lounge area.

It was done in art deco like the rest of the plane. Silver tea paper covered the walls. An impressive ebony bar snaked along the center, attended by a very attractive bartender with platinum hair that limped to her cheeks and curled at her throat. She was dressed in a bellboy style uniform. The bartender put a twist of lime and a red plastic swirl-stick in a Coca Cola and handed it to me.

I said, "Thanks," and turned to find Hastings.

Truitt had moved to a group of mohair chairs with white piping along the edges of their cushions. The chairs were bolted to the floor with impressive clamps made of the same bronze metal used to anchor the lounge's floor lamps. The lamps shot rods upward, then fanned into octopus tentacles with suction cups holding a glowing alabaster bowl. Light from the bowls brought the tea paper ceiling alive and then floated softly down, with just enough force to let a passenger read. It certainly didn't feel like I was inside a jet. Only a line of small windows let me know I was in a plane.

Hastings gestured to a chair. "Take a window seat, why don't you?"

I slid by him and sat down, putting my drink on a white cube between the mohair chairs. Nervous, I poked around with my hands and discovered a remote control was Velcroed to the edge of the seat. It had everything on it I'd expect to find in a plane, but it also had buttons for a TV and DVD. Marv Logan had said that A United Tomorrow was always prepared. He'd also said that was how they won. Not good for me, I thought, but then I had the FBI on my side. Why didn't that comfort me as much as it should?

Truitt Hastings sat opposite me, a diplomat's smile on his face. Truitt crossed his legs and folded his hands on the sharp crease of a pant leg. "How's your drink?"

"Fine." To pass the time, I asked, "How long have you been with A United Tomorrow?"

"Five years and three months. It's a pretty nice job, providing the jet lag doesn't get to you." He smiled the perfect teeth again.

I sipped my Coke. The familiar taste and carbonation melted my stress a bit. "Go all over the world?" I asked, surprised I was able to find two innocuous questions in a row. It's not easy for a news reporter to make idle chit chat.

"Not the world," he answered, "just the U.S." You're the one with the really exciting job. I envy you. You must meet a lot interesting people. I just finished reading a bestselling Wyndham & Dorset book, *Scandals*. You edited that one, didn't you?"

"Well, yes." I put the drink down and focused on remembering my cover story. To protect myself from making any mistakes, I turned the spotlight back on Truitt. "Did you work in publishing before coming to A United Tomorrow?"

"Not exactly," he answered. "I joined A United Tomorrow from a PR firm in Boston. It's been a great career move."

"What did you do at the PR firm?" I shifted in the chair. It was comfortable, but I felt too uneasy to sit still.

"Actually, I handled A United Tomorrow as the PR firm's client. I made sure AUT was written up in national magazines and such. I look back on that job fondly. It was a lot less work."

I smiled sympathetically. I picked up the drink and looked out the window. Service trucks were moving across the tarmac towards us. A ground crew member was skipping rope over the microphone cord tethering him to the aircraft. I sipped again from the drink and turned back to Truitt. He'd been waiting patiently.

Hastings smoothed a pants leg and glanced down to inspect the result. "We've been talking too much about me. You're the special guest here. In fact, Marv has a half-day introduction planned for you. Speakers will cover the structure of A United Tomorrow and how Jonah uses it to support philanthropic projects worldwide." He pointed a finger at my glass. "Would you like me to freshen that drink?"

"No, one's my limit when flying," I joked.

Hastings played the good host and laughed at my lame humor. He stood up, adjusting his pants and blazer. "Excuse me a minute, Drew. I hear our other guest arriving. I'll be right back." Hastings vanished down the spiral stairs. Indistinct but jovial conversation welled up the staircase.

I was too restless to sit, so I went to the bar. The bartender was pouring red wine in a goblet the size of a small bowl. I put my Coca Cola glass down and spun on the barstool, looking out the aircraft's windows. There was a slight jolt of the plane. The air conditioning hiccupped with the lights, then resumed humming. Through the windows, the hangers and equipment began to move away from me. I realized the plane was getting ready to taxi on the runway.

The bartender moved to where Hastings and I had sat, mopping up with a cloth. She placed the goblet of wine on the white cube between the seats and the wine rocked slightly as the plane jiggled over seams in the concrete apron.

Hastings levitated up the stairway, followed by a stockbroker-type in a brown suit with tan wingtips, a flashy tie and square glasses in ultra-thin titanium frames. He looked like he'd just graduated from a fancy Ivy League business school with an MBA. They walked over to me and the stockbroker-type shook my warm hand with his cool, limp one.

Hastings announced, "Drew, let me introduce Nick Zeradakis to you. Nick is one of the top organizers of Senator Noland's re-election campaign and press secretary for the Senator."

I nodded and smiled deferentially.

Hastings continued the introductions. "Nick, this is Drew Morrissey, a senior editor with Wyndham & Dorset. She's considering a bio on Jonah. Drew's flying to Malibu so she can meet with Jonah for the first time."

"I hope all goes well, Ms. Morrissey," Zeradakis said. "Senator Noland thinks a lot of Jonah Cameron and all he's done, here and abroad. A bio sounds like a very fitting tribute. When do you think it will be out?"

"Well, that's hard to say," I evaded. "Usually it takes a year from concept to publication. Some bios take much longer."

Zeradakis scowled, putting deep furrows in the forehead of his boyish face. "Couldn't rush it a bit? Get the bio out before the presidential election?"

Truitt intervened. "Nick, we've got some of that French Cabernet you love, decanted and ready for you. Why don't we take a seat? The plane will be taking off soon."

We moved to the mohair club chairs. Nick Zeradakis picked up his goblet and made a production of trying the wine, swirling it in the glass and then sipping a bit, swishing the tablespoon around his mouth. "Fabulous, as always, Truitt." Zeradakis took a much hardier swallow and eyed me. I let the awkward silence continue.

The plane slowed, then jerked to a stop. There was an abrupt jolt as the tractor disengaged. Zeradakis deftly swiveled the wine glass, but he still got a splash on his hand-painted, gaudy tie. "Damn," he muttered.

I suggested, "Don't worry, Nick. People will think it's part of the design."

"Thanks, I think." He gave me a wary glance.

I avoided eye contact, reminding myself I wasn't there to spar with jerks. I looked at Truitt. He found seatbelts at the side of the club chair, so I groped around, found mine and buckled them. The bartender shut the cabinet behind the bar and went downstairs. An artificial bell chimed and the pilot announced that the crew should prepare for takeoff. The no smoking and seatbelt symbols appeared.

The plane rippled faster over tar strips seaming apron, then braked with irritating squeals and began a ponderous turn. I heard the engines winding up and felt the plane strain against its brakes. The Airbus lumbered forward and felt myself pressed into my seat.

"Nick, there's something I don't understand," I said.

Truitt's eyes lost their soft focus. I ignored his admonishing stare and continued. "Why is Senator Noland interested in getting the endorsement of A United Tomorrow?"

"Who says he is?" Truitt Hastings intervened. "We just have many compatible viewpoints, a symbiotic relationship, so to speak."

Zeradakis put his glass down and pressed his fingertips together. He began tapping the fingertips lightly against each other. Zeradakis glanced at Truitt Hastings. "I don't think we need to be so coy, Truitt. The press release has been finalized." His eyes brightened as Zeradakis told me, "There's going to be a dual announcement by Cameron and Noland next week. Jonah's going public as founder of A United Tomorrow and Noland is backing Jonah for President." He spread his hands open in pronouncement like he was giving a sermon.

The pieces fell into place – Cameron for President, Senator Noland as his VP. No wonder Zeradakis wanted the bio out so soon. I felt their eyes on me and fumbled for a question. "Why does Cameron think he can come out of nowhere and be elected President?"

"Simple arithmetic, Drew," Zeradakis explained. "A United Tomorrow is much larger than most people think. They've been very active in the last five years." Zeradakis wiped his glasses with a handkerchief. There was a red stripe on the bridge of his nose where the glasses had been. He put the handkerchief away and fitted the glasses.

This was a great opportunity to pry. Nick Zeradakis had a little wine and a huge ego feeding his mouth. I couldn't resist asking, "How big is A United Tomorrow?"

Truitt intervened again. He spoke in his most soothing and professional voice. "Unfortunately, we don't publicize our membership, Drew. I personally think we should."

Zeradakis ignored Truitt's hint and answered my question. "AUT has more than twenty million members, concentrated in states with a lot of electoral votes, like New York and California. Plus, A United Tomorrow is a very evangelical organization, so their reach extends beyond direct members. Each member is being asked to influence at least two friends to vote our way. We're talking about swinging a sixty million Americans, a third of the registered voters in the country. You see the obvious benefit to us. AUT will clearly be the deciding factor in the election."

Truitt Hastings squirmed uncomfortably. "This is off the record, Drew. None of it is for public dissemination."

I nodded. In my mind, the nod meant I understood Truitt's request, not that I would keep the information secret. After all, if anyone knew about Elijah, it was Jonah Cameron. It wouldn't be good to have a President who hired pro hit men. An icy chill trickled along my spine.

I asked the next question out of my fears before I had time to realize how risky it was to raise this topic. "But what about all this violence at election headquarters? What does Cameron think about that?"

Hastings' polished veneer suddenly vanished. His face became stressed and his lips were pressed in a thin smile. "A United Tomorrow doesn't endorse violence in any form. It operates strictly within the law."

"Of course," I reassured him. I felt the pressure building in my ears as the plane began rapidly ascending. The engine noise seemed more distant. The pressure in my ears meant I could barely hear Zeradakis when he talked.

"But Truitt, you must admit, the violence actually benefits A United Tomorrow. It makes you look moderate. Radical groups doing violent things and isolated fanatics shooting people are tragic." He shook his head for emphasis that he didn't endorse such awful things. When he'd waited the proper, calculated moment, Zeradakis continued. "Yet, they actually help us, give us momentum. The violence pushes middle of the road people toward us because they're afraid." He spun his forefinger. "It's what I call the spin effect."

"The what?" I asked in amazement.

"The spin effect. It's what will put us over the top. The spin effect from these acts of violence is that right wing groups appear moderate when fanatics commit atrocities. You see?"

"Yes," I said, "It's all very clear." It was clear that having a personal empire wasn't enough for Cameron's ego. He needed to be President. To aid him in that quest, Jonah created a cult following, A United Tomorrow. Then Cameron found AUT didn't have enough power because they were viewed as too fundamentalist. Enter Elijah, professional killer. A few massacres at election headquarters and A United Tomorrow looked sane, even middle of the road. Now I'd heard the motive behind the killings, straight from the sponsors. Regrettably, I didn't record Nick Zeradakis because the FBI hadn't wired me up.

I had to fix that problem before more valuable evidence was lost. But I wasn't going to get help from Balducci. I had the sick feeling Jake wasn't interested in bringing Cameron down or catching Elijah. I was concerned Jake Balducci was using me as bait for another agenda, one I wouldn't discover until it was too late. That intuition made it all the more important I protect myself by finding a way to hide a recording device on my person.

It was a stroke of luck that I was staying the first night at the Hotel Bel-Air and not in Malibu, under the noses of Jonah's security people. I was hoping to slip out and get some recording equipment from a techie named Leo Bendel. A narc once told me about Leo and all the gadgets he could get for you.

First, the FBI would have to let their guard down so I could get away. It wasn't pleasant to think about the FBI being sloppy. Any mistakes by the Fibbies meant Elijah had an opening to kill me. But if they didn't let me sneak off, I'd never bring Cameron down and be free of Elijah. Either way, I was frightened.

25

A United Tomorrow drove me to the Hotel Bel-Air in a stretch limo. I checked in and was greeted by a pair of local FBI agents, Jorge Gonzales and Denise Mallory. Jorge was about twenty-five, athletic yet skinny under his oversized jacket and baggy pants. He was wearing a black shirt and a western tie. His face was covered with acne and a goatee was all that stopped him from looking like a teenager. Denise had a cute, wholesome face and curly hair. She was a bit older, but still in her twenties. Denise wore a tweed jacket and corduroy pants with walking shoes that looked frumpy and out of it, but were all the rage in L.A.

It took a lot of cajoling to persuade them, but I finally got the pair to take me shopping in Santa Monica Place, which was only a few blocks from Leo Bendel's address. In Nordstrom, I loaded myself with twenty cocktail dresses, from a baby doll glam to a strapless pinstripe with boned corset bodice. They came from designers like Galtier, Escada and Dior. It was one of the few perks of being used as bait for the FBI. If the worst happened, I'd be the best-dressed body in the L.A. County morgue. I dragged the collection into a dressing area and hung some of the garments on hooks, piling others on a bench. Then I peeked to see what Denise Mallory was doing.

She was sitting at the entrance to the women's dressing area, on full alert, like a good FBI agent. I spotted Jorge five racks from the entrance, thumbing women's jackets and scanning the store. They were too alert. I was never going to get away from them. I had to bore them to death.

I tried on a half dozen outfits, trotting to the mirror, asking Denise her opinion, turning them down for different reasons. This dress made me look too fat. The next one was sexy enough on a model but made me seem dumpy. Besides, it was too racy for a business engagement, definitely a hotel rendezvous dress. Finally Denise yawned, then stretched and told Jorge she was going to the bathroom. He nodded and moved to the door, turning his back so he didn't appear to be peeking into the women's dressing area.

I slid quietly to the fire exit and pushed on it, fearing an alarm. My luck held and the door opened without a problem. I stole a quick look at Jorge. He was leaning against the door sill, softly whistling. I let the door close fully and stepped out.

I found myself in an abandoned storefront that was being remodeled. Light scattered into the empty shop through windows soaped to hide the renovation from mall shoppers. Overhead, the false ceiling was gone, exposing metal ducting with remnants of yellow fiberglass hanging from the air conditioning tubes. Sprinkler pipes and electrical conduit flowed in a maze around the ducts. The gray walls were dappled with spackle and paint buckets were stacked in a corner. Near a stack of old light fixtures, a workman's equipment belt hung from a metal two-by-four.

My suede boots scuffed across the concrete floor until I got to the front door and walked into the mall. I went from eerie calm to sensory overload, dizzied by flashing lights above storefronts and heavy smells from the fast-food court. Looking over the railing, I spotted the street entrance below a waterfall of escalators. I jogged to the moving stairs and began descending, glancing nervously at my watch. I only had a few minutes to find Leo Bendel and buy what I wanted.

Once on the street, I started jogging, something I wasn't very good at doing. In a block I gave up and did a fast walk. In another block, I went past a new concrete and glass condo painted with tropical colors. The next section was from the days when Santa Monica was a sleepy beach town, a string of clapboard bungalows with tar paper roofs and sagging porches. I rounded a corner and spotted an industrial building that fitted the description of Bendel's "emporium." On the surface, it was a high-end body shop where you brought your dented Bentley or scratched Ferrari for repair.

Dust lay on cars like a death sheet stretched over a corpse in the morgue. Fine sandblasting grit powdered hoods and frosted windshields. The white dust sifted through broken windows, layering on cracked leather seats like makeup on an old face. The cars were packed along an aisle of dirty asphalt. The narrow driveway led to a low stucco building where an air compressor fought to keep up with a hissing paint sprayer.

I made my way along the car aisle toward the pungent smell of automotive paint. There was a huge dog panting in the driveway, drool on its jaws. It rose and stretched, stood in my path, trying to instill fear in me. I hesitated, then decided I had no choice. I swallowed my fear at getting bitten and kept going, but sweat dripped along my ribs and it wasn't from the muggy heat. The dog stood its ground as I walked at its huge jaws. At the last moment, the black mongrel turned to let me pass, sniffing at an ankle. I waited until it got bored enough to leave me alone. I sighed in relief, happy that my ankle was still intact.

I looked around, trying to find Leo Bendel's office. There was a Rolls Royce in a spray booth, windows and chrome masked with tape. In a bay next to the Rolls, a Mercedes was getting its fender painted with gray primer. Nearby, Hispanics in blue coveralls glided wet sandpaper over a V-12 Jaguar. They ignored me, but their boss with a clipboard kept a fixed stare on me. I smiled at him and he turned away.

The paint booths had one stall closed-in with stucco where a sun-bleached door was faded to dirty pink. A small oval sign on the door said, "Leo Bendel." Sun beat on the door varnish, splitting veneer at the bottom into a grass skirt. The doorknob blistered my hand when I turned it. I quickly let go of the knob and let the door close itself. Despite the heat outside, Leo's office was icy cold. It was difficult to see anything in the dark after walking through bright Los Angeles sunshine, but Leo Bendel was too big to miss.

Bendel was an ex-professional wrestler. The Tiparillo stuck in his thick lips looked like a toothpick. His two-hundred-sixty-pound frame was leaning forward and his rodeo-style belt buckle was pressed against a glass display case. A dozen turquoise rings were clustered on the long fingers Leo had spread across the glass top. Bendel's fingertips were an inch away from an automatic pistol. The gun lay on a rubber pad with a white price tag strung on the trigger guard.

Across the display case from Leo was an intense man in a three-piece suit, staring at the handgun. His hands were jammed in his pants pockets, bunching his coat. Smears of white cuffs slashed across his dark, nicely tailored suit pants.

I stood in silence, my eyes adjusting to the dim light, wondering if my narc friend had misremembered the kind of items Leo Bendel sold "off the record." I'd thought Leo sold eavesdropping gear, but maybe his repertoire was untraceable guns. Then again, maybe it was both.

One of Bendel's massive hands moved to his face and plucked out the Tiparillo, knocked ash in a plastic tray with a beer logo in its center, then speared the Tiparillo back in Leo's face. Bendel broke the silence. "It's the biggest gun we can fit in a hidden compartment. The newer Benzes are smaller than the old ones. You could step back in time. Got sedans on my lot from the 1990s that'll take an Uzi under the dash."

"I got two years left on my lease." The customer thought some more in silence. "It's a lot of money for just a handgun. You sure it will do the job?"

The Tiparillo wove up and down as Bendel spoke. "What job you got in mind? It won't stop three guys with assault rifles. But it's got thirteen rounds in the clip. You spray those around to keep their heads down and it buys you time to get the hell out of Dodge."

The guy hesitated. "Well . . . It's a lot of money."

Bendel asked, "What you do for a living? Attorney? Shrink?"

"Yeah, I'm a psychiatrist."

"So you can afford it. What if that accident hadn't been so accidental, huh? I mean, some gangs bump you off the road, then work you over. When they're through, you'll wish you was dead."

"I never fired a gun." The shrink said it like a surrender.

"You *never* fired a gun?" Leo said it with deliberate overkill.

"No."

"Well, you don't got to. If you want, go to a gun club and get instruction. Otherwise, just do what I said. Spray around a clip and leave. You don't kill nobody. You only get in trouble if someone notes your license plate. You don't got a personalized one, do ya?"

"Well, yeah."

"Hell, you just give the custom plates to the DMV, get new ones. Let me help you out. You had a little accident with the Benz and a friend said take it to Leo, am I right?"

"Yeah, sort of."

"You take it to Bendel 'cause Leo does a good job with the bondo and the spray. Hell, lots of guys do that. But Leo also sells you peace of mind. So I'll do this for you. I'll bury the cost of the gun and the hidden compartment in your bill for the fender. After all, your car is a Benz. We'll say you needed a new taillight assembly. Got smashed in the accident. Your adjuster ain't been here yet. You didn't take the car into them, did ya?"

"No . . ."

"So you only gotta pay another four hundred dollars outta pocket and you got peace of mind – plus a new lookin' car. Whatta ya say?"

"Let me think about it . . ."

Leo shrugged and turned to me. "Can I help you?"

"Yeah," I said. "I'm in the market for some electronics. You carry that stuff, or only guns?"

"I got all kinds. Whatcha want? Something to tail your boyfriend, a locator you follow in your car? I got those, plus supermikes for picking up heavy breathing two blocks away and through a bedroom window."

I smiled at him. "Not exactly what I'm looking for. I need something to record an interview without the other party knowing. I need to carry it with me, but not trigger any metal detectors. It can't show even if they x-ray me or search me. Worse, it can't give off radio signals they can detect. I was told you had such stuff. Am I right?" I hoped I was. I wasn't going to get another chance to buy some. I glanced at my watch. I had to get back to the Fibbies.

Leo looked at me like he was undressing me. I wondered if the price tag for his electronics included something I wasn't about to do with him.

Bendel nodded. "Yeah, I got what you need. Take off your boots."

"What?" I asked, wondering if he were kinky.

"The boots." He pointed at my feet with his Tiparillo. "Microphone and transmitter go in the boots. They can't see anything with x-rays 'cause it's all made of plastic and composite fibers. Antenna's carbon, not metal. Strip search you, they won't find nothin' because it's in your boots."

"Can't they detect the radio waves from the transmitter?"

"Nope. This is the same stuff used by Special Forces behind enemy lines. The frequency skips around randomly so nobody can tell you're transmitting. Only your receiver can pick up the signal, because it's doin' the same random dance."

"How do I turn the recording on or off?"

"You poke a switch in your big toe to start, again to stop. Doesn't record for very long, though, 'cause you're runnin' on juice from solar cells that replace the buckles on your boots."

"How much?" I asked, not that it mattered. I'd weaseled three thousand in cash from Saul and he'd delivered it to me at the pay phone near the donut shop. We met the night before I left on Cameron's jumbo jet. I'd given him the key to Karen's safe deposit box.

"Fifteen hundred, unless you want to negotiate a discount with me in the back room." Leo arched his eyebrows suggestively.

After the discount, I'd need to be checked by a doctor who specialized in venereal disease. "I'll skip the discount. How long will the gear take to install?" I was terrified he'd say I had to come back tomorrow.

"Only twenty minutes. Helps you wore the right kind of shoes in here. Most people don't."

"I can't wait twenty minutes. I'm staying at the Hotel Bel-Air. If I leave my boots at the desk, can you do the installation this evening, around midnight?"

Bendel sighed. "OK, but it's two hundred more for the inconvenience."

"Deal. Five hundred now, the rest on proof the gear works." I peeled off five Ben Franklins.

Bendel scooped the bills in his pocket and turned to the other customer. "You want the gun or not? Unregistered handguns ain't that easy to come by, you know."

The shrink cringed. "Can't you come down on the price?"

I rolled my eyes and headed for the door. As I touched the red hot doorknob, I heard Leo say, "I come down a hundred."

I left them to belly-bump price on an illegal handgun and dashed for the mall. A block away, I spotted a drug store and made an impromptu purchase. It only delayed me two minutes, then I ran like crazy into the mall. A group of elderly shoppers crowded the escalator. I slid around them on the first landing and sprinted up another escalator. I made it to the soaped-up windows and tried the door. It was locked.

I banged loudly and waited. It had been almost half an hour since Denise Mallory went to the restroom. They were going to kill me, after they called off the helicopters and the bloodhounds. The door opened and I saw a puzzled workman in jeans and a faded blue shirt. I said, "Excuse me," and pushed around him, ignoring his questions.

He left me alone, fortunately, and I flew to the back of the empty store, where it faced the dressing area. I opened a door into the angry face of Jorge Gonzales.

"Where the hell have you been?" he demanded.

I showed him my drug store purchase. "Got my period and had to run out for a box of tampons. Couldn't try on dresses when I was bleeding. I'd stain the fabric. Right?" I gave him an endearing smile, feeling rather proud of my ad hoc reason for being absent.

With that excuse, Jorge couldn't murder me, but he sure wished he could. Gonzales stood with his hands on his hips, feet spread. "You should 'a told us. We got five agents tearing this mall apart, looking for you. You don't care if I get fired, huh?"

"Jeez, Jorge, I didn't know. I'm sorry." I tried to look angelic and harmless as I could possibly conjure.

Denise Mallory appeared in the dressing area. "You found her," she exclaimed.

I said lamely, "Uh, sorry."

Mallory glowered at me and told Jorge. "We're never letting her out of our sight again. Balducci will kill us if she gets away."

"Yeah," he replied, cocking his head. "I guess that means you're gonna get a boat ride."

"Huh?" I mumbled.

"Denise and I are supposed to go scope out the Cameron place, using a fishing boat. You were gonna get a nap at the hotel this afternoon, but not anymore."

"But I get seasick," I stammered.

He reached in his pocket and pulled out a little round bandage. "Put one of these behind your ear." He peeled off the plastic backing and roughly jammed the patch on my neck.

"Ouch," I exclaimed. "Take it easy."

"I did," he said, grabbing me by the arm and pulling me along.

"But," I protested, "I haven't bought a dress for dinner at Cameron's estate."

"Oh yes, you did," Denise said. "I picked one out while you were cruising the mall."

"Where're we going?" I squeaked as the pair manhandled me out of the department store.

"Marina Del Rey," Jorge grumbled. "To go fishing, man. And I hope the sea is rough."

26

Trying to quiet my stomach, I sat at the stern of the boat and watched the horizon, that distant seam where the Pacific Ocean meets dirty L.A. smog. The problem was that I couldn't look at the horizon without seeing a sea and sky filled with motion, none of it to my stomach's liking. Birds swirled above glistening waves and teased the brilliantly colored sails of pleasure boats, pitching across a rolling sea.

Jorge Gonzales had slapped a round Band-Aid on my neck. It was a skin patch containing scopolamine, a motion sickness drug. Unfortunately, the patch was far better at making me drowsy than it was at calming my stomach. I was paying the price for running off, visiting Leo Bendel's gun and gadget "emporium." As a result, Denise and Jorge insisted I go "fishing" with them, which was really a stakeout of Cameron's beachfront compound.

The boat's engines changed pitch to a low growl and the frothy wake behind the trawler shortened. The boat rolled even more when it slowed to a crawl. A crewman came to the stern and sat in a fishing chair next to me. He reached in a bucket and began chumming bait into the water. Seagulls flocked to the boat and swirled overhead, slicing down to grab free meals. The diving gulls and smell of bait hit me in the stomach like a fist. I grabbed a salt-crusted handrail, leaned into diesel fumes and added my lunch to the bait trailing behind the boat.

After vomiting, I lurched toward the cabin, grabbing at pieces of the boat to steady myself. To think my father once suggested I go to Annapolis instead of Columbia. He told me a career in the Navy would be good for me, straighten me out. Cost him a lot less, too. I busted my butt for a scholarship instead. How much scopolamine does the Navy buy, I wondered?

I knew going inside the cabin would be worse because I'd lose sight of the horizon. But I forced myself down a short flight of steps so I could wash vomit from my mouth. I looked in the bathroom mirror and laughed at my greenish appearance. Opening the medicine cabinet, I found another patch and slapped it behind an ear. I had to try something or I'd never endure another four hours on this trawler.

When I came on deck, Denise Mallory slapped a packet of crackers in my hand. "Try these. Salt helps."

I mumbled, "Thanks," and sank into a lounge chair. I ignored the crackers. Any thought of food wrenched my stomach. After a few minutes of baking in the hot sun, I changed my mind about the crackers. I nibbled at one, then let my hand sink to the deck. A scopolamine-induced sleep fell over me.

When I awoke, the rolling of the boat no longer bothered me. I was grateful for that miracle until I realized my hands and face were painful with sunburn. I no longer thought of scopolamine as a miracle drug. I looked aft and spotted Denise Mallory. She was in one of the stern fishing chairs, dressed in cutoffs and a halter top. I envied her tolerance for sunburn. Gonzales was next to her, sweeping the Malibu shore with a pair of huge binoculars.

I got on my feet and rolled with the boat toward the stern. Putting a hand on Denise's chair braced me against the heaving motion of the boat. I asked Jorge, "Has Cameron arrived yet?"

Gonzales replied without taking his focus off the beach. "Yeah. Cameron's yacht docked two hours ago. You can't miss his ship. It's about the size of a guided missile cruiser."

I yawned and stretched in the chair. "You see anyone on his yacht besides Cameron?"

Jorge laughed. "Girl with big tits in a string bikini." Denise Mallory elbowed his ribs.

"Ouch. Hey, watch out girl. I'm doin' something important here. Government business, you understand?"

"Yeah, right," Denise snorted.

Gonzales was keeping his binoculars pointed at one spot, fixated on something. I asked him, "What are you watching now, stud? Couple under a beach blanket?"

"Better. They got no blanket," Gonzales laughed. "Want to see?" He offered me the binoculars.

Ever the curious reporter, I thanked Jorge and took the glasses. I swept the beach but didn't find the alleged couple. All I saw was surf playing over gray sand mottled with clumps of grass. There were no buildings for a mile on either side of the Cameron compound. His complex was a sweeping collection of low buildings done in white stucco with blue-tinted windows. I kept wishing for Superwoman's x-ray vision, but it didn't materialize.

I judged we were about a quarter mile from the beach. The trawler was slowly cruising the shoreline, going through the motions of fishing. I asked Denise, "Why didn't Balducci come with us?"

"Jake said he'd be along tomorrow. Got some business in San Francisco." Mallory was holding a rod and reel outfit. She let the rod dip, then slowly pulled it up, making it look like she cared about tension on the line.

"Strange," I muttered. "I thought Jake would be here today, making sure everything was set up right. You got anybody inside the compound?"

Denise responded without looking away from her fishing. "No. Before this, we've never had a reason to penetrate their organization. Cameron has a lot, I mean a lot, of clout. If we got caught, Cameron would have our scalps unless we had good reasons to be inside." She pulled sunglasses off her hair and put them over her eyes. They had a corny heart shape, with red lenses. Apparently those frames were a trendy retro-thing at Malibu. Maybe they were an homage to Gidget-goes-surfing, but on Denise Mallory, they looked geeky.

I pointed at hills overlooking the area, covered with homes. "Why didn't we do this watching from one of those houses?"

"Renting one of those houses costs my annual salary for just one month."

"So rent a few days," I suggested.

Denise shrugged. "I tried that. Because of the sea view, they won't take even a one month rental. They want you to lease an entire season, four months minimum. Jake wouldn't foot the bill and our L.A. office sure as heck doesn't have the budget."

I fidgeted. Her answer didn't make sense. The FBI could have pressured a rental agent into helping them. Besides, this was supposed to be the Director's pet project and was costing the FBI quite a bit of money. So why scrimp at this crucial point? Stranger and stranger, I thought to myself.

I heard crunching and turned to look at Jorge eating pretzels and drinking a Pepsi. Man, what a stomach. To get away from the food smell, I moved to the other side of the boat. I leaned over the railing and looked at the sea. Most of the sailboats were gone, but an industrial-looking ship was anchored a hundred yards from our trawler.

People in scuba gear were climbing into the long ship. I decided it must be a diving class. In the distance, I saw a gray speck flying over the waves. Engine sounds from the gray speck came to me in bursts. The buzzing noise intermittently cut off when the boat sank behind a swell. Something about that gray speck bugged me.

I put the binoculars to my eyes and scanned for my target. A loud motor led me to the gray speck, hopping over a wave. It was a rubber zodiac, a large raft with twin tubes forming its hull, like a catamaran. When the zodiac crested a wave, I could see its flat bottom. There were powerful twin outboards at the back.

I pointed to the approaching craft. "You know who owns that zodiac?"

Jorge shielded his eyes with a hand and peered in the direction I was pointing. "Probably the Navy. I'm guessing it's from Point Mugu. The Navy runs exercises along the coast. Drug Enforcement Agency gets regular calls from home owners saying drug traffickers are sneaking in.

Turns out to be a mock commando raid by Navy SEALs. DEA and the Navy almost got into a gunfight one time. It was just luck someone didn't get killed. Now the Navy informs DEA before doing anything."

"Oh, I see." I relaxed and tracked the Zodiac with my naked eyes. The raft peeled a sharp curve out to sea and spun on its own wake, coming to a quick stop. The Zodiac's motor died and a pleasant quiet returned to the area.

But the quiet was soon displaced by a guttural snort from diesels on the scuba training vessel. The big boat got my attention as it chugged in a wide turn. When I looked back at the Zodiac, I saw a man in a wetsuit donning scuba tanks. Next to him was a long bag, resting on the zodiac's flat deck.

I commented, "Kinda late to go diving, isn't it? Even for the Navy?"

"Yeah, well, some guys like night diving. Different fish come out." Jorge was munching on half of a ham sandwich. He pushed the other half toward me.

I wagged my head in a "no."

"I'll take it." Denise snapped the sandwich from its paper wrapping.

I ignored their cast-iron stomachs and brought the binoculars up, training them on the zodiac diver. For the briefest moment, I caught a flash of the man's face before his scuba mask was put on. There was something familiar about the face. I kept the glasses on the diver, but the mask didn't come off again. The diver bent over and yanked on the long bag. It was obviously heavy. Then he spun over the zodiac's side, tugging the bag with him into the water. The Zodiac lingered a moment, then flew away, skipping over wave tops.

The diver's face gnawed at me, even though I hadn't seen it clearly. I brought the glasses down. "You got any guns onboard, just in case?"

"Service pistols. Nine millimeter automatics." Jorge gave me a puzzled look.

"That's good. But how would you rescue me inside Cameron's building complex?"

"We can't." Denise's flat reply didn't make me happy.

"Why not?" I asked hotly.

Mallory's stare bored into me. "Look, we can't gate-crash Jonah Cameron without a warrant. Get real, will you, Drew? If one of us were inside, there wouldn't be any rescue. What's the difference between you and us?"

I snapped, "The difference is that I didn't volunteer for this party you're holding. I got trapped into it by some killer who's still on the loose and probably will be forever, the way Balducci is playing this one."

Jorge scowled at me. "What do you want us to do? Fly over Cameron in a helicopter every fifteen minutes? That'd be real subtle, Drew."

I grumbled, "It would be better than just sitting in a boat, watching."

Denise tried to console me. "You'll feel better once you get off this boat. Your seasickness is making everything seem worse than it is." She began winding in her fishing line. Mallory pointed at the sun approaching the horizon. "Can't stay any longer without being too conspicuous. Probably stretched that even now."

The boat's engines rumbled and we did a slow turn into a parade of waves approaching the shoreline. The trawler rocked over swells until it finished swinging toward Marina Del Rey. The skipper let the throttle out and the boat surged ahead, moving toward the spot where a Zodiac dropped the scuba diver.

"I don't get it," I wondered aloud.

"What now?" Jorge snorted.

"Who's going to pick up that diver? His boat left."

Jorge scoffed at my concerns. "The diver probably parked a car on the Coast Highway. He'll walk to the car after he gets ashore. Or a friend is meeting him. You worry too much, Morrissey."

I glanced briefly at Jorge, then leveled his binoculars at the beach, scanning it. I was about to put the glasses down when something in the surf caught my attention. There was a black ball floating toward the shore. I focused on the ball and it became a man's head. Then the diver surfaced, walking to the beach through surf, carrying a heavy bag.

I put the glasses down and looked at Cameron's villa. The diver was walking ashore on the other side of a bluff, where he couldn't be seen from Cameron's buildings. Was it because Cameron's security staff had threatened to prosecute for trespassing when the diver had previously come ashore? But didn't California have a law about coastal access that blocked harassment of divers?

I kept my binoculars trained on the man as he laid his bag down and shrugged off his oxygen tanks. The setting sun painted orange on his diving mask. The diver peeled back the mask. He shook water off and stood there, admiring the ocean.

I felt my knuckles tighten around the binoculars. "Oh no," I gasped. "It's Elijah."

27

Our trawler spent almost two hours plowing an ocean lit by the speckled light of homes densely packed along the Malibu coast. The twinkling lights were a reminder that Malibu wasn't a beach. It was only where Los Angeles ran out of overpriced real estate. The rolling ocean flattened to a calm pond when the fishing boat entered Marina Del Rey's floodlit harbor channel. The trawler cautiously made its way toward a large berth in the power boat section. A blast of air horn forced a skiff with drunken teenagers to veer from their collision course with us. The giddy drunks waved to me but I didn't wave back. I was too scared from seeing Elijah to indulge their partying.

Street lights over the docks pasted dull glow on fiberglass hulls and teakwood decks. It would have been romantic, if I'd been in the mood. I wasn't. Our ship's wake rocked neighboring boats and the gray slip jutting toward us. The diesel engines coughed in a forward-reverse dance that finally docked the boat. A crewman jumped from the ship and pulled a rope until white hull cushions pillowed against the dock. The engines died in a final plume of diesel exhaust, many hours too late for my tastes.

I didn't wait for a gangplank to be rolled out. I put a hand on the railing, swung over the boat's side and jumped to the slip. Grateful I didn't sprain anything in my leap, I wiped chalky dust off my hands from the ship's oxidized paint. I started toward a metal grill door protecting ships from unauthorized visitors.

Jorge Gonzales sprinted to catch me. He shouted, "Where you goin'?"

I shouted back, "To call Balducci, two hours after I should have done it." I stopped at the gate and twisted its locked handle, shaking the metal screen door.

Jorge jammed his hand against the door. "Ship to shore is just radio, man, it ain't secure. I told you that."

"Yes," I said calmly. "We agreed. And I wouldn't use your cell phone because I'm paranoid about Cameron overhearing our conversation. We're on his turf and Cameron Industries specializes in espionage equipment. So he might have a way of intercepting our cell phone call, especially from a boat sitting next to his compound. I've waited two hours for us to reach port and I'm going to find a pay phone somewhere."

Jorge took his hand off the door. "Look, I'm sorry we didn't bring any secure communications gear. We didn't think we needed it. This was supposed to be a low key stakeout."

"That's right, Drew." Denise Mallory caught up with us. "We were just going to observe and report."

"Fine. I observed Elijah and now I'm reporting it."

Gonzales crossed his arms and looked sullen. "You saw a guy in a scuba mask, with the sun full in his face, on a bouncing ship, through binoculars. Maybe he's Elijah and maybe he's not."

"Jorge, it was Elijah. He took off his mask. The sun on his face gave me a good look at him. He wasn't on a bouncing ship. Elijah was on the beach. Now let me through so I can phone Balducci."

Gonzales refused to budge.

The trawler's skipper walked up. "Hey, get into fights on your own time. I'm outta here. Let me through. I got the key." We shuffled aside and the door was flung open. I crashed through, followed by the FBI agents.

"Where's the nearest pay phone?" I spoke at the back of the skipper, trotting ahead of me.

The skipper jabbed at a brightly lit restaurant where mariachi music scratched energetically from patio speakers. The terrace was filled with green and white umbrellas. "Go in the bar at Pancho's. Phone's by the john. Not a bad place to talk. Get a beer and mellow out. It'll do you good." The skipper threw his coat over a shoulder and walked away. I wished I could do that – just walk away.

"Come on, Drew. I'll buy you that beer," Denise offered. She tugged at my arm. Jorge picked up a duffel bag of gear and followed us.

Pancho's bar was hot, stuffy, packed and loud. People were shouting to be heard over the roaring music. There were mesh trays everywhere, holding corn chips coated in cheese and jalapeño sauce. The recipe was calculated to make patrons thirsty for another margarita.

Suddenly the mariachi halted and a PA system blared indecipherable names, declaring their table was ready. A foursome left their chairs and headed for the patio, elbowing past me. Jorge captured their booth, besting a pack of fraternity boys. When they tried bullying him, Jorge flashed his FBI badge and they quietly slipped away.

I slid over the sawdust floor and jammed myself in the tight space allowed for my stool. Anxious, I scanned for the pay phone and couldn't see it. My view was blocked by a pair of tight cutoffs wrapped with an apron. I looked up and saw a tapered linen shirt, open to the navel. The tan, smiling face of the waiter looked into mine.

I tried to order and realized it was impossible to be heard at any polite level of speaking. I screamed, "Just a beer. Any kind. I don't care." I heard Denise Mallory yell for a pitcher of margaritas and two glasses. The waiter started to leave. I squirmed around the table, caught his arm and shouted, "Where's the phone?"

He pointed and I followed him to the bar, where we became stuck in a logjam of hot, sweating bodies. There were enough flat, tanned stomachs showing to fill a glamour magazine. The outfits were unreal, women in black lace with the cut of underwear and men in rumpled pants that looked like they slept under an overpass, all the outfits costing my hotel bill at the Hotel Bel-Air. I squeezed through the sticky human barricade and made my way toward the bathrooms. The roaring din of the bar muted when I turned into a short hallway.

Disinfectant smell leaked from both the men's and women's toilet doors. In the middle, a dim spot sprayed light on a pay phone. The phone's sides were carved in graffiti. A torn yellow pages dangled on a too-short chain. Anyone using the phone book would have to be a contortionist. Fortunately, I'd memorized Balducci's cell phone number for use in an emergency. I dialed and waited. Jake wasn't available and I was transferred to an automated recording. A flush triggered in one of the toilets and rumbled along the wall, causing me to lose what the robot voice was saying.

I was frustrated enough to tear the pay phone from the wall when a kind voice said, "FBI, please hold." I waited, listening to classical Muzak with one ear and mariachi with the other. I leaned around the corner to see what was happening with Denise and Jorge. They were laughing and drinking from salt encrusted glasses. My beer was being wasted on the table top.

The kind voice returned and I said, "Jake Balducci, please. He's visiting from New York." I was informed that Mr. Balducci wasn't available but she would take a message for him.

I surprised myself by talking in a calm voice. "This is an emergency. Can he be paged?" I pressed a finger to my ear so I could shut out the Mexican band music and listen to her reply.

"Great. I'm at a pay phone. Just a minute, I'll get the number." I looked at the dial. The number had been scratched out with a knife blade. "Look, there's no number on this pay phone. Since you're the FBI, can you tell where I'm calling from, like 911 does? You can? Wonderful. Please have Jake call Drew Morrissey. Yes, I'll wait right here. Thanks."

I hung up and immediately broke my promise to wait. Jake wasn't going to call right away and a beer was becoming as much a matter of life and death as Elijah. I squeezed through the bar crowd, my eyes fixed on the frosted glass bottle awaiting me. When I got to the table, I pulled a sticky coaster off the bottle and took a long, cold pull.

"You get Jake?" Denise asked me when I surfaced for air.

I wagged my head sideways in a "no," then took another drink. I leaned over Denise's ear. "If that waiter comes back, please ask him to bring me another beer. I'll be using the pay phone."

Denise nodded. I took another long pull, swirled what was left of the beer in the bottle, studying it in the light, then headed for the bar. I'd get my own beer. Ten minutes later, I had the tops of two beer bottles trapped between my fingers and was navigating toward the phone. It was ringing. I pushed through the crowd, dropping "excuse me" as I went. I picked up the receiver only to hear a dial tone. Would Jake try again?

I decided to wait, in case he was redialing me. Two more swallows of beer were laced with the smell of urine and disinfectant. I was about to call Balducci when the phone rang. I snapped it up. "Jake?"

"Yeah. What's up?" He sounded disgusted.

"Elijah is at Cameron's. I saw him swim to the beach in a scuba outfit." I braced myself for a verbal assault. Instead, there was a long pause. I heard a toilet dripping on the other side of the wall. Someone ran a blow dryer over their hands. A guy yanked the men's room door open and came out. A blast of stench hit my nostrils. I covered the tops of the beer bottles with my palm. "Jake, you there?"

"Yeah. Just thinking."

"So I'm not going into the compound tomorrow, right?"

"Wrong. I just need to go over a few things with Denise and Jorge."

"Jake, this is too much for me. I want Elijah caught before I go inside Jonah's compound."

"Stop worrying, Drew. You can't be safer than inside Jonah Cameron's place. He's got a private army to protect you on the inside and we're outside. It's a perfect time to catch Elijah. If you're lucky, he'll resist and get killed. You couldn't ask for better."

"I don't know, Jake. Why do I have to go inside that compound to get the evidence? Why don't you do it?"

"I have to get a search warrant, that's why. For a judge to issue a warrant, I gotta have a reason, which you have to go find for me. Even with you testifying, I'll have a hard time getting a judge to issue a search warrant for Cameron's property. With Cameron's political clout, it'll be suicide for that judge in the next election. I also have to brief the Director so when Cameron calls the President, the Director and me don't get fired."

"Are you prepared to go inside the compound, Jake, and get me out if it's needed?" My fingers tightened on the receiver.

"Denise and Jorge will be offshore. They can land on the beach."

"Jorge told me they only have handguns."

"They were just observing today. Tomorrow, they'll have assault rifles. You weren't even supposed to be on the boat during the stakeout. If you hadn't wandered off, you wouldn't be worried now. You'd have never seen Elijah. Drew, the bottom line is, Elijah can't get through to you."

"What if Cameron wants Elijah to get through?"

"Why would he? Jonah Cameron is a political animal. Cameron's public image will take a big hit if murder happens in his compound. He doesn't want you dead. He wants you doing a flattering bio on him. Look, if Elijah was working for Cameron, he would have walked through the front door, not swum ashore from a boat."

I couldn't deny that logic, but it still didn't feel right somehow. I had the intuition I was being swept into a trap and couldn't find a way out of it. I muttered, "Are you sure this makes sense?"

"Look at your options. You can leave now, but you won't be any better off on your own, walking the streets of New York. You'll have no protection at all." He waited for me to absorb that I had no choice. I had a gun to my head and was forced to do what Balducci wanted. The gun belonged to Elijah, but my fate belonged to Jake Balducci and the FBI.

"You there, Drew?" Jake asked.

"Yeah, I'm here." I never felt more disgusted in my life.

"Go back to the hotel and get some sleep. You've got a busy day tomorrow."

I heard the dial tone in my ear. I hung up slowly. Suddenly, alcohol was the last thing I wanted. The beer bottles went in the trash. I went inside the woman's room and glanced at myself in the mirror. I looked red from the sunburn and very dazed. I splashed water from the cold tap on my face. It smelled of rust and chlorine. Lukewarm, the water didn't refresh me at all. I left my face wet in the hopes of cooling down and walked toward the tipsy Fibbies.

I tried selling myself on the idea that I was safe. All I had to do was go inside, get briefed on the grandeur of Jonah Cameron and meet the great man. The next day, I'd go over a draft bio with ghostwriters. It was completely innocuous, totally safe – and that was the problem.

On that agenda, I'd never find a reason Balducci could use for obtaining a search warrant. So why was Jake sending me in there? I concluded events wouldn't follow the sanitized agenda I'd been given. Something else was going to happen inside the Cameron compound.

I felt powerless and vulnerable, a puppet dangling on Balducci's string. But I desperately needed his protection. Alone, I'd be an easy target for Elijah on the streets of New York, certain to be killed. So I had no choice. My only chance was going along with Balducci, letting him use me as bait. Maybe I'd live through it – and maybe I wouldn't.

28

The next day, I swallowed my fears and rode in a limo to Malibu. I was far too anxious to enjoy the magnificent view of a sparkling ocean from the Pacific Coast Highway. After a long ride, the stretch limo floated into Cameron's estate, rippling over brown Spanish cobblestones. I got out and was escorted to the entry pavilion, a three-level atrium floating on an indoor pool. The circular lake shimmered in orange sunlight spilled from the atrium's enormous windows. A buoyant island of foliage drifted lazily across the pond, green and yellow plant leaves dipping into the reflecting pool. There were two furnished areas circling the lake and both seemed levitated in position without pillars or beams.

Nearby was the Malibu conference room I'd seen by video broadcast, at the Chrysler Building in New York. I was surprised how different the amphitheater looked in real life. On the ground floor was an enormous chrome and glass table, positioned so it ran diagonally across the room. That table formed the needle of a giant metal compass, inlaid at the center of a bleached wood floor. The needle pointed east, not magnetic north. I assumed the eastern orientation symbolized Cameron's ambition to occupy the White House and meant all efforts were to be aligned on this goal.

I sat at the table, shook all the hands, returned all the smiles, then settled into a two hour propaganda blitz on Cameron Industries. After a short break, I endured another saturation campaign aimed at selling me A United Tomorrow. Finally, I was shepherded from the conference room and taken to an executive area, where I waited for my first in-person meeting with Marv Logan.

For a while, I paced restlessly through the open offices of admin staff located on a third story balcony. The crashing of distant surf mixed with a typewriter's staccato chattering and the whir of a printer turning out pages. Despite being near the ocean, the building's air smelled only of coffee left on the burner since early morning. The burnt odor was sharply tinged with ozone from a copier. Light glowered at me from the copier's lid as it sucked originals in and spat out neatly collated duplicates.

I paused for a moment and pressed my palms into gritty stucco covering the low balcony wall. Everything felt so perfect and benign that my fears were melting away. Still, I needed to see Denise and Jorge cruising in their fishing boat, guns ready. I tried to spot their trawler through a sweep of tinted glass separating the atrium's cavernous interior from the beach. My eyes struggled with the glare of sunlight glittering off ocean waves. I scanned and rescanned the waves, but the FBI was nowhere. To quiet the anxiety swelling in my chest, I told myself Denise and Jorge were just outside my view. They were still close to me. Weren't they?

Fear would push me from the building if I didn't refocus myself. I tore my eyes from the empty sea and followed the balcony wall, curving seamlessly to a highly polished grand piano. The musical instrument sat against one edge of a seating area inside Marv Logan's office. Through a glass wall, I watched Logan chat with Nick Zeradakis. Finally, Zeradakis got up, shook hands with Logan and left. I heard Logan's admin say, "You can go in now, Ms. Morrissey."

I said, "Thanks," and began composing myself. I shrugged my blazer in place and checked my blouse to be sure it was tucked in my pants. When I entered, Marv Logan was at his desk. Behind him, a torrent of sunlight turned Logan to a black silhouette and nearly blinded me. I couldn't see any details in Marv's face as he finished signing a document.

He stood and I could finally see his features. Marv Logan seemed academic at first, but there was a sharpness in his eyes that didn't fit with the benign smile. Marv didn't get to the top of A United Tomorrow by being nice. There was a shark in him that made me wary.

He shook my hand. "Glad to see you're still alive after that multimedia deluge. The overview of Cameron Industries and A United Tomorrow is enough to drown anyone. I'm sorry I didn't have time to meet with you before they poured that on you, Drew. Would you like something to drink? Coffee or a soda? They can whip up a great cappuccino and bring it over."

"Thanks. I'll try that cappuccino."

Logan bent over his phone and buzzed, ordering a cappuccino for me and a mint tea for himself. He moved to the couch where he'd been with Zeradakis. Marv gestured for me to join him, sitting on an opposing chair.

I sat and there was a mild hiss of air from the plush leather cushions.

Logan crossed his legs and calmly said, "I talked with Wyndham this morning."

My blood pressure shot out of sight. I was frightened my cover had been blown. "Yes?" I said with a catch in my voice.

"Wyndham was very enthusiastic about the bio of Jonah. You did a great job selling him on the project. I wanted to thank you and let you know it won't be forgotten downstream. I understand Truitt has a nice plum waiting for you, media director for New York Ops."

I tried to seem embarrassed. I shuffled my feet and looked away. I was actually searching for the FBI fishing boat. Where was it? I forced myself back to Logan. "Yes, a very exciting prospect, that media director job. By the way, Nick mentioned on the plane ride that Mr. Cameron will be announcing his candidacy soon, for the Presidency."

"Oh, did he? That was a bit premature of Nick. But yes, it's true. Running for President should help sell a few books, don't you think?"

I didn't have time to answer because the cappuccino and tea arrived. I thanked the admin and sipped some foam, blotting my lips with a fine linen napkin. I peeked again at the empty sea.

"Tell me, Drew, what's your impression of A United Tomorrow?" Logan held his teacup but didn't drink.

I tried to be diplomatic. "AUT's a very impressive endeavor. Quite a challenge for Mr. Cameron to take on, especially after building Cameron Industries." There, diplomacy wasn't so painful, was it Drew? I took a nice, slow breath.

"Well, Jonah is a dynamic individual, as you'll find out this afternoon."

"Oh? When am I scheduled to meet him?"

"At dusk. He'd like you to go for a ride with him on the beach, just before sunset. It's one of his great pleasures in life. Sunset is the time of day he unwinds a bit from his intense schedule. Jonah thought it would give you a chance to know him on a personal level, before you have to wade through all they've written about him."

"Ride?" I had an image of a dune buggy, but it didn't go with this pompous setup.

"Jonah has quite a few prize horses in his stables. The grooms will have one prepared for you. Afterwards, you can freshen yourself in one of the guest bedrooms before supper. We'd like you to join Truitt and Nick for dinner with Jonah."

"I'm honored." Now I really looked hard for that trawler. I felt sweat forming on my palms.

Logan stood. "If you'll excuse me, Drew, I have a meeting. We'll be getting together tomorrow morning at nine, right?"

I also rose. "Yes, so I'm told. I look forward to getting started on this project."

"Great," he said.

I slid my hand across the blazer to remove the fear sweat and shook hands with Logan. When I left Marv's office, Truitt Hastings was waiting for me, ready to take me to lunch.

I was a robot at the luncheon table, moving food to my mouth with a fork, answering questions on autopilot. My own voice sounded distant to me, like someone talking in another room. My mind was on the beach, where Elijah landed. I'd be riding to him, an easy shot. Would Cameron do anything that blatant? It seemed impossible.

Yet the lunch room had a sweeping view of the ocean, practically from Santa Monica Pier to Ventura Harbor. Nowhere on that ocean was a fishing trawler like the one Jorge and Denise used yesterday. In fact, there were few boats in sight. None of them lingered nearby. It was clear there was going to be no rescue from the sea if I got in trouble.

After lunch, I wasn't alone for a split second, even in the women's lounge. Toward sunset, they showed me to a dressing room and gave me English riding clothes to wear. The clothes fit perfectly, like the trap they were springing. I knew I'd be riding into an ambush. There was only one question. Was I bait to catch Elijah or his intended victim? Walk away and I'd surely be Elijah's victim when I returned to New York. So I went to the stables, hoping I was just a lure and not the target.

Normally, bait goes on a hook. This bait was going to mount a horse and pretend she knew how to ride. Truth was, I'd never been on a horse in my life, not even a Shetland pony in Central Park. Maybe that would work in my favor, I thought. Perhaps I'd get lucky and fall, just before Elijah took his shot. God, I was scared.

29

A river of Spanish cobblestones swept me from the main house to the stables. At the horse barn, the cobblestone river fanned to a large plaza paved in whirlpools of reddish-brown stones. I found the circling patterns disorienting, adding to my edgy mood. Startled by a falling eucalyptus nut, I turned around, wary that I was being watched. I saw no one behind me and rolled my shoulders in a vain effort to release the stress.

Then I glanced up and saw a TV camera tracking me, its lens spinning in a zooming movement. I tried to ignore my anger at being constantly monitored. After all, Cameron's people weren't the only ones looking at me. I was always watching myself, afraid I'd make a mistake and reveal my true identity. I didn't like this undercover work.

I kept walking, my stride now tense and aggressive despite wearing long riding boots that came to my knees. They'd dressed me in skin-tight breeches, a white chambray riding shirt and herringbone show jacket. Quite the English country lady on the outside, just frightened little old me on the inside.

Past the stables, a white-maned thoroughbred was tethered to a merry-go-round of steel pipe. A groom in silk jockey's uniform was leading the horse in tight circles, walking him through a cool-down cycle. The groom untethered his mount and brought the thoroughbred toward me. I thought he'd lead the horse inside a stable. Instead, the groom halted nearby, in the shadow of a vast eucalyptus tree.

I said anxiously, "I hope he's not the one I'm supposed to ride. Mister, er?"

"The name's Charles, but I go by Chuck, if you please. And Samuel B. Taylor here is Mr. Cameron's personal horse. He's a bit much to handle, even for Mr. Cameron."

The groom tried rubbing the thoroughbred's nose, but it snorted and turned away. The sleek animal jerked its head, trying to pull its reins free. The groom snapped the head back and urged, "Stay-yyy, Sammy. Your master's on his way. You'll be going out again, soon." Chuck turned in my direction. "You see how fiery Mr. Taylor is, even after he's been run down a bit."

"Yes, I certainly see the fire in Mr. Taylor. What does Jonah Cameron see in him, though?"

"Sammy won the Preakness twice and almost the Derby. Missed by a nose. Now he's got enough of a lame hindquarter to keep him out of the big time. But he's still a thrill to ride, miss."

After that résumé, I was delighted Samuel B. Taylor would be ridden by Jonah Cameron and not me. Riding horses certainly was a strange way for Cameron to introduce himself. I obviously couldn't keep up with him on horseback, so there'd be no conversation.

Chuck threw a short blanket across the racehorse's back, followed by an English chase saddle. The thoroughbred whinnied, showing his pleasure. Chuck explained, "Sammy's happy because he knows Mr. Cameron's gonna ride him soon. They go out together everyday 'bout this time, when Mr. Cameron's in town." Chuck tightened the saddle strap under the thoroughbred's stomach.

I heard steps behind me and turned to see another groom walking up. He nodded curtly to me, opened a stable door and vanished inside. When he came out, he was leading a stocky, older animal. This horse was more my speed. I'd never thought of myself as destined to raise my sword and lead a cavalry troop into battle. That was Cameron's style.

"Harv's got your mount, miss," Chuck told me.

"She's even larger than Samuel B. Taylor. Hope I fit."

"Maggie's bigger 'cause she's a quarterhorse, not a thoroughbred," Harv explained. He dropped a western saddle on the horse's back. "Thought you'd feel safer riding American-style. No insult miss, but doesn't seem you've spent much time around horses."

"You're right. I haven't ridden a horse, ever. Not even a Shetland pony." I shuffled around the quarterhorse toward its face and gently stroked a white patch on Maggie's nose. She responded favorably, so I gave her a smile and another soft caress. I needed all the good will I could get.

Harv gave me a pixie-like grin and a wink. "Most folks ridin' with Mr. Cameron haven't the guts to admit they're novices. On Maggie, you don't have to be a good rider. She just follows Samuel there, Mr. Cameron's horse. You leave the reins loose and Maggie'll take care of you." He patted the mare's rump and she stirred slightly. "Would you like some help getting aboard?"

"Ah, yes." I gave him what was left of my smile, which wasn't much. "Truth is, I don't think I'd make it otherwise. Do you have a crane?" I pantomimed being hoisted over Maggie.

Harv laughed. "No, miss. We use a little stair for the ladies. The gents have to tough it – 'specially if I don't like 'em." He left me with the reins and went toward the blacksmith's shed.

Holding the reins felt entirely strange, but I pretended I knew what I was doing. Fortunately Maggie went along with the ruse. I didn't have a prayer of stopping her if she wanted to leave. I was doing fine until

Samuel B. Taylor started dancing. In response, Maggie shifted nervously. I purred at the quarterhorse, hoping she'd calm down.

I sighed in relief when Harv returned, but my solace didn't last. Chuck dropped a two-step ladder on the ground next to Maggie and I reluctantly stepped on the plastic block. Beside me, the quarterhorse shifted uneasily.

"Well, here goes." I hoped I sounded braver than I felt. I hooked a boot in Maggie's stirrup, bounced on a step and tried swinging my leg over the mare's wide girth. My leg didn't make a high enough arc and I kicked the quarterhorse's rump. Maggie jerked forward, leaving me dangling in air. When the mare steadied, I swung again, with all the gusto I could muster. I sort of fell into the saddle. My tailbone hurt from landing on hard leather. It felt like I was doing the splits across the horse's wide back.

Harv handed me the reins and yanked the plastic steps away, a silly grin on his face. Chuck was smirking at me too. It actually made me feel better, because they realized how scared I was. Strange how that works. The horse jiggled anxiously under me, ready to go on a ride. I certainly wasn't ready.

"There," Harv said. "Isn't so bad, is it?"

Momentarily, my old spunk returned. "Feels like being on rollerblades for the first time, but seven feet off the ground."

Chuck laughed. "Not to worry, miss. We have the finest doctors here in California. Top neurosurgeon is our neighbor. If you fall, he'll have you back together in no time."

I grimaced. "You're so kind." Actually, his ironic humor was relaxing me.

"Grab the pommel there and you'll be all right." Chuck patted the saddle's leather neck, rising like a snake's head. "Mr. Cameron likes to go fast on the outbound run. Maggie'll trot along behind. Comin' back, Mr. Cameron'll slow down, so you can talk."

Likes to go fast. Great. Sweat trickled down my ribs. I forced myself to breathe, then look at the horizon. I could barely see the ocean through a dense grove of eucalyptus. The high trees swayed in large arcs, tossing yellowed leaves on the stone paving. A hot wind was bullying away the cool breeze I'd felt earlier. Yellow smog rolled off the land, sullying clear air over the ocean and burning my lungs. It felt like someone was pressing an iron into my back. I ran my tongue over dry lips. They were beginning to chap. The wind put an ugly edge on my fears.

"Santa Ana's coming," Harv said.

"What's that?" I croaked. My mouth was already parched by the hot air.

Harv explained, "L.A. basin's got a sirocco wind that blows off the desert. The hot wind make people edgy. It lasts for two or three days. Then things cool down again."

The horses shifted nervously, pulling on the grooms. The thoroughbred whinnied and pawed the ground. Suddenly, both horses turned their necks toward the outline of a man walking toward us, silhouetted in the brilliant glare of a sunset. He was wearing a fedora hat and a long horseduster's coat, flapping against his boots.

"Steady, Sammy," Chuck crooned. "Here's your master. You're going out now." The groom moved away, letting the man jab his boot into a stirrup and swing aboard.

Chuck looked up. "Have a good ride, Mr. –" The groom halted, then continued in a surprised voice, "Have a good ride, Mr. Hastings."

"Thanks," Truitt responded. He fought to keep the high-spirited thoroughbred reigned back. The horse swirled in resentment at being checked.

Apparently Hastings was dressed in Jonah Cameron's riding outfit. That's why the groom had mistaken Truitt for the great man. I didn't have time to ask Hastings why he was there instead of Cameron. We immediately began riding, Truitt fighting with Sammy to go slowly. The calmer pace made me grateful Cameron wasn't there.

Once we cleared the eucalyptus grove, the thoroughbred broke into a trot, moving across sand dunes. I found riding on the beach was hardly the romantic image I'd seen in movies. Maggie fell in line behind Sammy and Taylor's rear hooves kicked bits of dune grass in my face. I pushed on Maggie's stirrups to ease the pounding on my lower back. Santa Ana wind blew fine sand in my eyes, forcing me to squint. Blowing grit trickled inside my dry mouth and down my blouse.

We moved to the water's edge and it looked like both horses were going into the sea. Abruptly, Sammy twisted and went along the wet sand, Maggie following him. When a rocky bluff blocked the wind for a moment, I glanced at where we were going. About a mile ahead, a ridge of land ran to the sea, blocking further progress. That appeared to be our destination.

We cantered along, Maggie directly behind Samuel B. Taylor. I turned my head seaward to look for the Fibbies. I saw nothing but a distant shape that might have been the stern of a fishing boat. The ship was moving away, heading toward Marina Del Rey. I wanted to believe it had been Denise and Jorge out there. But they were gone now, even if they'd been there. Denise explained that charter fishing boats didn't cruise after dark. So they'd look conspicuous lingering off Cameron's place at night. I wished Logan hadn't invited me to dinner that evening.

We kept trotting and though I urged Maggie forward, she refused to move alongside Samuel B. Taylor. I wanted to ask Truitt why he came on the ride instead of Cameron. Maybe I'd get the chance when we stopped to turn around at the ridge. Eventually, the ridgeline was no longer just a dark shape. Sharp rocks jutted along its sides. Finally, it was a half mile distant, then a quarter.

Perversely, the horses didn't slow as the end got closer. Instead they speeded up, racing for where the ridge spilled into the sea. Samuel B. Taylor finally clattered to a stop, skidding on wet rocks at the base of the ridge. He turned in neurotic arcs, his nostrils flared, breathing hard. Hastings fought for control of the animal. In a few seconds, the horses calmed and backed away from the ridge. We turned out to sea and actually stood for a moment, all of us panting.

Hastings managed a weak grin. "Beautiful sunset."

I had to talk between breaths. "Cameron always does this to guests?"

Hastings was about to answer when his mount whirled around. The thoroughbred tensed, quivering its nostrils at a point on the ridge above us. I twisted in my saddle and stared at where the thoroughbred was pointing. Maggie refused to turn. She whinnied and stomped sideways.

"Taylor seems frightened." Hastings tried to calm the animal by stroking his thick neck. "Probably there's a cougar on the ridge. We get them when the Santa Anas blow. They can't stand the damned wind. Come to the sea for some rest."

I knew this was the same ridge where Elijah landed yesterday. Was he here, now? I strained my eyes and caught a flashing piece of glass about two hundred yards away. Its orange glare winked at me.

Hastings looked in the same direction. He anxiously said, "We better get back." His next words were cut off when the thoroughbred reared on its hind legs. Under the flickering orange glass, a tiny puff of smoke came and went like a ghost. Taylor screamed a horrible, chilling wail. The racehorse spun, its butt colliding against Maggie's flank. Before my mount and I could recover, Samuel B. Taylor was tearing across the sand.

I barely had time to be grateful the colliding horses hadn't broken my leg, then I almost toppled into the sea. Maggie stumbled and came up pointed at the ridge. I caught the orange glimmer again for a split second. Then we were flying across the beach in vain pursuit of the thoroughbred.

My quarterhorse's hooves gouged deep burrows in the sand with its frantic rush. At first, it appeared Maggie was actually gaining on the thoroughbred. I furiously tugged on the reins to slow her. Maggie was frantic and tore the leather strings from my grasp. I felt a hot welt on the palm of my hand, where the reins burned my flesh when the horse yanked them free. I could only wrap myself along the horse's pounding neck. The saddle's pommel dug into my stomach like I was being punched, over and over again.

It felt like a miracle when the horse slowed, then stopped in heaving breaths, spent from its futile race. Sweat frothed on Maggie's flanks and shoulders. I cautiously unwrapped my arms from her neck. One of my hands was still clinging to the horse's mane with demonic fury. It took all my will power to let go.

At first, I was too drained to swing my leg over and dismount. I waited, panting with the exhausted horse for almost a minute. Then I dragged a boot along the horse's butt. It felt like my groin would snap from the stretch. I fell from the stirrup on hard, wet sand. When I staggered to my feet, I bent double to let my aching lungs drag in some air. What I breathed was the hot Santa Ana wind, laced with acrid smog.

When my body recovered, I grabbed the reins and stumbled toward the compound, leading the horse behind me. I staggered up weed-covered dunes, following Taylor's deep hoof prints until the compound's white buildings surrounded me. At the horse barn, I gave Maggie to a wide-eyed stable boy. "How's Truitt?" I managed through cracked, sand-caked lips.

"He's fine, miss. Do you need help?" The stable boy looked confused, alternately staring at my breasts, then averting his eyes.

"No. I actually think I can fix everything with a hot bath. Was Sammy injured?"

"Uh, no," he said, looking confused.

"Well, I'm glad no one got hurt. You'll take good care of Maggie?"

"Of course, Miss."

"Thanks." I walked back to the house, every muscle feeling sprained. In the guest bedroom, I unzipped the boots and flung them on the rug, enjoying the air conditioning. My body ached into its bones. I gingerly peeled off the tight riding slacks, threw them on the bedspread and started unbuttoning my blouse. I gawked at myself in the mirror. Now I knew why the stable boy had been staring at my breasts.

The blouse was spattered with blood across its entire front. I felt a pang of guilt. Was the blood from pulling too hard on the reins, forcing the bit into Maggie's tongue? Well, there was nothing I could do about it. Perhaps I could go to the stables later and check on her.

I poured myself a hot bath and sank in the tub. The steamy water loosened me up and I tried to understand what happened out there. The moment when Samuel B. Taylor bolted kept flashing in my mind. What caused the racehorse to scream like that? I had to assume he'd been shot, yet the thoroughbred ran like the wind afterwards. That orange reflection probably came from the telescopic sight on a rifle and the puff of smoke was a gunshot. On the other hand, the stable boy said everyone was all right. But it didn't seem anyone was hit, even though Elijah was an expert marksman.

After that frightening ride, I wanted to leave and return to the hotel. But I didn't see an easy way out of the dinner obligation. At least dinner gave me a chance to ask Truitt for his impression of the ridge incident. Maybe I'd get a straight answer and I needed one. So far, I had only questions, not answers. For example, why did Hastings ride with me, dressed as Jonah Cameron? From the viewpoint of getting some truth, dinner might be worthwhile. Perhaps Hastings would be frightened enough to spill some clues to what was really happening here.

30

Santa Ana wind came in gusts, brushing eucalyptus leaves against glass dining room doors. The dry leaves made a rustling noise, like mice crawling around an attic. Fine dust crept beneath the weather seal, forming a little sand dune on the tile floor. Inside the dining room, dryness from the wind made the skin crawl on my bare arms. I let out a short, tight breath. I hadn't had this much fun since my twelfth birthday party, when my mother invited all the kids I hated because their parents were important people. After that, I looked forward to braces and acne.

I stole a brief glance at myself, dimly reflected in the door glass. Cameron's people gave me a Versace silk evening gown to wear, with a string of cultured pearls and matching earrings. They even had a local hairdresser coif my hair into a perfect stack. Overall, it was quite an improvement over my normal looks, created in a morning rush-to-work scenario. Personally, I'd have been happy to forego all the dress-up and roast hot dogs on the beach, wind or no wind. But I was trapped inside Jonah Cameron's private dinner salon.

Cameron's dining room was surprisingly claustrophobic. There was seating for six only, at high-backed chairs. I sat erect in one of them, acting like I was a celebrity bio editor for Wyndham & Dorset Publishing. It was a surprisingly easy role to fake. Jonah Cameron had turned into a no-show. Each dinner course, covered by a silver dome, had been set before his empty chair. We were meant to think the great man would take his seat any moment, with profuse apologies for being detained. We were now awaiting dessert.

Our chit-chat had died many times that evening, fading into deadly silence. I forced a smile on my face and looked at Truitt Hastings, expecting he would restart the conversation. But even the extroverted Hastings was subdued. Truitt's normally self-confident eyes were dull, focused through glass doors at the moon, a quarter million miles away.

Nick Zeradakis was chatting into his cell phone, lost in his own self-importance. I doubted he'd overhear anything said at the table. It seemed a good time to ask Hastings about the horse ride. "Truitt, what happened at the bluff, when Cameron's horse bolted?"

Hastings looked startled. Then he regained his composure. "Oh, Sammy's temperamental and uh, … I yanked too hard on the reins. He's very high-spirited, you know. Well, Jonah likes the horse …" Hastings stopped abruptly. He fixed his eyes on the empty seat Cameron was supposed to occupy.

"Go on," I suggested.

Truitt put a hollow smile on his face, a thin imitation of his earlier pretty-boy facade. "Drew, I'm sorry Jonah didn't make it tonight. I saw him earlier and he was really intending to be here. I know I wasn't a good substitute." Truitt added hastily, "I mean, on the ride – and I haven't been much of a conversationalist at dinner, either."

There was an awkward silence. I kept my stare fixed on Hastings. I wanted him to feel uncomfortable. Maybe he'd break and say something he wasn't supposed to tell me. It wasn't nice, but then I wasn't in a nice situation. Cameron being absent meant something happened. Maybe I'd been found out and they knew I was helping the FBI.

Hastings turned away from my stare. He grabbed his fork, a massive gold-plated thing. Truitt pressed his thumb against the fork, bending the tines. His teeth ground back and forth slightly, like his jaw had a nervous twitch.

I was rescued from my Freudian analysis of Truitt by a white-gloved waiter sliding dessert in front of me. The waiter placed a dessert by Zeradakis, and finally served Hastings. I lifted a spoon and sliced off the corner of a jiggling cube, floating in a deep pool of chocolate. When the tiny sample melted on my tongue, it was delicious – until I glanced at

Hastings and saw how angry he looked. The dinner should have been a real treat. But tension ruined the evening and made even gourmet food seem tasteless.

I petitely blotted my lips and dropped the linen napkin on the table. Across from me, Nick Zeradakis ignored dessert and entertained himself with an electronic appointment calendar. Abruptly, Zeradakis pushed his chair back. He talked into a corner of the dining room, without making eye contact. "I have to call the East Coast before they go to bed. See you tomorrow."

I rose also. "I'm beat from that horse adventure. I'll join your limo ride to the hotel. I can sit with the driver, if you want privacy for your phone calls." I started to leave and Truitt put a restraining hand on my wrist. I felt sick to my stomach. Fear twisted my gut. I tried to slide my arm away and Hastings' grip tightened.

Zeradakis stared at my arm where Truitt was holding me. Nick gave me a puzzled look, then shrugged. "I'll see you tomorrow, Drew." He quickly exited from the dining room.

I tried to act like I wasn't scared. "What's up?"

Truitt released my wrist and smiled. "We've upgraded your accommodations tonight as an apology for the horse ride – and for Jonah missing dinner. We brought your things from the hotel so you could spend the night here. I'll show you to your room."

I walked with Hastings, moving stiffly, like a toy. My brain raced and went nowhere. It didn't seem I had any options.

Truitt led me along a hallway where spotlights highlighted abstract paintings, splashes of red and blue hanging on rice wallpaper. The decor was too antiseptic for a home. It belonged in a law office and felt about as comfortable.

Halfway along the corridor, there was a small elevator. Truitt held its doors apart in an unnecessary show of masculine concern. I went inside, leaned against a railing and anxiously examined ceiling panels, wondering what had caused this shift in plans.

Hastings made a point to crowd himself in a corner and not touch me. Truitt kept his arm pressed tightly against his side when he pulled out a key. He unlocked the top floor button and the elevator started upward.

I swung my back to the door so I could face him. "Truitt, there's something I don't understand. There was blood all over my riding clothes. If the horse just bolted —"

He raced to cut me off. "Sammy bolted because he was in pain. I jabbed the bit into his tongue and he spat blood, you see. That's how your clothes got stained." Truitt put a silly grin on his face. "I goofed. That horse is Jonah's favorite thing in the world." Truitt relaxed his face into a more natural smile. "I'll catch hell for my mistake. In fact, I already have. But the horse is all right."

"You're sure?" I was suspicious.

"Absolutely."

I felt the door whish open. I turned around and walked into a huge room, the penthouse of a tower I'd seen from the outside. There were blooming plants everywhere. Classical music drifted from the ceiling and seemed to float on the subdued lighting. Under the windows was a king-sized bed with moonlight shimmering on satin sheets. Thick Ficus trees intertwined to form a headboard for the bed. Tree branches played upward, spreading across a domed roof. My things from the hotel were there, put in all the appropriate places.

There was an odd, almost sexual tension to the room, like some lingering perfume that was too slight now to be identified. I half expected Truitt Hastings to put an awkward make on me. But when I turned around, Truitt was gone. The elevator doors were shut and cold metal panels stared at me.

Surprised by Truitt's sudden disappearance, I walked aimlessly toward the windows. My view through a sweep of glass panes caught the entire Malibu coastline. I walked to the windows and looked down. Moon-tipped waves came toward me on the sea below. Off to one side, I could see the stables. I pressed my fingertips against the glass and lightly pushed off, turning to encompass the room. This wasn't any guest bedroom. One whole wall was covered by flat panel televisions, probably to keep Cameron updated on news events worldwide. This was obviously his personal suite.

I sat on a ledge and leaned backward until my naked shoulders touched the cool glass windows. Why in the world did they put me here, I wondered?

31

Half an hour later, I still didn't know why they'd put me in Jonah Cameron's personal suite, instead of taking me to the hotel. I just knew how I felt – like bait in a trap. I didn't like it and was determined to get out. Escaping was probably impossible, but it was worth a try.

They were undoubtedly watching me through hidden video cameras. I wanted to change into clothes more suited to escape than an immodest evening gown. But I didn't want them ogling me when I undressed. So I found the light switches, a bank of dimmers near the bar. With a bit of trial and error, I turned off the room lights.

I slipped into a closet, leaving its door ajar for some moonlight, and unzipped the evening dress. It fell around my ankles and I kicked the gown away, then pried off the heels and kicked them after the dress. Jeans, T-shirt and boots replaced the formal evening clothes. I would have preferred my Nikes, but those were in a suitcase near the bed. I didn't want to leave the closet until I was ready to escape.

Simply taking the elevator was out of the question. Pressing the down button would alert them. They'd know I was trying to leave the room. So I slid along the walls to a bank of windows facing the ocean. I noticed a brass piano hinge along a window, but no handle was apparent. I pressed on the glass and the pane gave slightly, then stopped. It was locked somehow.

I looked along the window frame, but there was no indication of how the glass was secured. I lifted a long seat cushion below the window and began feeling underneath. My fingers hit the raised edge of a metal catch. I found a ring and pulled. There was a light snick and the window trembled as Santa Ana wind brushed the glass.

Cautiously, I stepped on a seat cushion and pushed the window, only to have it fight back when the gusting Santa Ana kicked up. I waited for the wind to subside, muttering what little I remembered of a prayer. The storm relented and I pressed the glass open. Outside was a narrow ledge with a three-story drop to sand dunes. Anxiously, I stepped on the ledge, grasping the window for support. It was thirty feet to the ground and I despised heights. My idea of a daring risk was jumping off our stoop when I was a kid.

Suddenly, wind slapped the heavy glass into my fingers, trapping my hand beneath the window frame. I stifled a groan of pain. My hand was bleeding. Another gust sucked the glass outward and I instinctively pulled my fingers away. The window slammed with a click and stayed shut. I was locked outside.

There was a metal fire escape a few feet away. But fine grit rolled like ball bearings under my shoes. I tried moving carefully, pushing one foot at a time, but my body twisted. One boot slid into space. I was falling and had to try something. I coiled slightly and lunged for the fire escape.

My body jerked off the ledge just as my sweaty hands found the metal hoops and closed on them. I slid downward and my knees hit stucco, scraping against the wall and colliding with the steel ladder. Sharp pain jolted my battered knees. Despite the pain, I fought to wrap a leg around the fire escape but didn't make it.

Dangling from my precious hold on the ladder, my fingers ached and then grew numb. I swung my legs again and this time found a rung with my boots. After testing the foothold, I gratefully released one hand at a time, letting my fingers regain their feeling.

I waited for a few seconds that seemed like minutes. Hot wind licked sweat off my back and billowed the T-shirt. A loose metal cap slapped on a roof somewhere in the distance and the ocean cast itself on the beach with dull roars. A bright moon etched black shadows of myself and the fire escape.

I took in a long breath and started down, carefully placing each boot on the metal rungs. My feet descended until I felt for a rung and found none. I hated looking down, but I had no choice. I was still ten feet off the ground. There was an extension that could be dropped by removing a pin, but that would make a terrible racket. I decided to keep going, letting my feet slip off. Soon, I was hanging with my toes five feet from sand. Closing my eyes, I let go.

I hit and rolled, happy the thud of my landing was muffled by breaking surf. I looked around. The stables were nearby, and beyond them, wind brought the sound of cars on the Pacific Coast Highway. Past the stables, tall brush led to a wall separating Cameron's estate from the road. I could keep going until I found a way over that wall.

I sprinted to the back of the stables. Along the building, brush was cut to bare ground and there was no concealment. Fortunately, I was in black shadow. I looked around and saw no one following me. The only sounds came from brush tumbling in the wind. Then a sports car squealed its tires on the distant highway.

It appeared safe to move and I began creeping along the wall. A roll of dry brush shot ahead of me and beat against the stables, then made for my shins. I had to push the brush away before continuing. I was in the middle of the stables when scraping noises came to me. I stopped and listened. It appeared someone was moving toward me, creeping stealthily.

There was a door ahead, in the very center of the stables. I twisted the knob and pulled the door slowly open. There was a slight creak from the hinge. I darted inside and closed the door behind me, trying to be quiet as a stalking cat. Moonlight flowed into the stalls from the open tops of Dutch doors. The stalls were partitioned by boards running shoulder high on a horse. Support posts were cluttered with tack, bridles and reins hanging from nails.

When my eyes adjusted, I recognized Maggie in the next stall. She put her head over and nuzzled me. Apparently I hadn't injured her on the ride, as I'd once feared. The blood on my clothes must have come from Sammy, just as Truitt Hastings indicated. But where was Samuel B. Taylor?

I saw an English riding saddle on a stand and realized it was the one Truitt rode on Sammy. I must be in the stall for Cameron's horse, Samuel B. Taylor. Hastings said the horse was fine, yet his stall was empty and there was a funny smell in the air. What was going on here?

I decided to move into the dark area beyond the stalls, where I could hide for a while and think. When I tried to lift a foot, my boot clung to the floorboards. I kicked away hay, bent down and touched the floor. My fingers smelled of the medicinal odor that was in the air, plus something else. Horse blood? It appeared the floor had been blood-soaked before it was mopped and covered with fresh straw. There was a five-gallon paint bucket in one corner. I went to the can and found rags heaped inside, soaked in blood.

Questions shot through my brain like I was inside a video game, running through a bizarre landscape of threats and obstacles. Why all the blood? Answer – from a gunshot wound, which is why the horse bolted. The thoroughbred was shot, presumably by Elijah.

Samuel B. Taylor reared on his hind legs, then screamed from being wounded. Apparently, Elijah aimed at Sammy's rider but shot the horse instead, when Sammy reared up. Why would Elijah aim at Truitt Hastings when I was there, a perfect target? I wasn't moving. At the time of the gunshot, I was absolutely still, sitting on a winded, old quarterhorse. Did that mean Elijah wanted to kill Hastings more than he wanted to kill me? That idea seemed nonsense. There must be another explanation, but I didn't have time to find it.

Suddenly, bright light flew the length of the stables. High powered flashlights swept the area. I recoiled and spun around. A half step pressed my chest into the barrel of an assault rifle pointed at my heart. There were guns all around me, held by men swathed in black uniforms, like a SWAT squad. My heart stopped briefly, then began pumping so hard it slapped against my ribcage. I felt dizzy from it.

The rifle was pulled out of my breasts and pivoted up. A radio crackled on the lapel of a commando-style uniform. "We've got her. In the stables. We'll bring her in."

I shuddered, terrified and relieved at the same time. For a split second, I'd been convinced Elijah found me.

The man stood with his feet spread, the butt of his assault rifle pressed into a hip. "What are you doing here, miss?"

I blurted the only excuse that came to mind, even though it was idiotic. "I lost an earring on the ride. I wanted to get some air, so I came into the stables to look for the earring."

"You climbed down a fire escape to get an earring? The sheriff's department warned us there was a wacko in the area with a grudge for Mr. Cameron. We're on full security alert tonight, miss. In the future, please use the elevator and we'll escort you. Better yet, wait until morning, for your own safety."

"Sure. I didn't know." My heart slowed to a mere sprint pace. Maybe I'd just been paranoid. I'd misunderstood Cameron moving me to his compound. It had been done to protect me from Elijah. Then I glanced at the can of blood-soaked rags. No, I wasn't being paranoid. Something screwy was going on here.

"We'll take you back now, miss." The man in black grabbed my arm and pulled me toward the stable door.

I jerked my arm away and glowered at him.

"We can do this the hard way, if you insist."

There was no point in getting bruised. I walked sullenly ahead of him, moving toward the main building. I heard my boots clicking on the paving stones, mixed with the softer tread of men behind me. Everything had a surrealistic intensity from the adrenaline rush. When I saw water trickling into a fountain, each drop seemed to take minutes.

In the courtyard, the cloying scent of night-blooming jasmine was overpowering. The wind twisted my hair into knots and blew dust in my face. I moved a hand to shield my eyes and caught a glimpse of a man on a balcony, tracking us with a rifle. Like the others, he was dressed as a black shadow.

The building door was opened and I was marched down the hallway, past now-familiar watercolors. One man stayed outside when the elevator doors closed and another accompanied me. I rode in silence. At the top, the commando-type pointed at Cameron's bedroom.

I stayed in the elevator. My voice was hoarse with tension when I spoke. "I'd rather go for a walk."

He didn't smile at my little joke. He put his hand on my back and pushed me into the room. Then he gave me a smug, grim smile. We stood there watching each other as the elevator doors closed.

When the metal panels touched, I stuck out my tongue at him. Then I examined the bedroom. The seat cushion was lying on the floor in front of the fire escape window. I went over and looked for the brass ring I'd used to open the window. There was no ring, just a torn scar in the board where they'd ripped out the lever. Didn't take them long to determine how I escaped, did it?

I went to the elevator and pressed down. The light didn't go on. The elevator was disabled. I was right where they wanted me and I wasn't leaving. I put my back against the cold elevator doors and let myself slide to the floor. Sitting on the carpet, I tried not to panic. But it wasn't easy. In my mind, I kept seeing the image of a goat tied in a clearing, bait to lure a hungry lion. The doe goat was bleating in fear. She smelled the lion coming.

32

It was past 3 A.M. when I assembled enough of the puzzle to know I was dead. I just hadn't been killed yet. I wondered how much longer I had to live? Huddled behind Cameron's private bar, I was seeing everything reflected in a mirror. In the smoked glass, faint starlight sifted through the dome above. All color was washed from the room. In the dark, brilliant tropical flowers looked like gray fingers. The bleached carpet led like a freshly mown lawn to a panorama of curving glass. The night sky and a frozen ocean were painted on the sweeping glass. The angled window frames looked like a spider web.

My heart jumped. In the center of the web, Elijah stood pressed against the glass. At the base of the glass wall, explosives detonated in a crisp snap. The glass vanished and Elijah was instantly in the room. He stood over the bed, firing at the silk comforter where it huddled into a lump. I watched his unerringly quick, precise movements with terror.

I cringed, feeling icy cold in the overheated room. Elijah's hand closed on the blanket and peeled it back, revealing pillows I'd found in the closet. I saw astonishment flit across his face and then rage. His eyes raced across the room, a pair of searchlights seeking me out.

The Santa Ana wind carried away the slap of waves on the beach and left the room eerily silent. I stopped inhaling so he wouldn't hear me breathing. A digital clock flipped its crisp numerals with a light click. A spigot for draft beer leaked a tiny drip into the stainless steel sink. I had to breathe soon. In that silent room, I was sure even soft inhaling would be audible.

There was a light snap behind the bar mirror. Reflected in the glass, I saw Elijah freeze, one hand on the bed covers, the other holding a small pistol with a silencer. A delicate rumbling trembled under me. I watched a wall panel swing open, blocking entrance to the bar, sealing me in the serving area. I forgot how much I wanted to breathe when I heard footsteps move along the panel. Someone was standing on the other side of the partition. I again felt a strange, almost erotic tension. I'd first noticed the feeling when I entered the bedroom with Truitt Hastings.

A disembodied voice I'd never heard commanded, "Put your gun on the bed and turn around, Elijah."

The professional killer let his hand slip from the covers. But the gun didn't move. Elijah's body went rigid. "No, Jonah. I want the satisfaction of knowing you'll have to explain why you shot me in the back."

"Have it your way." The disembodied footsteps continued into the room.

In the mirror, I saw the back of a man close in stature to Truitt Hastings. I knew at once it must be Jonah Cameron. The resemblance between Hastings and Cameron explained so neatly why Hastings went with me on that violent, crazy horseback ride. Jonah Cameron took no chances.

Cameron turned and moonlight etched his features. Jonah Cameron's face was flat with a receding chin. His prominent nose jutted over very thin lips. Cameron's looks weren't remarkable. In fact they were a disappointment, certainly not commanding and presidential. Only the eyes gave away Cameron's intensity. He radiated a strange aura, similar to the erotic tension of a new lover stripping off your panties.

Jonah was carrying a hunting shotgun. He circled the room, getting closer to Elijah. The professional killer twisted, keeping his back to Cameron as Jonah stalked the room. As a result, they were both facing the elevator when its doors opened. A rectangle of light flashed across the surprised features of Elijah. Cameron looked smug.

I heard a gun snapped from its leather holster. Jake Balducci's voice barked, "Freeze!"

From behind the FBI agent came Karen Shaw's soft exclamation, "Oh, shit."

Their footsteps slapped out of the elevator and became muted shuffling on the carpet. The elevator's doors remained open, lighting the room. In the bar mirror, I could see Karen shifting uneasily. Balducci grabbed her, dragging Karen forward.

"Hey, what the hell," was Karen's unhappy response.

For a terrible moment, all three men were a snapshot in the mirror. Then I saw Cameron let the shotgun barrel drop. He closed on Elijah. "I'll get the gun," Jonah told Balducci. I saw Cameron stop and cradle the shotgun under his arm. He pulled a latex glove from his pocket. I felt faint as I watched Cameron forcing the glove on, one finger at a time.

In the mirror above me, Balducci's face grew pale. Jake tried to wet his lips and speak, but couldn't.

The glove was only one finger from being on. Cameron shifted his shotgun when it slipped a bit. I nearly vomited when I realized why Jonah was donning a glove. Jonah wanted the glove so there would be no gunpowder when he pulled the trigger. He wanted to kill Karen and me with Elijah's weapon. The glove made certain there were no gunpowder traces on his fingers, putting the lie to his alibi.

I wasn't safe behind the bar. Cameron probably knew I was hiding there, had spotted me on one of the video surveillance cameras. I had to turn Jake Balducci around somehow. I had to try. I felt crazy terror numb my body when I spoke, my voice floating over the bar. "Jake, you can't let him do it."

In the mirror, I watched every face twist in my direction. Oh shit, I thought, what have I done?

I stammered when I said it, but I had no choice. "You aren't leaving here alive, Jake. You know that. I don't know what Jonah's got on you, but disgrace is better than dying, Jake."

"That's ridiculous," Cameron snapped. "Just keep Elijah covered. Everything will be fine. You'll get a promotion." Cameron's words were smoothly poured out, like maple syrup on pancakes. Jonah moved toward Elijah.

"Jake, shoot Cameron if he tries to get Elijah's gun," I pleaded. "Jonah can't leave you alive, Jake. Cameron's got all the leaks in this room. He has to eliminate them. That means you, too."

I watched Balducci's tongue run over his thick lips. The FBI agent flicked his gun toward the bar. He told Karen Shaw, "Get over there with Morrissey."

Karen stumbled toward me. She collided with a bar stool and sent it clattering to the floor. The metal stool rang for a while and died. I thought Balducci wanted us together for an easier kill. But Jake swung his gun to cover Jonah Cameron.

Cameron snorted at the barrel of Jake's automatic. "Don't be an ass, Balducci." Jonah edged toward Elijah's gun.

"That's close enough," the FBI agent said quietly.

Cameron stopped, but brought his shotgun up.

I knew it was time to play my last card – if I had a last card. I put a hand on the bar shelf and tried to pull myself up. My legs buckled with fear. I cursed silently and tried again. My head cleared the bar top and I saw all of them, frozen like statues. The shadows of billowing eucalyptus trees danced over their immobile bodies.

My voice cracked when I spoke. "We're all here, Jonah, just like you planned it." It got easier as I went on. "But your scheme wasn't quite perfect. Elijah didn't kill me in the bed. That's why you put me in your suite, so you could claim Elijah came here for me. The glove is so you can use Elijah's gun to kill Balducci and Karen and me."

Cameron showed absolutely no reaction to what I said, but Karen Shaw nearly fainted. Karen sat on a bar stool with such force that the room echoed her loud plop. It looked like she was going to fall off the stool.

I couldn't stop to help her. I continued, "Have I got it right, Jonah? You kill us and tell the cops you arrived too late to help. Shot Elijah in self-defense after he'd murdered us. Huh, Jonah?" I knew Cameron was too smart to kill Jake Balducci. Still, I had to hope Balducci could be bluffed to my side.

Cameron finally cracked. He shouted, "Bullshit." Jonah aimed his hunting shotgun at me.

"No, no," I taunted him. "Can't use that gun on me. Must have Elijah's pistol."

Cameron's face twisted with rage. His hands clamped and loosened on the shotgun.

"Can't do it, Jonah," I explained. "You shoot me and Jake shoots you. Scenario one, if you will." I flattened my hands on the slick bar and my sweaty palms felt glued to the varnish. I forced saliva around my mouth so I could speak.

"Scenario two. Elijah shoots you, Jonah. Well, that doesn't go well for Elijah. Jake will pump Elijah full of bullets." My voice was better, but my hands trembled on the bar.

Elijah put a quirky smile on his face, indicating I'd gotten some respect from the pro killer. He prompted me, "Why would I want to murder Jonah Cameron, our next president?"

"Why?" I echoed. "Because you can run but you can't hide. Not in this modern interconnected world. Let's say you escape to a third world country. The FBI isn't a real threat. FBI has to extradite you, which won't happen for decades with your bank account. But Jonah Cameron is a different story. Jonah doesn't want blackmail threats arriving at the White House, so he'll have Elijah terminated. For Elijah to retire safely, he must first kill Jonah."

Elijah didn't say anything. But he gave me an appreciative look. We were building a relationship of sorts. Now, he'd kill me and regret it. Before, he'd have just killed me.

I looked at Elijah's small body and another piece of the puzzle snapped into place. "You knew Jonah goes riding at sunset. How? You worked as a jockey in Cameron's stables. That was before you were trained as Jonah's private hit man. Am I right, Elijah?"

He didn't answer me. The professional hit man just tilted his head slightly. His eyes sparkled. Elijah wasn't going to incriminate himself. He changed the subject. "You told us about scenario one and two. Is there a scenario three?"

"Yes, scenario three. That's where Jake starts it. Kills you, Jonah, out of spite for what you've got on him. That doesn't go well for Jake. Elijah gets the split-second advantage he needs to grease Balducci. Jake wants to live, don't you?"

Balducci didn't reply to my question. His eyes darted from Cameron to Elijah and back again. His tongue raced in tight circles around his lips. I could see how much Jake Balducci wanted to blow a very large hole in Jonah Cameron. Jake was calculating if he could do that and live.

I had to do something fast before Balducci tried shooting Jonah and everyone wound up dead. I moved my cold fingers along the bar and lifted a phone off the hook. The dial tone buzzed loudly across the room.

"Stalemate," I announced in a slightly quavering voice. "Three men with guns, but none of you dares pull the trigger ... plus little old me." My fingers hit the phone's key pad. I dialed three numbers.

"Just me ... and nine-one-one. Hello? We have a little trouble in the Cameron compound. FBI needs help. Bring your SWAT guys. Do it fast ... please." I gave a sad laugh. "Yeah, I'll be here. Trust me. I can't possibly leave."

33

A month after Sheriff's deputies burst into Jonah Cameron's bedroom, I sat in Carnegie Deli. My bare arms rested on the cool Formica of a table shared with Saul Morgenthal. The small table was crowded by a jar of pickles, silverware worn dull by countless mayonnaise-covered fingers and a battered vinyl menu holder. Still, I was pleased to be there. In Saul Morgenthal's world, asking you to lunch is like knighting you. When he invited me, I was shocked. I was more disoriented at Carnegie Deli than I'd been in Daniel, where I lunched with Truitt Hastings. It felt like years passed between then and now. There'd been so many changes since my encounter with A United Tomorrow.

On the good side, Elijah was in prison without bail. Sadly, no charges were brought against Jonah Cameron. But he'd dropped his bid for the presidency, probably forever. My job security had improved and I'd authored a series of articles appearing on the front page. They were carefully edited by Saul, then laundered by *Chronicle* attorneys. Still, the public could read between the lines and see the relationship between Jonah Cameron, A United Tomorrow and Elijah. I was shadowed day and night by FBI agents, lest Jonah decide to eliminate me. How long protection was needed, I didn't know. A month of it already felt like years.

FBI agents watched me from a nearby table, while I watched Saul carefully read the menu from top to bottom. He grunted over the typos and finally chose a pastrami with Swiss on rye. I looked up to see the waiter standing over us, an unmistakable presence.

He was a huge man with the moon for a face, wearing old trousers that were ironed to a glazed sheen. His stained apron was a palette for the deli's menu, yet his shirt was starched so much it crackled when he moved his arms. "What'a you have?" he asked.

"Roast beef, cheddar, on toasted wheat," I said.

The waiter looked at Saul. "You want your usual, a pistol. Pastrami on rye. Am I right?"

Saul allowed himself a shy smile. "Yeah."

The waiter pointed at the entry, where an ancient cash register topped a refrigerated dessert case. "You guys want some glazed cheesecake?"

"Nah." Saul looked at me.

I shook my head. "Not for me. I can't afford the calories."

"OK, pistol and a RB with cheddar, toasted wheat, comin' right up." He wrote the order as a smear on a little green pad, stuck the pencil under his greasy hair and spun away. Despite his bulk, the waiter danced gracefully around a customer standing in the aisle.

I opened the pickle jar and used tongs to pluck one out. I offered it to Saul.

He shook his head. "Nah, those things are salt mines. I gotta watch my blood pressure."

Avoiding a pickle was ironic considering the salt level in his pastrami sandwich, but I didn't press the point. Instead, I dropped the pickle on my dish.

Saul leaned over the table, so the Fibbies nearby couldn't overhear. "What'd Cameron have on Balducci?" Morgenthal loved gossip.

I nodded. "This is totally off the record, OK?"

"Yeah," Saul grunted. Off the record was better than nothing.

"Balducci had a gambling addiction. He lost $20,000 at Atlantic City and covered it with the petty cash fund. Somehow Cameron found out and gave Jake a loan to avoid disgrace and termination. The payback was that all FBI data on A United Tomorrow was passed to Cameron. They can't prosecute Cameron on blackmail, because Balducci won't testify, naturally. Jake doesn't want to incriminate himself as a spy. So that one's a stalemate."

Saul asked, "Why didn't you get anything juicy on Cameron with those boots? I spent twenty-two hundred to have your shoes wired."

I had to pay back my mother's loan, so Leo Bendel's $1,500 became $2,200 on my expense account. Fortunately, nobody in accounting called Leo to verify the amount. "I was under a little pressure, Saul. Remember?"

He glowered at me. "You forgot to use the wire."

"Not true," I pushed back. "I tapped the 'record button' with my big toe, after I stood up. But the microphone couldn't pick up much of the conversation. I was standing behind the bar."

"You didn't get *anything* on Cameron?"

"Saul, I had one pair of $2,200 boots. Cameron hired a dozen $2,200 an hour lawyers to pour through every scrap of dialogue."

Saul forgot his blood pressure and grabbed my pickle. He bit off a piece and chewed. From the look on his face, I could tell that instant heartburn had set in.

I tried to console him. "Hey, look at it this way. You stopped Cameron's bid to be President, with a loyal cult following carrying him into office. That's what Cameron was setting up with those election headquarters killings. You squashed all that." I tapped the Formica with a forefinger for emphasis.

Morgenthal still looked upset. Whether that came from heartburn or wasting money on Leo Bendel, I couldn't discern.

The waiter gently shoved a thick ceramic plate in front of me. My sandwich looked delicious. The waiter followed with a pastrami mountain for Saul.

I mumbled through my first bite. "It's Elijah I really want. With him, it's personal."

Saul mumbled back. "Did the Connecticut State Troopers ever link Elijah to the Porsche?"

"No. The evidence conveniently disappeared. They ran an internal investigation and everyone was innocent, as always. Official report blames the Post Office for sloppy handling of the mail."

Saul chomped and talked at the same time. "Any other way to convict Elijah?"

"Yeah. I think Elijah will get sent up, based on my testimony and Karen Shaw's. Karen had more in that safe deposit box than she let on. She actually had a note from Elijah telling Richie he didn't need to learn how to use the gun. Elijah would take care of the killing. The handwriting guys tricked Elijah into a sample and established the note is authentic. I think Elijah will be cooling it in Attica for twenty years before a parole board lets him spend his offshore trusts. I'm sure Cameron's giving Elijah even more bucks to keep him quiet."

"Nice bunch. By the way, I heard from George Halliday that all's forgiven. You can visit George on Long Island anytime. Just call first so he can empty the trash. He doesn't want you poaching more of Senator Cort's invitations."

I laughed. "Good old George. I'm glad I didn't give him any real trouble."

"Hell, he's happy. A United Tomorrow's membership dropped by two thirds since I ran the articles." I noticed my authorship of the stories had already vanished from Saul's memory. They were now his articles.

Saul looked at his empty plate with longing. His food appetite was like his never-ending hunger for a headline. "You know, Drew, it's been a while since you did something big."

I was indignant. "A while? My series finishes today, Saul."

"Yeah, well, that means it's history. I got some dead space on page one I need filled. A friend at the DA's office gave me a lead on a scam for getting expensive perfumes into port without paying tax. The Russian mob's behind it. I want you to poke around, see what you can find."

"Great, Saul. A United Tomorrow and Jonah Cameron aren't enough enemies for me." I rolled my eyes.

"You can handle it. Everywhere you go, you got backup." He pointed at a pair of FBI agents forcing thick sandwiches in their mouths.

The waiter interrupted. "You want anything else?"

We both wagged our heads in a "no" and the waiter dropped a plastic tray with the chit on our table. He waddled off, whistling softly.

I dragged my 1950s naugehyde and chrome chair away from the table. I warned the FBI agents, "Guys, I gotta get back to work." Saul levered his bulk up and we headed for the door. I didn't wait to see if the agents were following. They'd been glued to me for thirty days and weren't likely to get lost.

I pushed the front door open and waited for Saul to choose a toothpick. The sun was shining brightly yet it wasn't humid, a rare day for New York City. I hoped that was a good omen. I needed luck to snoop around the Russian mob, even with FBI shadows tacked to my back.